"DUNCAN, CONNOR... NEST!"

❧❧

Duncan's eyes flew up the main mast to the crow's nest, and as lightning linked its way across the sky he saw two women there, and by the strong presence, he knew they were both Immortals. "Amber!" shouted Duncan, but the wind would not carry his voice. He saw the glint of steel. Who the other woman was, Duncan had no idea. But they were fighting. Lightning filled the sky and Duncan saw the mane of red hair, just like that of Khordas, the Salamander.

Duncan shouted out to Amber again and began to run for the main mast, but now he saw Connor wrench one hand free from the wheel of the *Rosemary* and thrash at him furiously. "No!"

"But . . ." Crashing waves. The two women were pitched in battle in a space no wider than a tabletop. "She's not ready!"

"No!" Connor snarled again, over the elements. "You may not interfere! It is forbidden!"

Lightning crackled once again, and the two female figures were silhouettes against the gray clouds. Duncan heard the Salamander cry, "The God will be avenged, Highlander! I *own* the elements and will not be denied my due!"

❧❧

HIGHLANDER™

THE ELEMENT OF FIRE

JASON HENDERSON

ASPECT ®

WARNER BOOKS

A Time Warner Company

WARNER BOOKS EDITION

"Highlander" is a protected trademark of Gaumont Television. © 1994 by Gaumont Television and © Davis Panzer Productions, Inc. 1985. Published by arrangement with Bohbot Entertainment, Inc.

Aspect is a registered trademark of Warner Books, Inc.

Warner Books, Inc.
1271 Avenue of the Americas
New York, NY 10020

Ⓦ A Time Warner Company

Printed in the United States of America

First Printing: October, 1995

10 9 8 7 6 5 4 3 2 1

For
Douglas Vaughn Henderson

HIGHLANDER™
THE ELEMENT OF FIRE

Prologue

In a year without number, because all years were alike, in a land that would one day be called Scotland but was then called simply the World, the Children of the Salamander sang:

Khordas, we have come to please you,
Khordas, we have come to serve. . . .

The Time of the Return had come. With each beat of the drum the mud vibrated, with each pellet of hard rain the surface splashed, and ripples moved in muddy rings around the form of the god who slept. The god awakened in his sleeping place and opened his eyes. His Children were calling.

Khordas, hear our prayer!

On the surface of the mud lay the mask of the god, and now it lifted from its resting place, the form of the god bubbling up from below. The mud filtered away from the god's eyes and he saw through the mask, and became the mask, as he rose from the holy pit.

The Children of the Salamander danced, and now the god saw their forms, lit up by a lightning chain that linked its way across the sky. All of them were painted deep blue, like the mask of the Salamander. The rain ran along their muscles, beading on the paint, their glistening bodies moving in answer to the drums, for Khordas was their god, and they feared him.

Khordas threw out his arms to the beat of the drums and the clap of thunder, and mud flew all around him, splattering on the blue dancers. The god chanted in the tongue of the Children, answering their prayer: "Fire and water are my domain! Who dares call Khordas, the Salamander?"

We are not puny, like our babes,
Nor weak, like our enemies across the hills. . . .

Khordas leapt from the pit with a hiss and landed in the mud, surrounded by the dancers. The drums grew stronger now, and it seemed, so did the rain.

We are your Children, Khordas,
And because we fear you, we are feared!

Khordas slithered before them, crouching, moving his head like the Salamander, and now he reached into a pouch and drew out something the blue people did not see. Khordas slapped his hands together, and between his palms something flared and burned in the night, brighter than the lightning.

"The water can kill the weakest of you, in great amounts, but you control it, for I am your god.

"But fire is greater still, and even this, I use at my pleasure!"

Khordas, we have come to please you,
Khordas, we have come to serve. . . .

The fireball flew from Khordas' hands, and fell before him on the ground, and a ring of fire grew, too strong even for the rain. And even the dancers, who had experienced this since they were children, cowered at the sight. "Why," cried the god of fire and water, the greatest of things, the elements of power, "I should destroy you for even thinking you could serve me!"

Khordas, we beg your mercy,
Khordas, we wish to please. . . .

"And what will you give me that I might not destroy you? What will you give, that I might look fondly?"

We give you these baubles, poor though they are, but to us, they are great things.

And now they came, two at a time, all the Children of the Salamander, heads bowed, with offerings held before them. Each pair came to the edge of the fire circle and tossed the offering inside the circle, for none would cross the barrier, and certainly, none would approach the god. Slain animals, trophies of hunts, packages of meat and fish, even jewels—a great sacrifice, made only by the greatest of the Children.

The god danced the dance of recognition of the offerings, and soon he stopped dancing, and stooped low. "Your god is not happy."

The god is not happy, what have we done?

Fire rain down, tides wash us away!

"Your god lives in his pit and wants to know the deeds of his Children! Through the mud he cannot see what his Children do!"

We serve you, Khordas.

Khordas, the Salamander.

"Khordas will join you for this year, and walk among you, his Children, that you may do him reverence every day."

Every day we do Khordas reverence.

Every day is his, lest we be destroyed.

"Join you I shall, walk among you I shall! Eat from your tables, sleep in your beds!" Now the god twisted on his ankles, smiling, staring at his Children. The Children danced back a bit and one of the priests sang:

Unfit are we, to be joined with the god,

Khordas would tire of our home.

The god grew angry, hearing these words, roared from the circle, and approached the sacred hut near the pit. "Now before me I find this house, the home of one of my Children. I ask for shelter and companionship and I am denied it, and I will mete punishment!"

And the Children cowered, and sang of their fear, remembering the great destruction the god had once seen fit to send them, as the god threw something at the hut, and it burst into flames.

And now Khordas turned and sought out he who had been planned for, and this man he seized.

"Lonely is your god, and angry. . . ."

The man looked like any other, painted blue as he was, and great was the fear in his eyes. Khordas seized the man, and the Children of the Salamander danced and cried out in terror, remembered and real, as Khordas tore the disciple apart with his hands, saying as he did so, "But Khordas does not wish to be angry, he only wishes to be with his Children," showering the mud across his body with the blood of the victim, and now he returned to the ring of fire that surrounded the holy pit.

A priest emerged now, from the back of the congregation, and the sea of Children parted to let him pass as he sang his part:

Take then, oh Khordas, this my daughter, Nerissa.
Take as your Companion her lovely frame,
Her perfect soul, her worship is yours.

Khordas' blood rushed from his face as he felt her come near, her father pushing her into the clearing. What was this? What manner of . . . in all the years Khordas had been god he had never seen so perfect a portrayal of Nerissa, her hair such as he had never seen before, white as snow, skin utterly without color, her eyes pink. The creature wore no paint, and the mud splashed up and made holy images on the white skin of her bare feet. But more than this was a feeling he had never had before, of the air getting thick, smoke on his brain, and the pink-eyed creature looked at him, and sang with the Children.

"This companion your god accepts," said Khordas, as always he said, as every year he said again. But this time he knew there was something different, that made his mud-laden belly quiver, a force that bonded her as no sacrifice had ever bonded to him before. "Your lives I spare, as I have before."

Khordas . . . Khordas . . . Khordas . . . Khordas . . . the drums pounded as the Children danced and the god took the girl by the hand, and led her backwards, through the ring of fire, and into the pit of mud, and he covered her face with his hands and pulled her below. Bubbles flew from her mouth as she pitched, and it was minutes before she drowned, and he remained with her below the mud for the night, before slinking away with the offerings in the morning.

Khordas did not know who the first Khordas had been, but his mind clouded at the thought. He was Khordas, and so he always had been. The stories, the songs were about him. The sacrifices were to him. And now he had been Khordas for three generations of Children of the Salamander. He was surely the god.

He knew this, also, because the Nerissa whom he took into the pit, the pink-eyed girl who had affected him so, rose the following morning from the dead as he did. And thus Khordas knew that he was the real god, and she the real Nerissa.

Gods of fire and water. Gods of power. The oldest gods.

And every year for generations Khordas and Nerissa received their sacrifices, and they danced in the blood, and her pink eyes shone under the offering.

And when all the Children of the Salamander were gone, there was no one left to worship them.

And Khordas and Nerissa were very sad.

And very, very angry.

Chapter 1

1625

There are beings in the world known as Immortals. Nomenclature aside, dying is not impossible for them. Each dies twice—the first death is practice—but the next death, the final one, head torn from shoulders and all years poured out on the ground, is difficult. Most avoid it vigorously. The Immortals skim along the surface of the years like stones on a stream, now and again halted, the stone tumbling to the depths, the Immortal journey complete. In second death, the years stop skimming by; epitaphs can be carved again. Dying is difficult, though some wish for it.

Dreaming is easy.

Where do I come from? Duncan cried, but his father would not listen. He cried again, pleading, *Where do I come from?*

Father was staring at him from atop his horse, and he looked at Duncan as if Duncan were not his son, and said as much: *On the night my lady wife gave birth to our only son, stillborn, there was brought to her chamber by a peasant woman a boy child to replace . . .*

No!

. . . to replace that which was lost . . .

No! I do not believe you, (no, it cannot be . . .)

. . . and the midwife looked into your eyes, and said you were a changeling child!

(But Father, if what you say is true . . .)

. . . you are no bairn of mine! You're not my son!

But where did I come from?

"Where did I come from!" Duncan cried again, and then something had him by the shoulders, shaking him briskly, and he awoke.

"You're a bunk-mate from hell, *that's* where you come from," said the dark form that stood over him. Duncan could hear the crackle of the fire nearby. He had awakened Connor.

Duncan rubbed his eyes for a second and pushed his hair out of the way. "I'm sorry, really. It won't happen again."

Connor shrugged and sat down by the fire, leaning back against the mossy stones of the crumbling castle wall. Over Connor's head the wall stopped, jutting here and there with a rotting post. The stars shone bright where once there would have been tapestries instead.

The flames cast an eerie glow on the teacher's ruddy face, and the Immortal looked every bit the Connor MacLeod of legend. Connor, who had died in battle generations ago, and who some said rose from the grave like the Phoenix, like Christ—and, some said, walked the hills to this very day . . . Duncan had once laughed at those stories, and shuddered, and dreamt of the Immortal MacLeod. Here he was. And he had flesh, and he had blood.

"We are the same, Duncan MacLeod," the Elder Highlander told him, that first day. Connor had found Duncan like Prometheus waiting in vain for death, wedged between the rocks on the shore, as if he could drown. "We are *brothers*!"

And now Duncan sat up and looked at Connor, who had become his teacher, and who was trying not to be annoyed with him. Connor picked up his sword and began to run it across a whetstone. "You say it won't happen again, Duncan," said Connor, "but you lie. You dream the same dream each night, and I am forced to listen to it."

Duncan felt his cheeks flush. He hated embarrassment. He had endured more punishment from this new "brother" of his than he had ever received in his thirty years of natural life, and he still felt abused by Connor's every word. "I cannot help what I dream."

"Perhaps not," Connor closed his eyes and nodded, the sword scraping against the stone in long, even strokes. Connor seemed to be listening to the sound of his sword before he said, "Have I told you how I came to leave Glenfinnan?"

Duncan leaned on an elbow and grabbed a folded skin, unwrapped it and retrieved a piece of bread. He tore into it with his teeth and chewed.

"Close your mouth," said Connor.

"What?"

"Your mouth. Close it. My God, we're pigs, aren't we? Just trust me on this one, close your mouth when you chew. So I was telling you about how I left Glenfinnan." Connor laughed, then, that strange staccato laugh of his. Nearly a hundred years old, Connor must have been strange even when he was mortal. Now, there was something downright alien about him. The light glinted in Connor's brown eyes and sank into his dirty-brown hair in such a way that he seemed like a walking storage, hoarding energy and giving off little, saving the energy until it erupted in a violent burst. Duncan was glad Connor seemed to have decided to like him, because there was something fearful about him. Something dangerously efficient, as if Connor were on a plotted course and had no intention of allowing divergence.

Duncan watched his mentor and wondered how Connor had come to be this way. Perhaps it was the time Connor had spent with *his* mentor, Ramirez. Duncan had heard little about Ramirez, but he knew that the Egyptian-cum-Spanish Immortal was one of the truly old ones. Yet Connor MacLeod was a kinsman, Duncan could tell, by his harshness, his brogue, his familiarity with the land of their fathers. And so Duncan would listen to what the Elder Highlander had to say. After all, without Connor, he was alone.

"How you left . . ." Duncan clamped shut his lips, of

which he was now painfully aware. Close them while you eat. You have to open them to speak, though, right?

"So ask me."

"Oh," said Duncan, after swallowing hard. He sat up straight and imitated a clansman asking the advice of a proud chieftain. "Connor, how is it that you left Glenfinnan?"

"I am glad that you asked. I was driven out."

Duncan only stared. He had never heard this before, although a few things Connor had said over the weeks they had been together had given him an inkling. "But you're a legend . . ."

Connor leaned in and stared back. "The Scots, the MacLeods, are a fine and proud people. I say that first so that you may understand that although they drove me out, stripped me legally of my name, called me a child of Satan and a devil's servant, strapped a great plank to my shoulders, and threw rocks and dung at me as I forced my tortured legs to walk out of the only place I had ever called home, although they did these things, I forgive them, for they could do no other. It was their way."

Duncan had no response to this.

"You are racked by the pain of your separation, are you not? You died in battle and there was great wailing and gnashing of teeth. The women tore their clothing, all of them. Then, oh! You've come back to life. Different story, then. Get out. Unnatural. Go." Connor peered deeply into the shining steel of the katana, Ramirez's legacy to him. Duncan could tell Connor saw something not unlike salvation in that sword.

"Yes," said Duncan. "Exactly."

"They know no other way. And do you know something? They're right."

"What on earth do you mean?"

Connor lay his sword in front of him. "What I mean, brother Duncan, is that these things work out in roughly the way that they are supposed to. What if you had stayed in your village rather than being forced out?"

"I'd still be at home," said Duncan. "I'd like to be at home."

"I do apologize for my lack of proper accommodations," said Connor, regarding the lean-to hut that Duncan and he had been sleeping in. The lean-to was supported by the bricks of a kiln, the sole standing part of the ruin that surrounded them. "She was an old forge by the time I found her, and I fear she couldn't take a powerful Quickening. But in Scotland," he sighed, "there is no better place for me." He seemed lost in thought for a moment. Then the warrior's eyes glazed over and refocused on Duncan. "We would all like to be at home. But what would that do? So the whole town accepts that you came back from the dead. Big trouble for the priests. And what do you learn? Nothing about the Game, I assure you. Everything has a purpose. By casting you out they can remain themselves, and you can learn what you are."

"But why can't they accept that we're not like them and let us live with them anyway?"

"Be careful, Duncan. This is humanity you're talking about."

"I don't understand."

"You will. You must learn to hide your special gift."

Duncan shook his head. "But I don't want to hide. This is a wonderful thing, this life. But why can't I stay where I have love?"

"There will always be love. But there is danger, Duncan. You learn the rules of the Game, or you die. No question."

"Die of what? We've spent the last two weeks slashing at one another, and not an enemy in sight."

"Oh," said Connor, as he looked around at the ruins of his adopted castle. "There are enemies about. You'll find them soon enough. Or . . ." he trailed off for a moment, his whisper harsh and then simply melting away. Connor was always thus—intense, burning. Fighting for calm and trying to teach it. Duncan knew there were flaws in his teacher. But so far Connor was the only teacher Duncan had.

"Or what?"

"Or they will find you," said Connor, and the light from the fire bounced off the sword and strange shadows danced on the Immortal warrior's face.

Several months into Duncan's training, he and Connor went to Aberdeen. Connor had business there, and so Duncan got to see the harbor for the first time. His mentor had placed a large sum of money into several sailing ventures, and he went to the port to check their progress and withdraw a sum "to keep us for a while." And as Connor spent the day doing these things, Duncan was busy making friends with a lovely creature he met at the pub where he spent the better part of the afternoon. The pub was called the Quarry House, and the quarry was fine indeed. Her name was Nerissa.

Duncan was waiting outside the pub when he sensed Connor draw near. Duncan looked up and saw the older Immortal, clad in his best clothing, walking toward him. Connor raised a hand. "Ho, brother."

"Connor," Duncan smiled, sheepishly.

Connor stopped beside him and looked into the pub. His narrow eyes crinkled as he surveyed the crowded room through the door. "I'm in the mood for a game of darts. Did you arrange lodging as I asked?"

Hence Duncan's sheepishness. "In fact, I . . . no."

Connor nodded. "Something come up?"

"I have someone I'd like you to meet," said Duncan.

"The other Immortal," said Connor, evenly.

"Ah. Of course, you sensed her."

"Her? I begin to understand." Connor scratched his chin, looked down the street, and sighed. "For what it's worth, I have an innkeeper friend in town, so we . . ." Connor stopped because the loveliest creature had just leaned out the door of the Quarry House and was tugging on Duncan's arm.

Nerissa was the picture of an angel, a waif of an Immortal with a shock of hair so blonde it was almost white. Her dress was white, as well, and hung loosely on her, an afterthought of cloth. "Duncan, my lovely new friend, won't you come back inside? It's cold and your lager is getting warm." She stopped and smiled sideways at Connor, flicking the white locks away from her face to get a better view of him. "What's this? Another one? What a fine time we'll have."

Connor gave a slight bow. "I don't believe I've had the pleasure."

"Nerissa," said the Immortal waif, extending her hand. Connor took the tiny extremity and gave it a slight kiss, then let it go.

"Charmed," said Duncan's mentor. "Connor is my name."

"Well," said Nerissa, the word rolling deliciously from her pale mouth. "Duncan had been entertaining me; I've heard a great deal about you."

"From Duncan?" Connor smiled, but only half-way.

"From Duncan. Of course," she said. Nerissa had a way of tucking her chin and speaking from the top of her eyes with a delightful scolding look. "We're celebrating my birthday a few days early."

"Oh?" Connor shrugged and scanned his student, and Duncan knew he was more or less forgiven. "And how old are you?"

Nerissa laughed, gently. "Old enough, Highlander. Would you care to join us at our table?"

"In a moment, but first if I might have a word . . ." Connor tilted his head toward Duncan. Nerissa smiled and then shrugged, a bit drunkenly, and disappeared back inside, singing, "Don't be too long."

"Been here all day?" asked Connor when the waif was away.

"Most of it," said Duncan, turning to look in again. "Lovely, isn't she?"

Connor shook his head. "Oh, you'll be a dangerous one." The Immortal leaned in and said, in all seriousness, "you should be careful of female Immortals."

"Really? Up until now I had no idea there were female Immortals."

"Ah! Of course you would think so, wouldn't you? That never occurred to me, but I compliment your logic, Duncan." Connor tilted his head, scratching his chin. "We can't have children, so I suppose you're right in that we don't seem to actually *require* two sexes. Just the same it's a pleasant variation."

"Aye," said Duncan, as he wistfully turned back to look after Nerissa.

Connor continued, "But I'm just pointing out—every Immortal uses his—or her—gifts in the Game. My tools, you are familiar with, or you will be eventually." He cocked his head toward the crowded pub. "Her's you may never know."

"My God, Connor," Duncan sneered. "You treat me like a child. I'm not as much a fool as you seem to think. . . ."

"No, but you are a young Immortal and you will listen to me. These things I say may sound like the rambling of an old maid with too much advice to give. But I want to make sure that you keep paying attention. You haven't been Immortal a full year yet, Duncan. Sword work is only the beginning. *Pay attention.* It would be a shame if a pupil of mine didn't last his first decade." Connor turned to enter the Quarry House. "And in the future, if I give you an assignment, even a simple one, do it. Understand."

Duncan nodded and put on a charming smile, but Connor seemed unmoved by it. "Oh, aye," Duncan said. He couldn't help thinking that perhaps he would have been better off on his own. But somehow, he knew he was following the right path. Especially now, since that path led back to Nerissa's table.

Connor had settled into a chair across from Nerissa. "So," his teacher was saying, "you're not a Scot, lass, what brings you to Aberdeen?"

Nerissa smiled. "The same that brings you," she said. "Business."

Connor looked at Duncan and Duncan winced inwardly. He could never tell if he had broken the rules, and Connor seemed to like to keep him guessing. "I told Nerissa that you were seeing about our sea ventures," said Duncan. His eyes were imploring.

Connor grinned. "*Our* ventures . . .?" He turned his head slowly to the younger Immortal, drawing from Duncan a look that resembled that of a begging dog, before Connor continued, "Yes, we have many. So I take it, then, you're not out for sport?"

"Sport?"

"It is the hunting season, I hear."

"Not tonight it isn't, Connor MacLeod." The sweet face narrowed and the smile did not disguise the look that would be clear to any Immortal: *And you'd know by now if it were.*

The conversation lasted perhaps half an hour more, because Connor's arrival had a distinct dampening effect. Duncan began to get the impression that Connor trusted few Immortals and therefore had great difficulty in a friendly conversation with one he did not know. Nerissa too became less talkative after his teacher arrived, as if she had been caught doing something she should have known better than to do. What that thing could be, Duncan hadn't the faintest idea. But as he looked back on the conversation that had taken up the afternoon, Duncan realized he had done most of the talking, and that he knew nothing about her.

Duncan was finishing his beer when he felt the alcohol curdle in his stomach. A presence. Another Immortal. He breathed deeply, as Connor had instructed, to keep from getting sick. Connor looked away from the table and out to the street. There was no one in sight.

Nerissa shrugged and smiled. "I must go. My companion is here, and we have . . ."

Connor said, "Business?"

"Of course," she said, and the two Immortals stood as she rose. Nerissa squeezed Duncan's hand and thanked him for the lovely conversation, then turned to Connor. "And to meet the celebrated Connor MacLeod. Truly a joy. You have excellent taste in pupils."

"Don't we all," Connor replied, eyes narrowing. "Farewell, Nerissa."

"Farewell," said Nerissa, and she disappeared out the door.

When she was gone Duncan said, "Who is the . . ."

"I don't know," said Connor. "But I caught his presence in the harbor. Whoever he is, he was staying out of sight." He raised his eyebrows as he downed the last few drops in his mug. "I had the pleasanter company today, I think. We should retire. I thought we could rise early in the morning for our exercise before mass."

"If you say so," said Duncan. He had been hoping to sleep in. He leaned back and clasped his hands behind his head. "The celebrated Connor MacLeod?"

Connor smiled. "New to me," he said. "Try this one: '*Our sea ventures.*'"

The following morning, Duncan was forced out of bed by Connor an hour before the cock so that Connor could lead him in training, which generally involved hacking at one another with swords until Duncan lost. And he always lost, in those days. The town square filled with snow as Duncan and Connor dueled, and Connor's jeers filled the wind and stung worse than the frosty air itself.

You use your sword like a man putting on a play, Duncan. Who are you trying to impress? Me? Get in close. Use your body; stay inside. Be sticky. Confuse me. Focus. Where are you looking? Stay balanced.

And when you fall on your arse, try not to look like such a bloody fool. No wonder you died in battle.

And Duncan took his daily beating with a sullen pride, and he did his best to hide his embarrassment. And he tried to hide his smile when Connor repeated what he said every morning, as he pulled Duncan up from the ground: "Good. You were better today. Tomorrow, you will beat me."

On this particular morning, Duncan and Connor strode away from their practice towards the inn, breathing in the crisp air, and Connor stopped for a while to look at the snow that covered the ground. "Beautiful," he said, as he leaned on the wall of the inn, and he gestured for Duncan to stop with him.

Duncan leaned against the wall and panted. "I've seen enough of it," he said, for he was soaked from having rolled in the snow several times this morning. Connor waved off his complaint. There was snow in his hair, and for a moment it cast the illusion of age that the Elder Highlander would never really show.

"The feeling in your stomach when one of us approaches," said Connor. "It sickens you, I know. Some people are hit especially hard by it in the early days. I am not a poet, Duncan. My mentor was, and I wish I had his words. But as we stand here this morning I want you to look at the snow and remember it. This snow you will never see again in just this way, you panting there and I here. This morning will be gone by this afternoon. But that which binds us all will endure, and it carries with it all that we survey. We feel this in a way that mortals cannot, God save them. Even though it makes you sick right now, I want you to be aware of your gift, of what a great gift Immortality is."

Duncan nodded. He did not understand.

"Come," said Connor. "It is St. Valentine's Day, and we

have a mass to attend, and I think we will meet a friend of mine afterwards."

"A friend? An Immortal?"

Connor laughed. "No, he's a sailor. They only think they're Immortal."

Three hours later, Duncan was listening to fish stories. He didn't care, though, because he had never seen so much food in his life.

"Lad," said the smiling Captain Carmichael, "you have quite a teacher here. Quite a teacher."

Duncan pulled away from a turkey leg to emphatically nod his agreement. As Connor had planned, they had met Carmichael after mass and had been invited to join the captain for his own Feast of St. Valentine's. The Feast was a glorious exercise in gluttony, and Duncan found himself stuffing his belly among mountains of meat, wine and cheese, in a large, torchlit room in a house that, although he remained unsure throughout the Feast, must surely be a brothel. (Or else the help were simply friendly in the extreme.) There were sailors everywhere: men from Carmichael's ship, as well as mates from other ships that happened to be in port that February. According to Connor, Carmichael was notorious for his feasts, which he funded out of his own pockets, God knew how. He probably starved for it the rest of the year. But what a gesture!

Carmichael was every bit the cliché he wanted to be—a grizzled sailor with stringy white hair and some of the most god-awful scars Duncan had ever seen on a living man. He was a drinker and a happy drunk, a man with a limp from something he wouldn't talk about and a crew who liked him very much. But for all his joviality, Duncan felt sure the man was a tough man to work under.

The three lay like Roman Senators on the rug in the torch-lit room, surrounded by platters of food in various states of consumption. Carmichael clapped his fingers together and one of the more voluptuous denizens of the house cantered by, and caressing his chest, bent down to pass a grape into his mouth from between her teeth. Carmichael patted the girl on the rump as she disappeared and turned his fat and happy visage back to Duncan. "Let me take you back, now, fifteen years," said the captain, and Carmichael looked at Connor to validate the time. Connor simply sat quietly and smiled.

Connor never ate much, but he seemed to enjoy attending feasts. Connor simply liked to watch mortals, Duncan had decided. Once, he asked his teacher, "why are you so fascinated by what the mortals do, when we can do the same, or most of it, and more?" Connor had replied, "Not true. Every bite, every lovemaking, is different when the sands are running out. When with every one you get older. That is what fascinates me."

"Fifteen years ago," Carmichael continued, "I was first mate on a vessel called the *Jugleor*. And Connor here—and not a day younger, I might add, but that no longer surprises me—we picked him up off Cape Horn, of all things. Said he'd work on our ship if we'd drop him off the next time we hit Scotland. Now, Captain Farrell was a crusty old son of a bitch, but we'd lost a few off the side and Connor looked fit enough, and so Farrell hired 'im on.

"Naturally I was surprised to find a fellow Scot out in the land of aborigines, so I tried to get to know the lad." Carmichael looked around for effect. "Never a more kept-to-' imself sailor did I see, but what strength! One night, the strangest thing happened after Connor had been with us for five weeks. We hit a nasty storm, the kind that had already swept away five good men. One of the sails broke its rigging and the beam went swinging across the deck. I remember looking across the deck and seeing that beam punch the captain himself in the gut, and send old Farrell flying into the water."

Connor sighed audibly. Duncan wanted to hear this.

"Now, mind you, this is freezing water. Winds to take your head off, and we all figured Captain Farrell for a dead man. But then silent Connor did the damnedest thing. Around his waist he ties a rope, which he then lashes to the rail, and into the water he goes like a dolphin! And here we all stand, agape, I content to stay at the wheel and try to keep the ship under control. I want you to picture the water, Duncan: deep furrows of black waves, lit up by lightning, and forty yards off, Captain Farrell, quickly succumbing but still waving, and then Connor, swimming towards him, diving under to try to cut the current of the waves. Presently he surfaces, moving like lightning, and grabs the captain and waves, and we can tell that he's signalling to us. Two or three sailors go to the rope and start to pull." Carmichael stopped to take a draught of wine, wiped his lips, and sighed.

"Go on," said Duncan.

"Well." Carmichael had obviously waited years to hold forth before so eager an audience. "It can't be done. Two big men weighing near five hundred pounds between them? The crewmen are pulling against the current and the wind, and it just isn't happening. So then I see Connor unlash himself and tie the rope around the captain, and disappear. We pulled the Captain in easily, then."

"So where was Connor?" Duncan asked.

"God, Carmichael, I can't take this," said Connor.

"You'll take it and love it, MacLeod; you don't fool me. So, Duncan—we don't know. Old Connor's lost at sea, brave soul. Even said a prayer myself for him, although by his bravery he'd kept me from becoming captain sooner than I'd planned.

"Next day, calm as far as the eye can see. We drop anchor and have a memorial service, the latest in a long line, and met with great sorrow by the crew. And I'm taking the honor o' the eulogy, because I spoke to Connor perhaps three times and he was a countryman, and no one else knew him. Oh, it was a fine speech. To hear me tell it, you'd think God himself had sent the angel Michael to us to serve as a sailor and then had taken him overboard and back home again after saving the captain."

Duncan grinned at his mentor, who simply drank his beer and listened, legs crossed calmly, propped on one arm.

"And as I wrap up this fine speech, the cabin boy hands me a bundle, the extra suit of clothes that Connor wore, which were wrapped with a stone, and we went to the side of the ship to commend it to the sea in place of his body.

"So I lean over the side, grim and mournful, and all the men gather around me. I toss the bundle, and it lands by the anchor chain and sinks. For a second we all just stand there, silent, watching the calm water, a beautiful day for such a sad occasion. Then slowly we turn to go back to our duties, our memorial concluded."

Connor said, "I think I'm going to go find some whiskey. . . ."

"Stay where you are, Connor. So, Duncan, we're dispersing as we will, and over our head comes flying a dark object, which lands on the deck, and then I see that it's the bundle of clothing that we'd just thrown in. Then, a splash. We all run back to the rail.

"I look down, and what do I see but a brown head of hair coming out of the water, all drenched in sea weed, and then a dirty pair of arms, climbing the anchor chain, until presently this man of moss climbs to the top of the chain, stops at the chain portal, grabs the rail, and climbs over. And collapses on the deck."

"It was . . ."

"Connor MacLeod. A miracle. He could have told us he'd been living in the belly of a whale and we would have believed him. Aye, there was something odd about this man for sure. After that, the Scot had great favor on the *Jugleor,* and I did my best to try to get to know him."

"Not easy to find a ship after a storm," said Connor. "But she was a good ship, and I missed her." Carmichael laughed heartily in agreement, sending wine spraying through the air. Now another of his plump little friends came up and dipped a finger covered in berry juice into Carmichael's mouth.

"I thought you said we must hide what we are," Duncan whispered to Connor.

"Sometimes situations call for different tactics."

Duncan laughed. "I don't believe a word of it," he said loudly—louder than he meant to in fact, for he found he was having trouble controlling his volume.

"Oh, believe this one," said Carmichael, as his friend scampered away. "It's true."

After that, they drank and ate even more. Carmichael told more stories—some of them more true than other—and they lay merciless waste to the feast before them, until, exhausted by gluttony, they all fell asleep on the floor of the brothel, and slept like babies, or mad sailors in a storm.

* * *

Duncan and Connor put off their return to Connor's ruins until after they had seen Captain Carmichael off. Carmichael was moving grain and whiskey, mainly, down to England, along with some large sacks of money for a few special clients, and he was anxious to ship out. The day was crisp and cold, and the three met for supper at mid-day and spent the afternoon on the harbor. Carmichael complimented Connor on the fine student he had chosen, and Duncan was pleased to hear his mentor praise Duncan generously, which he rarely did, except when he said every morning, "You were better today. Tomorrow you will beat me."

And occasionally, Connor's unseen friend became palpably Present, around a corner, always out of sight. And every time his presence was felt, Connor would look at Duncan, survey the area, and shrug.

Carmichael left at dusk. Connor and Duncan stood on the shore, waving as Carmichael's vessel *Crossover* moved off. That was the moment Duncan would never forget: the ship gently rocking in the harbor, the sun going down at Duncan's back as he and Connor watched Captain Carmichael go. Presently a figure waved from the deck, and Connor waved back. Duncan thought it was a trick of the light at dusk that caused the curious effect that he saw, like a cloud of dust over the deck and among the sails. Then there was a small flash, like a torch coming into view and out again, somewhere towards the back of the ship.

Connor said, "What in Hell . . ."

And then, Duncan saw the waving figure of Carmichael disappear in a blinding flash, as the air over the ship turned orange and flowing, and Carmichael reappeared for a brief moment on the distant, fiery deck as a black stick man, like a child would draw in the sand, the stick man still waving as the orange cloud tore through him and the ship and the sails.

The two Immortals stood completely still, in awe of the ship that now resembled a funeral barge. It had caught and become engulfed in the time it took Duncan to take a breath. Duncan found himself taking an involuntary step backward, as if in fear that the air around him might rupture and turn to flame as well.

And then Connor began to move, wading into the water furiously, calling, "Carmichael!"

"What do think you're going to do?" Duncan ran after him, grabbing his mentor by the shoulders. "Please, Connor, what are you going to do?"

"I . . ."

"What are you going to do?" Duncan spun Connor around and looked into his eyes. The fiery Immortal looked stunned, and then grasped his pupil's forearms.

"You're right," said Connor, who looked back at the ship. The fire was going out now, as quickly as it had caught. All that remained was a black hulk, with goods and grain flowing out its side like ship's blood. There was nothing of a deck, nothing to recognize. Nothing to save. "What am I going to do?"

The awkwardness was palpable. There they stood, knee deep in water, Connor's friend had just been utterly obliterated and they could do nothing but stand there, feeling the cold as the sun went down behind them, and presently Connor nudged Duncan and the two waded back. Connor mumbled, "I wasn't thinking, I'm sorry, the water's very cold, I shouldn't have— *What in Hell just happened?*" he screamed, and turned back towards the smoldering hulk, and fell to his knees. "Someone . . . someone . . ."

Duncan knelt down beside him. He felt woefully inadequate trying to be useful to his mentor; the role did not suit him. He had no idea what to say. "Connor, I . . ."

"No, Duncan," said Connor, who reached up his hand and patted Duncan on the shoulder. "There is nothing to be said. It happens. If Carmichael were an Immortal I could swim out there right now, pull his remains out of the wreck. Give him time, and he would rise. In time. Days. Hours, perhaps, if he were strong. And he would sail."

Duncan nodded, and took Connor's extended hand and helped the teacher off of his knees. There were new sounds, now, the anguished cries of a few pitiful mortals who happened to be on the harbor at dusk. The sound of mortal anguish rose, but Connor began to speak and kept his voice low.

"Time is something the mortals do not have, Duncan,"

Connor whispered, his voice hoarse and mournful. The Immortal rose and looked at him, looked deep in Duncan's eyes as he always did when he had something serious to say. "Remember this. Seldom will you see it so clearly, seldom will it be so dramatically illustrated. Make no mistake. In the end, they will all be snuffed out. All of them. That is their nature."

Something in the calm of the Elder Highlander's voice gave Duncan the bravery to ask a harsh question. "But then," he asked, "why do we mourn? Why do you care?"

"I don't know, Duncan," said Connor. "I honestly don't. But it hurts every time."

The sound of a cracking whip split the air and a coach came barreling down the beach. Duncan felt a presence on approach. As the coach passed them he looked up and saw the person whipping the reins, her face barely revealed by the hood she wore. It was the white-haired waif he'd met at the Quarry House. "That was the albino. Nerissa."

Nerissa stopped her coach about three hundred feet from the two Immortals, not a full length from the water's edge. Connor and Duncan turned to watch her, and Nerissa held up her hand toward the water. A glint of light flashed, probably from a hand-held looking glass, and presently Duncan spotted a small answering flash on the water.

Duncan remained perfectly still. He whispered, "Beware of the female Immortals." Connor had been watching all of this. He nudged Duncan, and the two began to walk towards Nerissa's coach.

They peered more closely at the dark sea and saw a small boat, with a man rowing. Nerissa's horses were nervous, and she scolded them repeatedly to calm down. The woman looked out at the rowboat, and now seemed to notice Duncan and Connor for the first time.

The rowboat reached the shore and its passenger, dressed in a black outfit that was soaked but seemed also to be smoldering, jumped out and was dragging the boat. As he did so Duncan's gut curdled, and he knew this wading sailor had to be the hitherto unseen Immortal. When the smoldering man had made it all the way onto the sand and could drag the boat no further he motioned to Nerissa, and now he began to throw something, a large, black parcel, into the coach. This was followed by three more such packages, and then he ran around to the front of the coach and began to climb in.

"Nerissa . . ." Duncan held up a hand as they drew near.

The angelic eyes looked at him from beneath the hood, and there was no friendliness in them. "Duncan."

"Business?" asked Connor, and Duncan could tell his teacher was about to explode.

"Pleasure."

"Pleasure." Nerissa looked over her shoulder to see if her partner had made it into the coach.

Connor was drawing his sword. "You!"

The black-suited man had a leg up on the boards and now turned his head and shoulder, hanging on. "Yes?"

"I challenge you! You must answer my challenge!"

The man in black took off his cap and a long mane of red hair flowed out, cascading over his shoulders, as he stepped down for a moment. "What on earth for?"

Connor said, slowly, still in his challenging stance, "You have killed one who was important to me. I call on your honor to accept my challenge!"

"I am not armed."

"Arm yourself."

The strange man's eyes narrowed. "Khordas answers to no challenge from those who should bow to him. Go away, little man. We have had a fine evening, and we must be gone."

"Wrong answer," said Connor, evenly. He was moving forward now, and Duncan began to wonder if he was about to see his mentor behead a man in cold blood. Could he? But "Khordas" was climbing on the coach again and signaled for Nerissa to go. The albino cracked the reins and the coach began to move.

"Khordas!"

"Connor MacLeod!" came Nerissa's voice, "Khordas is not armed. But I am." Nerissa turned a bit in her seat and Duncan saw the Italian pistol in her hand, hammer drawn back.

The man shook his head, the hooves pounded in the mud, punctuating his words. "Not today, MacLeod!"

"But—"

"I always make it a point to light a fire on Nerissa's birthday. So sorry if one of your mortals got in the way." And with that, the coach sped up, and Duncan heard Connor cry, "No!" and now the teacher was running for the horses, grabbing onto the reins, dragging the leather straps back. The horses pitched and reared as Connor managed to get a leg up onto the sideboard.

"You . . . will . . . *answer* . . . to *me!*"

"Nerissa," said Khordas, "get rid of him."

Duncan saw the albino point her gun down at Connor. A shot split the night, celebrated by a puff of smoke and the pungent smell of sulfur. Connor sucked in air and fell back, sprawling, and Nerissa cracked the reins again. And Duncan ran to his teacher's side as the horses picked up speed.

Connor still grasped his katana and struggled to get up, but he was dying, for now, and no amount of struggling would stop it. Within seconds, he was dead.

And by that time, the coach was gone.

Chapter 2

———

February, 1632

There is a mountain in the Highlands called Beinn Bahn. At its height it rises three thousand feet above the neighboring Inner Sound, saluting the Isle of Skye which lies on the Sound's far side. In February of 1632, when Duncan had been with Connor nearly seven years, it was here, on Beinn Bahn, that Duncan MacLeod the Highlander finally stopped losing.

Connor had been running Duncan ragged on the mountain for nearly a week. They had come all this way to play what amounted to a war game. The Elder Highlander could disappear for days while Duncan searched for him, trying to track him on the mountain as best he could. It would be years, indeed, before Duncan would become a master tracker; now he searched more by guess and by God, looking for broken branches, prints in the sand—all of which he felt sure Connor left deliberately just to keep the trail fresh. And then he would catch Connor's presence, and suddenly Connor would be on him, closing in like a wolf, descending sword-bared from the trees or from behind a pile of rocks. But each time, Duncan was more ready.

Stay relaxed. Let the enemy come to you. Surprised? Out of control? Off balance? Rebuild yourself before you move again. Duncan heard the words go through his head and suddenly, on one day he never could recall exactly, when Connor's presence loomed and his mentor came running through the woods, something fell into place.

Duncan saw Connor's head come over a small mound of brush and he did what he had never done before. No gasping, no shocked raising of his sword in a panicked sweep. Connor was half-way over the top of the hill and coming fast and Duncan took his surprise and banished it from his mind. *Here we are. Around me, there is wind in the grass, there are tiny animals I cannot see at my feet. My ancestors walked here on their way to war, and fought off the daring Romans who tried to take this land. I am at home here, in these Scottish hills, and there is a century-old man with a sword coming at my head. I am surprised by nothing. Do your best, old man.*

Duncan stood still with his sword unsheathed and waited. Connor growled and came at him, swinging his katana at Duncan's neck. Duncan breathed again and could actually feel the air moving past his limbs, his feet moving in complementary union, as his sword came up, an extension of his body, to meet Connor. Connor was ready for this, allowed Duncan to swat his blade away, and kept coming, and Connor's face came close enough to kiss and the teacher hit him hard in the ribs with his elbow. Connor liked to play close. Duncan staggered a bit and saw Connor spin, his boot a blur as it came up with his pivot.

Duncan felt the boot hit his chest and he was thrown back, off balance, and he allowed himself to breathe and in an instant rebuilt himself, back together. Connor came at him again, bringing his sword down at an angle across Duncan's torso. Duncan matched his blow, watching the sparks that flew from the metal as the blades clashed, claymore against katana. Duncan dropped slightly and moved in, striking like an animal, hitting Connor with his shoulder, lashing out and landing his palm in Connor's face, moving back quickly. For once Connor fell back, too.

The teacher was bleeding from his mouth and with one hand he reached up to wipe away the blood. Connor wore an eerie grin, his breath slicing through the air, and suddenly he pounced again. Duncan let fly his sword and slashed at Connor's blade, then brought it down and around and back, moving in, and he felt a slight resistance that he knew from battle to be the soft resistance of flesh against metal. Quickly he brought the claymore back, almost guilty for having connected.

Connor seemed both angered and pleased, and he flew at Duncan, glancing Duncan's sword away and slamming head to head. Duncan found himself falling, ground coming up to meet him, and as Duncan's back struck the forest floor he curled a bit and brought his feet up to kick Connor in the face, jumping to his feet again as he did so. Connor staggered back and Duncan saw the next move before it even happened. Connor's left fool hit an exposed root and the Immortal staggered again, and Duncan tore at him, aiming for his sword hand. Down and up again, a lightning arc, and Connor's sword left his hand and flipped through the trees.

Connor looked around and found his balance, but not before Duncan brought the claymore down and back to Connor's throat.

"You and me, Connor. The Final Gathering. Think of it, teacher," urged Duncan, "would you take my head?"

"Heh," came the staccato, breathless laugh of Connor MacLeod. "There can be only one."

Duncan saw Connor jerk backwards, dropping, going for the kick. Duncan caught Connor's boot with his left hand and Connor went down.

"Let's hope it doesn't come to that. Teacher," said Duncan.

Connor lay on the ground and Duncan realized the Immortal was laughing, his bloody mouth in a delighted snarl. Duncan sheathed his sword and grabbed Connor's offered hand, and helped him up. When he rose, Connor stepped back and gave a foreign bow.

Duncan breathed, and he felt something like the close of

an era, a goal achieved and leaving him, and with it went his energy. He had been waiting to best Connor for years. And now, rather than elation, he felt only exhaustion, and a hint of fear.

"Very good," said Connor. "Today you have beaten me. I am very proud."

Fear of what?

"Let's go. It's time to camp. We'll head into Applecross tomorrow for provisions before turning south, homeward." Connor looked him up and down the way he'd appraise a mule and said, "You need rest." Then Connor added, "Of course, it's up to you whether or not you come back to the ruins."

Duncan wiped the sweat from his eyes and leaned against a tree, hands on his knees. When he absorbed what Connor had just said he shot his teacher a bewildered glance. "And what does *that* mean?"

"It's up to you, Duncan. There is more to learn than I can teach you."

Duncan nodded, and folded his arms, and stared at his boots and the grass. He looked at Connor. He wasn't sure. But somehow, he felt strong now, stronger than he had ever felt. Connor came over and took him by the shoulder and they began to walk through the trees. And that was the first time Duncan noticed something that somehow had escaped him: he was taller than Connor, by at least a head.

They were camping on a hill and Duncan looked toward the sea and the valley to the south and saw a strange light. "Connor, what is down below?"

Connor was lying back and staring at the stars, humming a tune. He turned his head idly. "Should be Applecross."

"It looks like it's on fire."

Connor frowned at Duncan and sat up, rose and walked over to join Duncan at the summit of the hill. Far below, in the dark valley, a sheet of orange lay unfurled across what looked to be a quarter mile of land. "It is," said Connor. "We'll be there in the morning."

*   *   *

Connor had been right. By the time they reached Applecross, it was dead, a town's carcass crawling with confused, human maggots.

Through the crowds the Immortals moved, as always, detached, slicing through the throngs of people like ships at sea. Duncan and Connor looked around them at the madness of the mortals as the two slid past grubby, stunned people pushing their way down the streets of Applecross. Sometimes it was as if the mortals did not see them: the Immortals were so different that if they acted correctly they did not blend in but blended right out, observant and invisible. Connor said that Ramirez said that the mortals looked for magic in the wrong places, so that they would not risk seeing it when it was present, and this was just as well. The Immortals were fearful of attention, and they were lucky that the mortals paid so little of it.

Here and there, tendrils of dark smoke rose from the charred remains of the buildings as Connor and Duncan moved on. The villagers were ghosts. Duncan passed a man who stood in what may have been a house and poked at bits of charred wood with a rake, as if he expected the wood to respond. The man looked up as Duncan passed and looked right through him.

Like most Scottish towns of medieval origin, Applecross was arranged along a central street, the buildings wooden and rectangular and stacked along the main street like vertebrae. To Connor and Duncan, who reached Applecross that morning after rising early, the spine looked to have been crushed.

"It looks like we won't find breakfast here," said Connor, looking around.

"Aye," said Duncan. He looked at a tavern as they passed it, simply a black skeleton, wisping curls of smoke rising. Connor pointed out certain darker patches on the wood, this was drying wine. Broken glass, everywhere. A tavern keeper, standing in the middle, staring into space.

"Oh," said Connor, "look at the church." At the end of the main street lay what must have been an attractive little chapel indeed. The smoking hulk loomed before the two Immortals and Duncan surveyed the wreck as they drew closer.

Duncan thought it strangely comic, that this church had burnt down, but the facade, and thus the arched doorway, still stood. The door, in fact, lay open. As the Highlander walked along towards the doorway he saw a man within the ruin, framed by the doorway. The figure stood where the congregation would have sat before at mass, the pews reduced to scattered wood and ashes. The man was strongly built, with white hair and a beard, and the robes of his Order draped over him like a second skin. He was crouched low, his hands clasped together, not in prayer but in concentration.

The priest looked up when he heard Duncan's feet crunch into the ashes and broken wood. There was no vacant stare here, although the man looked weary, to say the least. The priest rose, sweeping his hands together to rid himself of excess ash, then wiped his hands on his robe.

"Father," said Duncan.

"I'm afraid we have nothing, my son," said the priest. "Please be patient. I have sent an apprentice for aid from the neighboring villages."

"No need for aid," said Connor. "We were on Beinn Bhan and saw the fire. I am Connor MacLeod of the Clan MacLeod and this is my kinsman, Duncan."

The priest nodded politely. "Father Dumphries." Then he shook his head. "And I'm sorry that this is not the best time to visit Applecross. Good Lord. Good Lord."

The two Immortals stepped into the main area of the ruins. "What happened?" Connor took off his hat and looked at Duncan, telling him to do the same. Duncan did so, although it seemed odd.

Father Dumphries shook his head. "It started here."

Duncan frowned. "You saw it?"

Dumphries smiled briefly. "I saw it from the tavern. Well, outside the tavern."

"No storm last night," said Connor.

"No," said Dumphries, "and believe me, I'm not in the habit of leaving untended fires. No, no. Besides, I couldn't have—even lightning couldn't . . ."

"What?" asked Connor.

"I've never seen anything like it. I'd had a pint or two with some wayward brethren who needed a jawing, eh? So, when I was leaving, I was walking down the street, and I looked up, and the steeple of the church was clear against the moon, which was huge, as it will be when it's behind an object."

Connor smiled politely. Franciscans were mainly a teaching order, and it was a hard habit to break.

"And this is the strange part—there appeared something like a cloud, or a swarm of something . . ."

Duncan saw Connor react, if only slightly. Their eyes met briefly and Connor's spoke angry volumes. They really didn't need to hear the rest.

". . . and the cloud just erupted," Father Dumphries shook his head.

"Erupted?"

"I cannot say it better. One instant there was the chapel and the steeple, next, a wall of flame, a burst of orange, and wood flying down the street as if some great force had been unleashed."

Connor turned around where he stood and looked out the odd standing door and down the main street. The maggots still crawled back and forth across and along the street, poking at embers and crying to the skies. "And the fire spread by itself, all the way down."

The priest shook his head, violently, his fists clenched, as if he were ashamed of his anger. "No. This was not natural by any means."

Duncan squeezed his hat in his hands. "What do you mean?"

"I swear to you I saw a line of fire run like a finger of flames, a little growing wall, that someone laid from building to building, all the way down the street. And I ran for the church, to rescue the host." The priest looked at them, reliving the moment that Duncan and MacLeod had looked down on the night before. They had known it was bad, but it just didn't register from a distance. Duncan wondered if God might have a similar problem. From a distance, vision fooled you. *Stay inside.* "I didn't make it," said the priest. "That is my failure."

Connor said, "Father, I have something very serious to ask you."

"Yes, my son."

"Any new additions to the church collection? Valuable gifts?"

The priest nodded, thinking. "We were visited by the Bishop a month ago, and he presented us a gift of a coffer that he said belonged to Malcolm Canmore's Queen Margaret when she set about reforming the church in Scotland. Five hundred years old. A magnificent piece of work, inlaid with gold and jewels, and inside, and encased in amber, a piece of the true cross itself. Magnificent, as I said. A joy to behold." Dumphries shook his head. "Curse my coward's blood that I did not run in to save that, either."

Connor threw a glance at Duncan. "Have you seen it since?"

"No. No sign of it, my son. Buried in wood and ash, melted, stolen by a wrathful God, I know not."

Connor said, "Could you show me the place where it would be?"

The priest seemed confused as to the stranger's curiosity, but he had little else to do but show him. They walked to a separate pile of wood, near where the altar would have been, and the father pointed. "Here."

Connor knelt down, lifting a few boards. Nothing. He looked at Duncan and Duncan confirmed what he was sure Connor was thinking. No fire would destroy such a piece. Connor sighed and stood, then looked down with surprise as his foot knocked against a hollow block of wood, or at least so it appeared. "Hullo."

Connor snatched the block and lifted it, and saw that it was not a block but a wooden box the size of his hand. "Ever seen this before, Father?"

"No."

"Hm." Connor rubbed the top of the box with his thumb and realized that there was metal there, covered in soot, like the rest of it. He rubbed it away and read:

Gift of he who knows,
Breathes it—
Where no man goes,
Am I at home:

Their loss, my boon.
Their fear, my embrace.
In the heart of the flame,
The element of fire.

Father Dumphries said, "I don't understand."

The Elder Highlander raised an eyebrow and held the box before him and moved his thumbs to the lid. Duncan and the father leaned in to have a look, and both were silent, not even breathing when he opened it.

When the box lid swung open, both drew back in surprise. There, in a bed of red velvet, slithering to and fro, and then stopping to look up at them, was a salamander.

"Khordas," said Connor.

Chapter 3

Three months later

"This is as far as we can go with our mounts," said Connor, grimly. From town to town along the coast they had searched. Connor had said he could go it alone, as Duncan's training with him had more or less run its course, but Duncan had stayed on for the extra months. What else was there?

Along the way Connor and Duncan met many mortals, life and limb ravaged by the passing Salamander and his white-haired wife, a burnt house here, a ship in the harbor there. Khordas was acting carefully, Connor said. "His fires are small; he loots and burns. That's to keep satiated. Remember what he said to me? The big fires, he saves for Nerissa's birthday."

In Plockton, south along the coast from Applecross, an innkeeper had seen the two, but the next two towns delivered no leads, and Connor surmised they had either taken to water or gone deep inland—and the former seemed more likely, as Khordas liked water so much. A tutor in Gleneig, on the banks of the Sound of Sleat, had seen them, and had lost a student and a year's tuition to the Salamander's fire there.

"Here's the flash point," said Connor. "I don't know what he uses, but he douses the place in a cloud of incendiary matter."

"Gunpowder?"

"Maybe. If the conditions are right, it could be anything. Sawdust. Soap, even. And then a fuse and something to ignite and flash, then . . ." Connor shrugged, and he turned something over with his foot that looked like a human finger.

"Sometimes I think he knows we're looking for him," said Connor, standing in what had been a meeting house. "Sometimes I think he likes it."

"This doesn't sound like the way the Game is played?" asked Duncan. "Pick an Immortal and hunt him?"

"No," said Connor. "No, this is special."

And then something clicked when Duncan and Connor were in the town of Shonah, having a meal that barely fed them. Connor had not drawn funds for some time, and their bellies were beginning to show it. He was sitting at their table and studying the salamander box when a thought seemed to strike him. "Duncan?"

"Hm?"

"Where does the salamander like to be?" asked Connor, in a way that he might ask when the hunting season began.

"Khordas, or the lizard?"

"Amphibian. But think of both at once."

Duncan called for another loaf of bread and hoped he had the coin to pay for it. "Fire and water?"

"Right. Places men fear."

Duncan nodded. "Or where they prefer not to exist."

"Right," mused Connor. He shook his head. "We've been looking in the wrong place. We won't catch him like this."

"What do you mean?"

"The trail's gone cold. He could be hitting the other side of Scotland now. But he may not even be sticking to the coasts."

"A loch, then?"

"Perhaps." Connor reached into the pouch on the bench beside him and retrieved a map, and unfurled it over his empty plate. He swept his hand along the country. "But more than that, if you think of this whole land, what is the least passable terrain around?"

Duncan stared at Connor. "You have me there."

"All the elements, water and earth and impassability."

Impassable terrain, thought Duncan. Then, "Oh."

"Oh. Exactly. We're running along the wheel when we should be sliding down the spoke." Connor ran his finger around the country to illustrate, then brought it down in the direction of the center. His fingertip came down to a name, illustrated by a rendering of mud and trees, the home of a thousand murky creatures. "Rannoch Moor," said Connor. "And if I'm wrong you can tutor me."

There would be no negotiating Rannoch Moor on horseback. It could be done, but one had to know the territory. The moor swept over twenty miles of bog. Mud and muck and low trees made it nearly impassable with horses, and so Connor and Duncan dismounted at the southwestern shore of Loch Rannoch and proceeded on foot.

It was hard going, the home of a salamander if anything at all. With every step Duncan felt his boot slide into the muck, a dull sucking sound gasping out he retrieved it and stepped again, a rotten-root stench belching from the ground as he did so. Connor suffered the same but set the pace, and they moved quickly toward the center. After two hours they must have gone nine miles, an easy clip on dry land, exhausting in this drudge.

Connor stopped in a clearing and looked around, and Duncan took the opportunity to lean against a tree. A bit of moss swiped against his shoulder and he swatted it away. The sun was going down.

"Here," said Connor, as he knelt to the ground. "Footprints. Old ones."

"Those could be anybody's."

Connor smiled. "Yes they could. But I feel good about it just the same."

"Congratulations."

"So what are we looking for?" asked Connor, in the way

that he insisted on asking any question to which he already had an answer prepared.

"I was hoping you'd tell me," said Duncan, who was getting irritated. "Connor, it's getting late. . . ."

"We're looking for a camp, of course. The sun is going down. And if there is not one already, there will be a fire soon."

An hour later, Connor shimmied to the top of a tree and breathed deeply. After a moment he exhaled and said, "Aye. He's burning something. The slightest tinge of smoke in the air." Connor dropped down into the mud and indicated southeast, in the direction of the wind. "That way."

The moonlight filtered through the trees to give the moor an eerie glow, and Duncan followed Connor, who now seemed like a rodent hunting a snack, hunched low to the ground and snarling. After half an hour the ground sloped downwards a bit, and Connor stopped. "No presence yet, Duncan, but I think we're close."

Duncan nodded. As soon as they could sense Khordas, Khordas would be able to sense them. It was the Game's way of keeping things fair.

Over the slope and through a line of trees, and then Connor pointed at something. "Look."

"What?"

"In that clearing."

"What? The mound?" Up ahead was a mound of earth, like a burial mound but larger. How large, he could not tell in the light.

"Aye. There's smoke coming out of it," said Connor. It was true. What they were seeing was not a mound but a large hut, with a billow of smoke that came from what amounted to a chimney hole. As the two crept closer Duncan saw that the mound was larger than he had thought: the mud walls were at least twelve feet high, like an old *broch* that someone might use as a hunting station. They were strengthened on the outside by a layer of dried moss, and now bits of brown moss could be seen lifting slightly in the breeze.

"How big?" Connor whispered.

"I'd say a good forty feet in diameter. This took work," Duncan answered.

And then, as they crept closer to the mud house, the presence hit them.

"This feels . . . different."

"That's because there's two of them," whispered Connor. Slowly they drew their swords and advanced.

"Easy," said Connor. "Easy."

Duncan nodded and breathed and several things happened at once. He was watching Connor and the mud *broch* when both of them stepped an inch too far. Suddenly Duncan's feet were plunging through the surface, and the mud became thin and watery, and he saw Connor drop to his chest in mud as Duncan did the same.

Duncan reached out to grab for some sort of edge and then cursed himself, for somehow he was no longer holding his sword. The claymore must be at his feet, sunk into the bog. Duncan heard a noise overhead, and he looked up. At the top of a tree on a constructed platform stood a nimble figure with a shock of white hair. The creature was laughing. *Nerissa.*

Duncan's feet were just barely touching the bottom of the watery moat and he was scrambling for some sort of handhold at the edge when he saw something flare in Nerissa's hands. A brilliant light extended and burnt before her. As she drew it back he could tell by the movement of his arms that it was an arrow with a phosphorous tip.

Through the night, leaving a streak of brilliant orange light, came the arrowhead, and it found its mark in Duncan's side. He gasped once, falling back in the muddy water. The surface bubbled and belched when it met the burning shaft. Duncan's flesh was searing, boiling, and he gritted his teeth in rage and pain.

Connor had found the inside lip of the moat and was using a dagger to pull himself out. He rolled over onto the mud next to the wall of the *broch*. Duncan began to move toward Connor, and Connor was extending a hand to help him out, when something moved. Next to Connor's hand, at the edge of the moat, was a lump, a block of mud near his face. Duncan heard air sucking into someone's mouth as the lump opened its eyes. The head that was just barely above water laughed, and said, "Out of your element, MacLeods."

Connor was still pulling Duncan toward the lip when something kicked Duncan in the stomach, jarring the wound in his side. Duncan growled to realize that the damn thing was *still burning*.

"I've got this one, Nerissa," said Khordas, as the Salamander rose from the water and Duncan saw he was holding a short sword, and suddenly the sword was at his throat and Khordas' other hand went under the water. "Teach Connor MacLeod a lesson," Khordas shouted up. And then Duncan felt Khordas reach for his wound and grab hold of the arrow.

"Amazing, isn't it, young MacLeod, what a wonderful gift Immortality is. The wound you receive repairs itself shortly, gone. But what a delightful pain if you have something lodged in your gut while the wound rebuilds around the foreign body. You can feel it burn, over and over, and the pain never stops because you *just keep rebuilding*. Don't you?" Khordas jerked the arrow a bit. "*Don't you!*" Now Khordas leaned in, still pulling at Duncan's wound, and whispered in his ear. "Fool. Follow *me*? You are just an Immortal, MacLeod. Just a long-lived mortal."

"As . . . are . . . you."

"No. I am a god. And you have angered me, little MacLeod."

Duncan was no longer listening. He was watching Connor, who had taught him, *Feel no pain, take it in and expel it, breathe it out*. But the pain was rebuilding, over and over again, and now he looked at Connor and saw an arrow in flight towards the teacher's chest. Duncan's eyes were playing tricks, though, he was losing consciousness, he supposed, going into shock, and now he felt the handle of his sword at his toe, down in the muddy moat. He slipped the toe of his boot into, through, the rounded pommel. *Gloat, Khordas. Go on and give me time. . . .*

Nearby, Connor saw Nerissa's next arrow fly and he moved aside as the flaming tip scraped past him and struck the side of the *broch*. The wall of brown moss went up in flame, and suddenly the moor was lit brighter than day. Connor was reaching into his pocket and drawing a dagger, and he threw it, and Duncan heard a woman shriek, then the thump of a body hitting the mud.

So did Khordas. "Nerissa!"

Duncan was bringing up his claymore, his foot moving closer and closer to his stretching fingers. He felt the metal brush his fingers and the Highlander took the sword by the handle, and as Khordas shouted Duncan kicked the Immortal back. Khordas was still holding fast to the arrow that stuck in Duncan's side and as the red god moved backwards with the kick the arrowhead tore out of Duncan's body. The Highlander gritted his teeth and backed to the outer lip of the moat, drew his own dagger, reached up and scrambled out. Duncan lay on the ground for a second, feeling the mud in his wound being pushed out, and then he saw Nerissa standing over him.

Nerissa drew a rapier and was bringing it down at Duncan's neck but he rolled back against the tree from which she had fallen. Duncan found his feet and crouched, and saw the woman advancing. Connor's dagger was still sticking out of her shoulder, and this she jerked out and tossed aside as she came forward. "Lovely young man. Why have you been hunting us?" she asked.

"Because they wish to kill us," came the voice of Khordas, and Duncan looked over and saw Connor and Khordas against a wall of orange flame.

"It is not our place to kill the mortals," said Connor.

"Oh? And how would you know?"

"There are Rules."

"Not about that, Connor. You know better than that. Duncan, is that what your mentor has taught you? Nonsense! We kill mortals because they get in our way and because it is easy. They don't understand a thing. I've heard worse excuses."

Now Duncan saw Nerissa draw back her blade. "I've been waiting for this," he said.

"Such a beautiful Immortal," she said. "If things had been different," and now she lunged, "we could have been friends."

Duncan moved aside and brought his claymore down against the rapier, then back up. She met his blade again. Over his shoulder, he saw Connor and Khordas. Sparks flew, and Khordas' face was covered in blood.

Nerissa was the first female Immortal Duncan had ever seen, he told himself again, and now he was supposed to kill her. That was what Connor had trained him to do. *(When they come, kill them. We're not here to make friends.)*

(But you're my friend.)

(Count yourself lucky.)

Nerissa came at him again and Duncan knocked her blade aside, dropped and kicked her, and his boot made a sharp sound against Nerissa's breastbone and she fell back. Then Duncan thought of Connor, of the wolf in the woods, and pounced, moving in, overtaking her. Nerissa raised her sword but he was too close and he slammed his shoulder into her face and saw blood fly from her nose and stain her white hair.

And then Duncan stopped, for just a moment. *What in Hell am I doing?* He heard Connor snarling, Khordas and the teacher going at one another, dancing as if it were what they were made for, and here Duncan was trying to kill a woman with white hair and a lovely smile with whom he had spent a fine day drinking.

Before she destroyed Carmichael, Connor's friend. Before she shot me with a burning arrow. Duncan blinked as the rapier sliced through his tunic and into the flesh of his stomach. *Back to reality. What are you doing? You're not paying attention!* Duncan stepped back, feeling the blood flow over his abdomen, and he tried to ignore this new pain as he lunged at Nerissa with the claymore, hacking at her.

You're right handed, and your left side is weak, as if sometimes you don't see it. If I go there I have a tiny point in time when you lose me. Connor's advice, given on some calm afternoon. *And if you attack a strong box, you have to keep hitting the corners. Find the weak corner. Hit it again. And yet again.*

In to the left, hack, Nerissa turned and blocked and Duncan drew back. Moving in again, head-butt, in to the left, hack, and now she was a proper partner, back again, in to the left, hack, this time drawing blood from the left shoulder, don't slow down, back. Now Duncan kicked high and saw his boot connect with her face and saw the head snap back, and he brought his claymore hard at her wrist. Nerissa was better controlled than to lose the rapier just then, and Duncan moved in, and when she turned to meet him coming for her left side he drew back and brought his sword down and up and back from her right side, and he saw reflected in her eyes the light from the flaming wall as the claymore sliced through her neck and her head came ripping from her shoulders.

And then Duncan breathed.

Here it comes.

Nerissa's body crumpled to the mud and Duncan felt a wind pick up. This had happened before. But it never came easily.

Thoughts racing through his mind, Immortal heart pounding and guiding, his blood chanting a litany . . .

Now, the pain comes, now, crash to the earth as the wind rises, feel the shock of your knees against the earth . . .

This is your destiny, this is our gift. . . .

Now! Feel it, raise your sword above your head and catch it, feel the crackle in the air, the sparks that fly as the air heats and explodes around you. . . .

The gift must be hidden, but do not be ashamed; you are Immortal.

It is Nerissa who lies before you, remember her name, it is she who has passed his part of the gift to you, take it!

Somewhere in the world and not ten feet away Khordas was turning, Khordas was shrieking in horror, and Connor was sending him into the wall of flame. Pockets of gunpowder and fuses caught and ignited and an Immortal was screaming, raging, burning, and Duncan was lost in the moment.

Feel the pain and pleasure, do not fight, for this is what you are. . . .

Feel your mouth open and cry out in pain, feel the dust in the wind swirl around you and rub your skin raw, feel the lightning. . . .

The lightning will speak to you as it burns through you, remember the name of the presence you have consumed, for she is part of you now, and you will go on with her. . . .

Feel your shirt catch fire and smoke, to be snuffed by the ravaging wind, feel the blood pound, this is the gift!

Arcs of lightning lit through Duncan's hands, fusing his fingers to the hilt of his sword. A long, blue arc danced from the pommel of his claymore and into his eyes, electricity pushing through, and his vision was filled with sights Immortal. He saw the lightning, attaching him to the dead woman, attaching the dead woman to the mud in which she lay, saw the mud in the ground itself heat and expand, and an outward sheet of hardened mud exploded from the surface around him on either side, shards of hot clay slicing past him and into him. Duncan leaned back his head and felt the saliva in his mouth spark with lightning and screamed.

This is the gift, receive it!
This . . .
For in the end, Duncan MacLeod,
. . . is . . .
there can be only one!
. . . the Quickening!

Silence. Duncan fell backwards and lay still on the hot ground, not wanting to move. And he looked sideways, and saw Nerissa's head, floating in the water, staring open-eyed at him. On the other side of the tiny moat stood Connor with his katana before him, and something that did not look like Khordas was shrieking, for he was on fire. The whole of the man was aflame, flesh cracking and splitting, and Khordas dropped his sword and looked at Nerissa and called out her name, diving for her.

The flaming man hit the mud and the whole moat erupted in steam, and Duncan brought himself up to his elbows and stared. Khordas, moving slowly in the mud, roaring in pain, holding the dead creature to him. Steam bubbling as the mud around Khordas belched and hissed, hardening like a husk. Khordas was still moving as he turned over, mourning wails pouring from his encased mouth, and sank.

The *broch* that the Salamander built of mud and moss burned for several minutes before there was nothing left to burn on the walls and the mound began to smolder. Connor motioned to Duncan to follow him and they crept around the mud house until they found its entrance, large enough to duck through without difficulty. Inside, a small fire burned, and lit the clay walls. Duncan steadied himself against the doorway for a moment, still woozy from the Quickening. God, god, what a sensation. You could get drunk on it. It could warp you, send you after any head you could find, just to get another. Most of the evil ones were victims of that compulsion, and some suggested this was simply all in the Game. Duncan straightened himself up and pretended there was no chance of that happening to him.

As Duncan entered the *broch* he was struck immediately by the stench. "God, what is that?"

"Brimstone," said Connor. The room inside was larger than Duncan had expected, and deeper, for he stepped down at least a foot when he went in. In one corner was a trench of liquid like the moat outside, a bath of sorts. And when he turned his head Duncan was struck by the sparkle of jewels that littered the room, embedded in the walls and stacked throughout. "What an odd creature."

"Not a creature," said Connor. "An Immortal, like you and I." The teacher was standing at what appeared to be a small shrine. A number of small figurines, fashioned from earth and straw, stood on a shelf of earth. "Look at this."

Connor pointed at one. "I'd call this a priest of sorts. Note the raised arms, the scratchings before him, a rudimentary sculpture of a fire."

"Not a very good sculptor," said Duncan, regarding the stick-like figures.

"A face is not important for this man. He is his office." Connor tilted his head. "Look at those." Duncan's eyes traveled along the shelf to see other figures, and each one had more defined clothing, the folds in the robes more real, the bits of straw more like highlights than a necessary bond.

"What was Khordas?"

There was a small puddle before one of the priests, a man coming out of the puddle, sculpted flames upon him. Connor whispered, as if he were in a holy place. "Scotland is a very old country. The stock you and I come from is an amalgam of a great many peoples. Some of the old cultures, the Picts, the old Scots, changed very much even before the Romans came in from the south, or the Vikings from the north. We do not know enough," he said. "Fire and water are powerful tools."

"Like tools of gods."

"Like gods themselves," said Connor. "Anything can be a god. I don't want to make any haphazard guesses, but Khordas may have played a part in the service of his religion. Perhaps he was chosen by the priests to represent the god of fire and water, of destruction. Look at the figure of the man coming from the water."

Duncan looked closely. God, what work. "He has jewels in his eyes."

"Right. Probably given in offering. Maybe it wasn't jewels, anything valuable would have sufficed, I imagine. There's an image of a girl, there, too. Probably an offering also, a fair girl given as a slave. Our Khordas was a very important man."

Duncan's eyes refocused on the wall behind the figurines. There was an inlaid sculpture in the wall, bits of straw everywhere to highlight the muscles of a creature that stretched across the length of the shelf. "The salamander."

"Yes. A very powerful image. They say the creature embraces fire, and is rarely seen."

"Goes where no man goes."

"Right."

Duncan looked around and found an earthen chair, and sat upon it. He rubbed his chin. The pain in his side was nearly gone, now. "What happens when your culture is gone?"

"Good question," said Connor. "A strong Immortal can live a very long time. My teacher was Egyptian. But by the time I met him, he was Juan Sanchez Villa Lobos Ramirez, Chief Metallurgist to King Carlos the Fifth of Spain." Connor shook his head, remembering. "Dressed like a Spaniard, the peacock. What was Egyptian of him? Did this Immortal carry anything of the Great Pyramids under his Spanish bonnet? Hard to say. Humans grow old and die, and often by the time they are old world has changed so much that even if they were not old they could not go on living. But we have to go on.

"You're Khordas," Connor continued. "And your gods are

no longer gods, all your disciples are dead. All your people have changed. Do you?"

"I think so," said Duncan. "After all, I became a pirate and swordsman." Duncan saw a face staring at him from the shelf and took it down. It was a mask, painted deep blue.

"But did you change?" Connor held out his arms, studying the vat of mud where Khordas probably slept. "I don't think so. I think you adapted. I think you kept serving your gods, being the image of your god."

Duncan sighed, turning the mask over. There was a funnel on the inside for projecting the voice of the wearer. Khordas, Duncan noted in retrospect, had a spectacular voice. Not that it mattered. "Good riddance, then," he said. "It must be hard for the very old ones."

"Don't be over-confident. You don't know how much *your* world is likely to change."

Duncan thought of killing Nerissa and could not help feeling guilty. "You mean Khordas may simply be out of time?"

Connor's eyes grew narrow. "Careful. All in the Game, Duncan. You have to let go of *your* time, too. And more."

Duncan was thinking of his father, forcing him away. *You are not who I thought you were. You are not even who you thought you were. You are nothing, a mistake, a demon, you have no place.* But Duncan still considered himself a Scot. He had to be. He was *here*, wasn't he? Duncan put the deep-blue mask back on the shelf, and it continued to mock him.

Duncan had a sudden thought, an ugly one, that burned into him and hurt so much that he hated to ask it. "Connor," he said slowly, "what if there were no Game?"

"Now *I* don't understand."

"What if," Duncan shrugged, as if this were just a playful theological discussion, and it didn't mean everything in the world, "what if the Game came later?"

Connor was staring. "Go on."

"What do we know about this life? What if it's all a hoax? Maybe Khordas is right and there is no Game, no Prize, no Gathering."

"A cruel hoax? So 'In the end, there can be only one' is just some sort of joke to get us to chop one another's heads off? And who is playing this joke?"

"You tell me, Connor," demanded Duncan. He was entertaining the idea, now, embracing it, and he found he was getting angry. "Because I want to know the truth. *Where do I come from?* If it's not real, Connor, then what *are* we?"

Connor shrugged. "That line of thought will get you nowhere." Connor leaned forward. He paused and tried a different route. "Look, if you want proof, is the Quickening not proof? The fact that we sense one another before we're in sight?"

Duncan shook his head. "Only in our nature as Immortals, and you know that. The rest is faith. How do you know the Game is for real?"

"Ramirez told me so," his eyes deadly serious, "as I told you. Tradition is all we have. It's almost all we are."

"And what if tradition is *wrong?*"

The Elder Highlander took a deep breath. "Then you would be right. It would be a cruel hoax. No," Connor said. "I cannot give you the proof you seek."

"Fantastic," said Duncan. "Just incredible. All this life and death, an end that you've taught me to strive for, but that I might not even live to see. I could live for another thousand years and then die and never know what happened at the Gathering. But doesn't it bother you, Connor, that there might not even *be* a Gathering? Or worse, that the last few will get together, the last man will win, and nothing happens? No Prize, no grand Quickening, no eternal knowledge, none of that. Over. Finis. No more Game. And one lone Immortal, wondering what in Hell he wasted his life for."

"Let me give you this to chew on," countered Connor. "If there's even a chance that the tradition is correct, wouldn't you rather make sure you live up to it?" He shook his head. "I'm sorry, Duncan, but I must follow the Game." Now he eyed his student carefully. "And I hope you'll do the same. But if you become some doubting Thomas, I don't want to hear about it."

Duncan recognized this as a vague threat, but some urge he could not define made him speak on, embracing profanity. "I'm not saying, in fact, that I think there's no Prize. But it frustrates me that we run this course without ever knowing if it's the true way."

"It is for mortals, Duncan, and not for us, to choose faiths and ponder their existence. Yours was chosen for you when you became an Immortal. Go ahead, if you don't think it's real. Go beg an evil one to behead you. Too bad Khordas is down; you and he seem to have a lot in common."

"That's unfair," said Duncan. "Khordas was evil. He was killing people."

"All very dramatic," said Connor, "but hardly different. And at least he was true to himself, I'll give him that."

Duncan was staring at the mask. "So few answers, Connor. I don't know how much I can adapt. I don't know how much I *can* let go of."

"Then in the end, you will be like Khordas," said Connor. Then, as if admitting this had been harsh, the Elder Highlander said, "perhaps we all will."

Outside, Duncan crouched by the moat, staring at the mud into which the Salamander had disappeared. The curls of smoke from the smoldering *broch* wall still filled the air and flooded his nostrils.

"He should be weak," said Connor as he came out of the hut. "I think I could kill him if we dig him up."

Duncan dipped a finger into the mud. It barely made an impression, so dry had the mud become with the fire as Khordas dove in. His mind stretched for a moment before he said, "I'm afraid not."

"What?"

Duncan blinked. *How* . . . "He's gone."

Connor knelt by the moat himself, eyes meeting Duncan's. He closed his eyes and opened them, and Duncan knew his teacher had reached the same conclusion. There was no presence.

"What, is he dead?"

"No," Connor shook his head. "No." He furiously wiped his hands off on his legs as he stood. "We just lost him."

Far below, as far from the moat as his tunnel and his strength could take him, the Salamander clutched his Nerissa to his breast and moaned. He felt the bubbles of mud harden against his burning flesh, and he fought to move again. He called out to his limbs and received no response. In rage and pain he held Nerissa, until in rage and pain he slept. And waited.

Chapter 4

1853

Skimming along the stream, now, down through the centuries, focusing on *these* details and not *those*. An Immortal's life can be told in a thousand ways; which is right? Skimming along the stream, and no plummeting yet . . .

An Immortal feels pain, but his wounds heal quickly, and so Immortals suffer less physical pain than their former kinsmen. Duncan MacLeod was an Immortal, and at two hundred and sixty-one years of age what he had found was this: the physical pain passes, but the *aches* build up, layer upon layer, and every year was a new layer of spiritual aches. And two hundred and sixty-one years of aches will exhaust one, grind him down, flatten him. The Immortal walks around mocking himself—young of body, muscles springy and taut. And the aches laugh at the muscles and the young body and say, *remember thou art old. Remember thy aches.* Indeed, sometimes one wished one could die. Which, of course, was next to impossible.

In December of 1853, Duncan MacLeod made his second voyage to America. When Connor had announced, all that time ago, that Duncan was free to pursue his training elsewhere, the Highlander had had little idea that the world was so large. He had wandered, here learning to fight *this* way, there learning *that*. He learned to read in Italy, and had finally mastered English in a monastery in Europe, starting with "Macbeth," the Scottish tale. He had covered Europe and then visited the Orient, with all its wonders, and had met many more Immortals than Connor had ever given him cause to believe there could exist. From one master he obtained the sword he would use for centuries to come, the dragon-head katana, a gift from a man who died for him, when Duncan could die for no one. He saw many mortals die, so many, in fact, that he flirted with philosophy, with pacifism, with war. Pains came and went with fresh and quick-healing wounds, and the aches remained.

And in 1853, when he discreetly booked passage on board a ship for America, it was a different Duncan MacLeod that met the captain than the Duncan the captain had sent away. As the claymore had gone from his side, replaced by the katana, so had much of the wide-eyed youthfulness left him, replaced by an aspect of weariness. And Duncan was not surprised to see the change reflected ten-fold in his former master. The ship was the HMS *Rosemary*. Her captain was Connor MacLeod.

"She'll do," Duncan told Amber, his new student. He had found her only recently, and was now struggling with what to do with an undertrained Immortal.

Amber Lynn stared at him. "What kind of ship is she?"

"Gunrunner," said MacLeod, "but the captain is a friend of mine."

Connor smiled as he looked down the plank at his former pupil and his pupil's pupil. Once they were off, they settled into Connor's quarters and Connor drilled Duncan for information.

"Well," said Connor, "we have yet to be introduced."

Connor took the lady's hand and raised it to kiss, but Amber pulled it away. The young Immortal fidgeted, pushing back her yellow hair, and looked at Duncan.

"It's all right," said Duncan. "You can trust him. He's a friend. My oldest friend, in fact. This is Connor MacLeod."

"Of the Clan MacLeod, aye." Connor glanced at Duncan. "At least so far." Duncan was happy to hear that Connor was still Connor by name. He had received letters from the teacher, advising Duncan that it might be time for a change. When would Connor cease to exist, replaced by some stranger that looked just like him? Connor appraised Amber and asked, "How long an Immortal?"

"Two months," said Duncan.

"And you've gone in for taking on pupils, now?" Connor eyed Duncan carefully, and the Highlander was not sure how his mentor meant his statement. But then, he never really could tell what Connor fully meant by anything.

"Until I can find a better teacher for her," Duncan said. "But yes, for that matter, I have."

Connor offered Amber a seat. "You didn't tell me you wouldn't be alone. And a girl no less, oh, the mates will love that."

"Look, Connor, if it's too much trouble to provide us with passage . . ."

"Don't be ridiculous, lad."

"I'll hide," said Amber. "I'm getting good at it."

Duncan nodded. "Amber died . . . ah . . ."

Amber tilted her head. "I was drowned for being a witch."

Connor nodded. "Are you a witch?"

"I'm a midwife and an herbalist. The witchfinders wouldn't know a witch if they saw one."

Connor said to Duncan, "She's one of us, all right."

"Yes, milord."

"Polite, too. It is hard for a female to receive training, I must tell you," Connor said.

"She knows," said Duncan.

"She can speak for herself, Duncan."

"That I can," said Amber. "I trust Duncan. Twice I have been attacked by these men, Immortals as I am told I am, and only by wit have I gotten away. Duncan offered to teach me." Amber looked now at Duncan, and Duncan groaned inwardly. He caught Connor's glance and could tell his old mentor was thinking the same thing Duncan was—she was too beautiful for this to work. It just wouldn't do to take an attractive pupil. You went too easy on them.

Connor shook his head so slightly it was barely noticeable and looked at his desk. Duncan cleared his throat. "I have heard that Amanda is in America. She could do it."

Connor said, as he looked down at his desk, "What about Amanda?"

Duncan cleared his throat. "I have heard that the lass is in America."

"Oh." Connor smirked. "Of course. An excellent teacher. Watch your back," he said, as if he knew more about the ancient Immortal—and about Duncan—than he preferred to say. How Connor managed to gather so much information would remain a mystery for a good, long time.

Duncan allowed Connor his jibes against the Immortal thief. "Then we're all right?"

Connor laughed. "My god, man, the ship's set sail, what do you expect, that I'll feed you to the sharks?" And now he looked at Amber with a charming, for Connor, wink. "Settle in, while I find you a quiet spot. And Amber, I want you to stay in that spot. This is a long voyage. We'll be going to Asia before we head back to America, and I don't want the men getting so much as a whiff of you."

Duncan smiled. "Not until you learn to use a sword."

"As to that," Connor put a finger to his lips, "I say we start her training right away. We'll have to practice in the hold. Not much room, but close quarters is good for skill. That's probably where you'll sleep, as well." Then he looked again at Duncan. "As for you, it's bunking with the mates. You, I'm putting to work."

"That should be fine."

"Are you joking? It will be murder. But you're getting fat, so the work will be good for you."

It was idyllic, in fact, and for three months aboard Connor's *Rosemary*, Duncan got a taste of what seemed to drive

Connor, again and again, to the sea. Even Connor wouldn't stay on water forever, but he retreated there often.

"History is almost unknown out here," Connor said, a day after they left China with a shipload of guns and explosives. They were standing on the deck looking west at the sunset on the water. "This water will never change. It is fierce, it is kind, it is life."

Duncan looked down and watched the waves against the hull. "Are you in hiding, Connor?"

"In hiding?" The teacher eyed him carefully. "Been hard, has it? Why, are you thinking of going under?"

By going under, Connor meant leaving the Game. Planting yourself on holy ground and staying there. Like an evergreen monk. Duncan scratched his chin. He needed a shave. "I don't know. I've been fighting a long time."

"Aye," said Connor. "So have we all. Except your friend Amber Lynn. She has only begun to fight—although she shows promise."

"Your point being?"

"There is a point to it all, Duncan. Mark my words. You are a part of the Game and you cannot turn your back. You cannot escape it, even if you try."

"Even for a while?" Duncan saw a dolphin break the surface and jump, twisting its smooth body and slipping back into the water with barely a splash. It was peaceful out here. It was true. He was completely and utterly tired of fighting.

"Oh," said Connor, who was watching Duncan's eyes, "for a while, yes. But you will be followed. What you must not forget, Duncan, is that even if you take no interest in the Prize, there are others who lust after it passionately."

"Evil Immortals?"

"Some, yes. And it is those whom you are here to counterbalance. You *must* play the Game, Duncan. If I'm not around at the end, perhaps it will be you, or Grace Clandel, or Darius, or even your friend Amber. But if we lose faith . . ." Connor trailed off, for he did not need to run down the list of the other possibilities. "Guard the Prize, Duncan, even if you are not the final one. Protect it, or at the time of the Gathering, all will be lost. Can you imagine what would happen if the Kurgan is the last?"

A cold current ran down Duncan's spine. He still wanted out, but Connor was right. Then he said, "You still haven't answered my question, Connor."

"Which one?"

"Are you in hiding?"

"No," said Connor. "I'm just enjoying a little peace. I'll be ashore again, I think, in time. And it's not as if we can't be reached out here, you know. This is the sea, God bless her," chuckled the Elder Highlander, as he spread out his arms. "It's not Holy Ground, but it's close. Damned close."

Connor was right about something else: they *could* be reached.

One night, after a day of red sky, a storm arose, as Duncan slept in his bunk. He awoke to the sound of shouting men and rain slamming against the deck. And when he rose, he felt the presence of two Immortals who had not been there before.

Duncan rubbed his eyes and pulled his coat around him as he emerged on deck, and his face was chilled by a right smart wind that came whipping along the length of the ship.

"Heave to!" Duncan heard Connor cry, "Heave to!" The first mate steered furiously, trying to face the vessel into the wind. Connor was busy barking orders at the sailors when he saw Duncan and ran to him. The deck was slick, now. It had started to rain.

Duncan looked around. "Where did this come from?"

"Just old Davy," said Connor, raising his voice to beat the wind. "But we have visitors."

"How do you know?"

"A small boat with two Immortals on it."

"Who are they?"

Connor's face grew deadly grim. "They're hiding, Duncan. I think they were waiting for the confusion of the storm."

Duncan nodded. "I have to check on Amber."

Duncan ran to the hatch and opened it and dropped down into the hold. Outside the cave of wood, the waves churned, and he knew the storm was going to get worse before it got better. "Amber?"

No answer. Duncan stepped past the mortars and rockets and found Amber's pallet, which was in disarray. She and her rapier were gone.

"Connor! Amber, she's . . ." Duncan said as he emerged from the hold and slammed the hatch behind him. He ran towards Connor, who had taken the wheel and sent the first mate off. Connor was looking out to sea, trying to gauge the winds, which were pitching the ship violently, and now the teacher looked at Connor and opened his mouth to speak. Just then a crack of lightning filled the sky, and the air was sliced by a bloodcurdling scream. Duncan looked in the direction of the cry and saw a sight he would never forget.

The wind was powerful and thick with rain, but Duncan could make out a man, standing at the mainmast, a dead sailor at his feet. The figure was tall and gaunt, and Duncan could not see the man's face, covered as it was by a hood that draped over a foul weather coat. The stranger had his arms raised above him, revealing on his hands an outsize pair of gloves. In one hand he held a staff at least three times his own height, and this appeared to be made of metal. Its pointed end had been jabbed into the deck, through the breast of the sailor.

Duncan shouted over the storm to Connor, who had taken the wheel. "Connor—that's a metal staff—he's trying to attract lightning."

And then, when the stranger spoke, Duncan knew who it was.

"I . . . am the God . . . of fire!" the stranger cried, calling out to the rumbling, brewing sky. "I . . . am the God . . . of water! I command these elements, for they are mine!"

Christ, no, not you, how in hell. . . . A crashing wave sent the ship reeling and Duncan found himself thrust sideways, and he grabbed a lifeline and held on. "Connor, it's . . ."

"I know," cried Connor, "Duncan! The crow's nest!"

Duncan's eyes flew up the main mast to the crow's nest and as lightning linked its way across the sky he saw two women there, and by the strong presence, he knew they were both Immortal. "Amber!" shouted Duncan, but the wind would not carry his voice. He saw the glint of steel. Who the other woman was, Duncan had no idea. But they were fighting. Lightning filled the sky and Duncan saw the mane of red hair, just like that of the Salamander.

Duncan shouted out to Amber again and began to run for the mainmast, but now he saw Connor wrench one hand free from the wheel of the *Rosemary* and thrash at him, furiously. "No!"

"But . . ." Crashing waves. The two women were pitched in a battle in a space no wider than a tabletop. "She's not ready!"

"No!" Connor snarled again, over the elements, "You may not interfere! It is forbidden!"

Lightning crackled once again, and the two female figures were silhouettes against the gray clouds, and Duncan heard Khordas cry, "The God will be avenged, Highlander! I own the elements, and will not be denied my due!"

Duncan was running towards Khordas now, and he saw the Salamander's face, raised back in laughter, lit up by the intermittent lightning. "This ship is dead, MacLeod! As dead as you! As dead as your kinsman! As dead as your dear, young friend!"

"This fight is between you and me, Khordas! Call off your dog!" Duncan was within twenty feet of Khordas, and he was beginning to draw his katana from its scabbard, when he heard a sailor call, "MacLeod, look sharp!" and something hit him hard in the face and sent him sprawling across the deck.

Duncan reached his hand to his face and felt blood flowing freely where a lifeline had snapped and lacerated it. The line dangled from the mast and Duncan grabbed it, dragged himself to his feet, careful not to slip on the slick deck. If he washed over in this, there was no telling if Connor would be able to find him come morning. And more, there was Khordas.

"See, MacLeod! The battle goes badly! Say good-bye to your companion!"

Duncan looked up again at the crow's nest and saw the two women. He could not tell them apart, but one of the female shapes seemed to stagger now. Now a sword flashed and another one went flying into the ocean. Lightning struck again and Duncan saw Amber's yellow hair, electric, and though it was impossible he swore he could see her eyes. *Oh, Amber, oh, my pupil . . .*

Slow motion, now, the wind howling, Khordas' laughter filling the air, Connor snarling at the wheel, trying to keep his dear ship from capsizing, and another flash of the sword, and Duncan saw a shape rip free from its base, a yellow and white shape, tumbling through the air, and when it landed and rolled and rested against Duncan's boot, the Highlander did not have to look to know its identity. But he did. The eyes of Amber Lynn stared at him, imploring. Dead.

Duncan felt the hard rain against his face mixing with tears in his eyes and he roared, "No!" and as he threw back his head he saw the blue flame circling the crow's nest and the red-haired woman and the lump of flesh that had been the Immortal Amber.

Suddenly, all was calm, and the rain turned to mist, and Khordas was chuckling. "This ship, this life, like this abomination you call a Game, is dead. Just like your little Companion." The blue flame was spinning now, like Saint Elmo's fire, and the carcass was lifting off the deck of the crow's nest and into the air, and then, all at once, the storm returned. With a vengeance.

Lightning tore from the sky and through the levitating, spinning body of Amber, and a massive bolt of white-hot light burst from her severed neck and slammed into the red-haired Immortal, who fell against the rail and screamed. Lightning, blue and white, flying out in all directions, bursting the wooden rails, and Khordas' consort fell out into the air and stopped, floating on the winds, as lightning sliced through her and held her aloft.

"Yes, my Companion," cried Khordas, "we receive our due!"

And Duncan saw Khordas pull back the hood and his hair whipped in the torrent, and he laughed as the lightning that supported his Companion wrenched free a cord of pure white flame, and the cord burst forth in a violent arc, connecting with the rod that Khordas held. The lightning danced along the metal rod, arcing up and down its length, and slammed into the deck, bursting the chest of the impaled man, tearing into the boards beneath him with a fiery roar. Now Duncan could make out a gaping hole in the deck, and he saw a flaming board fall, into the hold, into the dark.

"Duncan!" Duncan tore his eyes away from the Quickening and saw Connor, who had let go of the wheel. Connor shouted to him, cupping his hand before his mouth, "Duncan! Go! Go! That hold is full of mortar and powder, there is no time!"

The ship was a nightmare of fire and water, Khordas still holding to his staff, and now Duncan saw the Companion beside Khordas, and all the deck was aflame, the rain only fanning the inferno.

"Abandon ship," Connor called out, "All hands, abandon ship!"

Duncan ran for Khordas, now, screaming at the top of his lungs, katana before him, and Khordas shouted out, "Another time, Highlander! I have caused you just a small portion of the pain you can expect from me!"

Khordas and the Companion turned and ran as Duncan heard a popping sound, far below the deck. The two Immortals threw themselves over the side, Khordas' laughter still filling the air, defying the storm.

Duncan looked around him where he stood on the fiery, pitching deck and he saw sailor after sailor running for the rails, and now Connor grabbed him across the chest and pushed. He and Connor tumbled, and Duncan's back hit the rail and they went over the side, Connor still holding on to him. They plunged into the crashing waves and began to sink, and Duncan was sure he could still hear the laughter of Khordas and the silent screams of Amber Lynn as the cargo of the HMS *Rosemary* exploded. Duncan saw Connor's face under the water, then lost the sight as the shock wave hit him and the waves swallowed the Highlander and the *Rosemary* whole.

When Duncan came to, he was alone, the Immortals having been thrown by the storm in separate directions, like the children of Babel.

It was many pains, and many layers of aches, before he saw Connor again.

Chapter 5

1897

Nantucket Sound

The years between the wreck of the *Rosemary* and Duncan's next meeting with the Salamander were busy ones, indeed. A lot can happen in forty years.

Duncan travelled America in that time, and even more mortals died. Tragedy became a timepiece. Now and again he saw Connor, who drifted in and out like the ghost he seemed on the verge of becoming. More intense, always. Duncan felt the intensity, too, the burning drive to go on, because there seemed no other option.

Connor was there, in fact, in 1872, when Duncan lit a funeral pyre for Little Deer.

Duncan had joined the mortals who called themselves Sioux; tired of revolution, he had loved their peaceful ways, their respect for the order of the world. He had adopted the woman, Little Deer, and her son, and they had lived as a family. He had come home one day to find them butchered along with the whole village, one and all, by blue-coated psychotics.

No, not psychotics, he corrected himself. Just the Army. And one mercenary scout in particular, the Immortal Kern. Just like MacDuff in the Scottish play, the first English book he had ever read, Duncan had been gone when needed most. *Front to front. At my arm's length set him. And if he 'scape, Heaven forgive him.* But that day had not come.

Ten years' isolation after that. Meditation. Burning. Near three hundred years of life for Duncan MacLeod had shown not a jot of hope in sight of the mortals. At the same time that they created their lovely articles of technology, the camera here, the steam process there, they continued destroying one another.

He travelled, and watched, always separate, but not always alone, and sometimes, as now, in love. Despite everything.

Gabriela pointed the child out to Duncan as the two walked along the deck of the *Andrew*. The little girl was skipping rope and chanting:

Did you ever think, as a hearse rolled by,
That someday, in it you will lie?

The rope slapped against the deck, in rhythm with the waves and the splashing of the steamer's great water wheel.

Gabriela Savedra leaned back against the rail, and Duncan watched her, his hands in his pockets. From under her tiny hat, Gabriela's brown hair was flowing in the wind, her olive skin tanned even in January. She reminded him of someone and he was trying to place it.

"Well, did you?" she asked. The sun was going down behind her, over the shore, where a thousand little lights were burning.

"Think of hearses?" Duncan tilted his head and moved to her, putting his arms around her to rest on the rail. "Not generally," he said. "Only in dreams."

Gabriela smiled, in that way that she did, a pouting smile that Duncan had come to love over the past week. "I never know if you're sad, or if you just want to look it," he had said, to which she had replied, "Life is complicated, Mr. MacLeod." Duncan had long since come to accept that people tended to speak philosophically when they were traveling, when they could be anyone they wanted to be.

But Gabriela was special. And she had a mind like a trap.

Duncan gave up on trying to place his remembrance; kissing the girl in front of him seemed like a better idea. He smelled chartreuse on Gabriela's breath, and he knew he tasted of Glenmorangie, and the tastes mixed and they lingered for a moment, until the sun was gone, and still the little girl skipped and chanted:

And the worms crawl in, and the worms crawl out,
And the worms play pinochle on your snout!

Duncan spoke as they embraced, into the rich, full hair that poured over her shoulder. "We will put into port soon."

"Back where we started," said Gabriela. The passengers on the *Andrew* were just drifting, now, having completed the trip down to the Keys and back. The ship would put in at Buzzards Bay in the morning.

Duncan cleared his throat and stepped out of Gabriela's arms to lean against the rail himself. "I'm closer to home now than I will be tomorrow." Then he smiled at what this sounded like, and added: "I have a boarding house on Nantucket." He gestured with his arm at the island, the lights of which were visible now. "Perhaps you would care to visit?"

"I might." Gabriela had the slightest accent, a lovely, lilting pattern which Duncan had placed early on and correctly as Argentine.

"How busy are you?" he asked.

"Not very," Gabriela said. "Father likes me to visit his ship, and so I do, and there's very little else to keep me busy."

"Ah," said Duncan. "Captain Savedra." He had met Gabriela's father all of once in the entire cruise. A pleasant man, but distant. A widower. Duncan had wanted to talk to the man, but what could he say? *Terribly sorry, my good man, I too have lost the near and dear.* Nonsense! As an Immortal he might lose love a hundred times over, but he had no idea if it was the same for a mortal. What was it like, he wanted to ask, if he could, what if you find the one true love and lose her, and you know your own days are numbered? Your time is running out, you have but a few years of loneliness before you go on, you know not where. What have I missed, what is it like to be mortal? Is your pain like mine? I fall in love again and again, and lose every one. Whose situation is better, Captain Savedra? Duncan cursed himself for playing at what his mentors had warned him about. *Don't get too attached. But try not to get too detached, either.*

So many lost loves, and now Gabriela's warm body beside his, her sweet-liquor lips near his neck, her dainty gloved hands clinging to his arms. And it happened every time, like that: he just couldn't help himself. The dead are buried and gone and the lesson is buried with them, it must be, because *damned if you're not falling again.*

Gabriela was watching the waves. The little girl's mother appeared and tempted her away with the prospect of dinner. Gabriela looked back at Duncan. "A boarding house, eh? I'm trying to fit that into my picture of you."

"I haven't owned it for very long," he said. "You might like it."

"I'm sure it's charming," Gabriela smiled, and she seemed to mean it. "And I would love to visit very much."

The tiny rowboat slowed in the dark waters and its Immortal passenger looked ahead at the cruise ship. *Andrew.* He thought he heard a chant carried across the waves, a little girl singing about hearses and worms. *Good lass,* the Immortal thought. *Keep your eye on the Prize.* The Immortal was dressed from head to toe in black, and his hands were smeared with the same dark substance that covered his face. He shifted in the small boat to inventory his tools for the last time. The *Andrew* bobbed ahead, slowly coming closer, and the Immortal slowed his rowing, letting the boat drift toward the cruise ship. There were small steamboats available now, and Khordas had been tempted to acquire one, but for now, nothing provided silence like a rowboat. Within minutes, the prow of the dinghy reached the starboard side of the *Andrew,* and the prow scraped against the *Andrew*'s wooden hull, water splashing up at the Immortal.

And then, as he was gathering the tools he would need and

putting them into a pouch, he felt a reflex, a shudder, and stopped for a moment to regain his balance. When the queasiness left him, he had to smile.

There is an Immortal aboard, thought Khordas. *This should be entertaining.*

Duncan and Gabriela were walking together towards the dining room when he felt the presence. As the two rounded a corner, something hit Duncan in the gut, or felt like it, and a wave of nausea flashed through his body and head. He nearly fell back against the wall before he stood straighter and looked around.

Gabriela took him by the arm and asked Duncan something he didn't hear. The wooziness had passed. The presence of an approaching Immortal was something that after three hundred years still took him somewhat by surprise, but he was better at it now than in the very beginning, when an approaching Immortal made him want to retch.

Bloody Hell. Not now. The Highlander looked around him, and saw nothing. Close. But where?

"Duncan, what is it?" Gabriela still had Duncan by the arm. She reached up to his brow and he moved the dainty hand away, trying not to look annoyed.

"It might be nothing," said Duncan, but he knew Gabriela could tell he was lying. "It's just that I . . ."

"Are you feeling alright? I could get you something."

"No," he said. Duncan frowned. The presence was still there, somewhere nearby. This was not a safe place. "Gabriela, go ahead to dinner, I'll be along shortly." With that, he moved away from her, striding along the deck and around the corner until he was out of her sight. Gabriela would probably be perturbed at his abrupt departure, but he couldn't think of anything else to say. It always happened that way, and after all this time he had not found a proper way to excuse himself to go look for someone who was likely to take his head off. He counted it one of the lucky things about mortals that they tended to invent their own reasons for the unexplained, and so he usually just left. He would work it out later. *Where are you?*

The *Andrew's* deck was sparsely covered with people, and

Duncan could see clear along the two hundred yard expanse of the promenade on the starboard side. Most of the people had gone to the dining hall on port. Duncan reached into his coat to touch the hilt of his katana, then scolded himself for being hasty. Just the same, it was a comfort.

In the small boat, Khordas was busy fastening a small dark packet the size of a man's fist to the hull of the *Andrew*. He worked swiftly, his hands smoothly performing their task while his tiny craft moved up and down in the lapping waves. All had to be timed perfectly. As Khordas smoothed the final piece of tape over the packet and began to unwind the fuse, he ran over the scheme of the cruise ship in his mind. The wood where he had attached his packet should be the wall of a servant's cabin. There would be screaming. That was good. Khordas lit a half-minute fuse and pushed away, moving down the hull of the *Andrew*. Soon he saw a metal cable hanging down the hull, and he knew he had come full circle. Khordas tested the strength of the cable and, satisfied, began to climb.

Moving along the lamplit promenade, Duncan had made his way to the starboard bow when he thought he heard a sound in the water, like a scrape of wood against wood. He looked over the side, peering into the inky darkness in the shadow of the *Andrew*'s hull. As his eyes adjusted he began to make out what appeared to be a small craft, floating freely about fifteen feet from the hull. It was a one-man craft, a rowboat. Strange. *Strange, and too damn familiar for comfort.*

Had Duncan looked down to the end of the promenade, whence he'd come, he would have seen a figure springing over the rail and onto the deck, turn briefly towards Duncan, and then go about his business in the other direction.

Then the packet blew.

Duncan felt the ship rock with the explosion as smoke and fire poured up past the rail near him. He leaned over the rail, looked down and saw a ten foot hole ripped through the hull. The rim of the hole was burning still, but there was little fire. Of greater concern was the water that was now rushing into the *Andrew* through her punctured side. The ship was still pitching violently from the shock of the first blow. The presence was still here, and it was going to be nasty.

Somewhere, somebody started to ring a bell. Duncan heard footsteps and looked up to see two officers of the cruise line running to the rail to look over. One of them shouted at him, almost accusing. "What happened?"

"Have a look." Duncan pushed past them and began running along the promenade. *All right*, Duncan sighed. *Where in Hell are you?*

There was a sailor, or so he styled himself, named Neville Thurow, who never quite had the stomach for long voyages away from all the finer things in life, such as wine. So after giving up on the merchant marine Neville Thurow joined the Royal Battalion Cruise Line, where there was wine aplenty, and where the captain never minded the crewmen having a nip or two, so long as they could stand to perform their duties. On the particular evening that the Royal Battalion Cruise Liner *Andrew* was invaded by the pyromaniacal pirate known by some as Khordas and by others as, simply, the Salamander, Neville was playing guard to the ship safe. This was generally a pleasant duty because it allowed one plenty of time to drink, if one did not mind the cold company of an iron safe. He was twenty-two, the kind of intelligent person who avoided work when there didn't seem to be enough gratification in it, not accounting for taste.

Neville Thurow was one-quarter shy of finished with the particular bottle of wine he was working on when the door opened and a man stepped into the safe room, dressed in black from head to foot, his face covered in dark paint.

"Hullo?" Neville looked up with a quizzical smile.

"If you please," said the figure, "Open the safe."

Neville laughed, and spat wine. "Why don't you have a nip instead."

"Thanks, but I'd rather see the open safe."

"Nah!" Neville waved a hand in a wide arc and nearly fell out of his chair. "Don't be ridiculous, I can't do that." He wiped his mouth and picked up a soiled wineglass which lay tipped on the desk. "Wine?"

"Why can you not open the safe, please?"

Neville managed to get out, "Because I don't even know the combi—" at which point he barely noticed the glint of metal that appeared so suddenly, as if from nowhere. The sword sheared off his head right below the jaw, and it tumbled to the deck next to the safe that Khordas had to waste an extra thirty seconds cracking himself. Luckily, he had set another explosive already, on the other side of the ship.

God, these mortals were stupid.

Duncan heard hundreds of footsteps on the deck, passengers catching wind of concern and beginning to move through the chill night air. The boat was beginning to list. He pushed through the crowd and found Gabriela near the dining hall as the second explosion ripped a hole in the bulkhead, near the shuffleboard. The two looked up and saw the upper deck in flames, and now a confused crowd flew into a full panic. "Find the lifeboats," he said. "Get on one." There was a sailor not far from them, waving and trying to get the attention of the people, directing them. The ship was pitching and Duncan could tell that the stern was already dipping too low.

"But where are you—"

"I'll catch up. Don't wait for me."

All right, friend. Come out, come out, wherever you are. Duncan pushed through the crowd, stretching, focusing his mind, hoping that the presence would grow stronger. He heard someone running past him, shouting, "Abandon ship! All hands, abandon ship!" As the man passed Duncan saw that it was Captain Savedra.

"Captain," Duncan shouted. The Argentine looked over his shoulder and Duncan met him, touching him on the arm.

"Please," said the captain. "Find a lifeboat and go."

"There's a small boat, a one-man craft, off the starboard side," Duncan said. "I think we have a visitor; have you seen him?"

"No," said Savedra. The boat was beginning to incline, now, and the captain had to hold to the rail to keep from slipping. The sad man looked around him. Duncan could tell the man was immune to panic himself—he simply seemed forlorn. "My ship . . . please, sir, we cannot control these fires or fix this kind of damage. You must leave."

Duncan looked down the promenade. Water was cascading over and onto the deck at the stern. Something fired off in his brain and he said, "Does the ship have a safe?" The captain nodded and the two ran for the stairs to the upper deck.

Within seconds they reached the door to the safe room, which stood open. Over the sound of fire and screams the captain shouted as he moved inside. "Thurow? Are you here?" then, back to Duncan, "I think the guard has run off."

Duncan looked around. The saferoom was small, about eight feet by eight feet, holding only a desk for the guard and the safe behind it. There was another door to his right as he entered, and through the glass window in the door he could see that it opened to a stairwell going down. Duncan looked back at the desk and saw a pair of feet sticking out from under it.

"I was wrong," said the captain, who had moved around behind the desk. There was blood seeping across the floorboards. "Neville has not run off."

"Someone killed him to get into the safe," said Duncan.

The captain shook his head. "He didn't even know the combination." The captain braced himself as the ship groaned and pitched once more. He then turned to the safe and began to turn the combination lock.

Duncan peered through the glass to the stairwell and was about to open the door when he looked at the hinge and stopped. Gingerly he pulled out his knife and ever so delicately dug into the wood next to the hinge. He had to shake his head in wonder. *Hello.* This was good work, for a man in a hurry. And he had to admit it now. It was better—a thousand times better—but it was the same. The moment the hinge moved, and the wooden door scraped against what had been wedged between it and the doorframe—boom.

Up until now it's been just another work of art. But now, Khordas, you've gone and signed it.

A chip of wood fell away as he dug into it and the flash detonator fell from its hiding place. The fuse curled out in his direction a bit, as if missing its partner. Duncan knelt and looked through the small glass window again and saw the explosive packet taped above the door. Praying silently that Khordas had had the patience to place only one detonator, he opened the door and stepped into the stairwell.

Duncan reached up and looked and began to remove the tape from the packet. *Could it really be him?*

There are moments in life when a person realizes that if he had acted a moment earlier, if the tiny electrical currents in his brain had connected with one another by the tiniest fraction greater efficiency, he could have changed everything. But it was only then, when Duncan was pulling the tape off the hinge of the door, that he thought about the hinges on the inside of the safe.

For a split second he saw the face of Pablo Savedra look back at him, annoyed, because Duncan was yelling. Only a split second—for as Captain Savedra opened the safe, the room exploded in flame, and the man disappeared in a cloud of crimson.

The blast blew the door off its hinges and sent glass fragments into Duncan's face as he tumbled head over heels down the stairwell. Duncan slammed into two feet of water and realized he was in the engine room. It was dark, but he could hear the churning of the steam turbines, wheezing as they were. A gaslight flickered on and off and Duncan forced himself onto his feet. He plucked a few shards of glass out of his face and felt the wounds healing already. *Damn.*

The presence was everywhere. Duncan rubbed the blood away from his mouth and said, "Where are you, Khordas?" As Duncan's eyes adjusted he scanned the area. The engine room was cramped, with tables and apparatuses of inconceivable use everywhere. Between the turbine and the wall the deck afforded no more than twelve feet of fighting space, tops. *Fine. Close quarters makes it more fun.*

Behind a churning turbine a voice rang out. "Duncan MacLeod," the voice said, chuckling. A figure slowly emerged. "What luck. What an excellent end to a perfect evening. However did you know it was me?"

"I know your work anywhere, Salamander."

"Little Highland fool. You mock that which you cannot possibly understand."

"I understand that you are fevered of mind, Khordas."

"Oh?" said Khordas, as he moved a bit into the light. Over his shoulders he carried a sack, presumably whatever he had recovered from the safe, and his "tools." Duncan heard a scrape of metal and saw that Khordas had drawn his saber. "Is this where we fight and one of us takes the other's head?"

"All in the Game."

"I have no interest in a Game which I did not choose. It is a higher Law that I serve. The Salamander will be appeased," he said, "and I will teach the impious the rites."

Duncan's own katana came into his hand by reflex, spinning into place, a part of him. He glanced down. The water was rising.

Duncan and Khordas circled around one another like two ships of war, the water splashing around them. "Do you smell smoke?" smiled Khordas.

"I smell a lot of things."

"I have quite a bone to pick with you, MacLeod," continued Khordas, as he shifted the weight of his saber. Light glinted off the metal and the water. Beneath the Immortal's dark cap Duncan could see the flaming hair of the pyromaniac, and he remembered what the man was talking about. Khordas' face took on a serious look. "Wht has it been now? Forty years? We have a great deal of unfinished business, you and I."

"Let's finish it," said Duncan, as he thrust forward with his sword.

"Ah-ah," said Khordas. "And here I thought you never attacked." And with that, the Immortal stepped into the stairwell. "You know, I wouldn't remain down here; it's not safe. Not for long."

Khordas ran up the stairs and Duncan followed. He emerged in the saferoom, still an inferno, and as he moved through the flames he felt the crunch of Captain Savedra's bones. Duncan had his handkerchief over his mouth and nose, his katana before him, and he moved out onto the deck.

It was like a painting. The deck of the sinking *Andrew* was awash, and every substance above the water was aflame. The clouds in the night sky reflected red. Duncan ran to the rail and looked around. The presence was fading. "Khordas!"

The Highlander caught sight of Khordas in his rowboat, racing away. The Immortal's arms pumped the oars as Khordas shouted from the boat. "Don't be sad, MacLeod. I'm on a very tight schedule. But now that I've seen you," Khordas cried, "I'll find you." The engine roared and the boat began to disappear in the night, and with it, so did Khordas' presence.

About four hundred yards away, six lifeboats pitched in the waves. Duncan looked up and down the burning promenade and realized he was alone on the deck. He decided the best option would be to join the rest of the passengers. He tore off his shirt and shoes and dove, swimming furiously.

Duncan stopped for a moment in the water to look back at the floating inferno that was Captain Savedra's *Andrew*. Just then a final charge blew, deep in the engine room, and the whole of the vessel burst like a flaming bubble, spewing steam and wood and fire on the water.

Three minutes later, Duncan climbed aboard one of the lifeboats, when he found the right one, and rested on the wet boards at Gabriela's feet. He shivered in the January cold and someone put a blanket around him, and somewhere among his thoughts he heard Gabriela asking him who did this thing, this thing the half of which she still did not realize.

And swimming in all his memories, spanning centuries, Duncan said, "His name is Khordas. He's a very dangerous man."

And we should have killed him, he thought, staring at the flaming wreck on the dark waves of the Atlantic. *When we had the chance.*

Chapter 6

Martha's Vineyard

Mrs. George Drake hated her name, but she used it nonetheless. She used it smilingly at the shops, she heard others use it as she strolled along the gaslit streets downtown. George Drake was the husband Lauren had chosen, and she had chosen wisely, but it disgusted her to attach his name to hers, because she wanted almost nothing to do with the man.

George Drake returned from work at six o'clock on the dot, as usual. He announced himself in the usual way, opening the door and dancing in as if he were on stage, his countenance beaming like a hard light. George was always smiling. He did something he considered terribly important and impressive at the Bank of Manniver and Trundle, and so he was a confident little toad who strode into the house as if he owned it, which he did.

On this particular night, by the time he arrived at their magnificent house—two stories, nine bedrooms, a swimming pool in an adjoined house all its own—Lauren had dismissed the servants and given them the day off and had fixed

George's dinner herself. She told the servants that she wanted to prepare for an evening at home alone with her new husband, which though it made her sick to say was readily accepted by their trio of servants, who would take the day off for any reason at all. She could have told them she was going to kill her new husband, which *was* true, and they would have skipped away just the same, cheery bastards.

In any event, dinner was prepared and waiting for George as he bounded into the house and threw his hat on the rack and embraced Lauren, who tried not to look like one whose skin was crawling. They had been married for three months, and she was glad that the whole affair would be coming to a close in a matter of moments. George's coat was spotted with rain, and Lauren turned away from his offered kiss and looked out the window. Lightning flashed. She stopped for a moment, watching the bolt link its chain across the sky, fire in the air. Lauren found herself aching for her love, for his fire and his ice. The lighthouse must be empty indeed without her, and she missed it.

George tried not to look annoyed that Lauren would not kiss him. He smiled and said something about how she must not be feeling well, and that being cooped up in the house must be torture. A vacation was in order. Lauren ignored him and told him his dinner was getting cold.

Turning into the dining room George stopped and looked back. "Why, there's only one place set. Are you not up to joining me, kitten?"

Ugh. "I don't think so, George. I ate early. Perhaps if your days were shorter you'd enjoy my company more." George barely registered, if at all, that this was an unfair statement. He disappeared into the dining room and Lauren strode regally to the den, where she had a fire burning. She sat down beside it and stoked the coals a bit, watching the flames. The embrace of fire, the control of it, was something these mortals could never understand. Oh, they tamed it, all right. But her love had shown her so much more. The element of fire was a force like the Immortals themselves. Ancient, never ending, and never changing. Ruthless and clean.

Lauren looked at the grandfather clock that George's eminent sire had given them for their wedding. Six-twenty. She picked up a small hand-held rolling machine and sprinkled a handful of tobacco into a paper, gave the machine a twist, and retrieved her cigarette. She lit the cigarette on a candle and stood by the window, watching the smoke between her and her pale reflection. Lauren appraised herself for a moment. She was thin, and stronger by far than George, although he made great drama of doing manly things about the place like chopping wood and brushing the horses. George was absolutely devoted to his new wife, even regarded her fierce physique as a child does a marvelous toy. George saw no threat in anything, although Lauren thought a million times that he really shouldn't use sharp objects near her.

Lauren took a phonograph record off the bookshelf— Berlioz, "The Walk to the Gallows," which was short enough to fit on a record and suited her immensely. She placed it on the Gramophone, gave the machine a crank or two, and stubbed out her cigarette. As the music began to play she went to a broom closet, removed a key from a pocket in her gown, and opened the closet door.

With a resolute thump the body fell at her feet. Lauren had chosen a prostitute who was tall and thin enough to pass for Mrs. George Drake and had tempted the young woman away with a packet of bills. "Whatever you want, darling," the woman of the evening, as society called them, had said. This was before Lauren burnt her face beyond recognition and ruined the woman's hands. The body had rested in the closet for the past few hours—it had stopped thumping some time around four—and now Lauren dragged it over next to the drapes and dropped it there.

Lauren had only to wait, now. If George acted according to type—and he always did—he would stay away from her and retire to his study to do something terribly important. Indeed, George did not disappoint her in this regard. And so at eight o'clock, when Lauren was finishing yet another cigarette, she felt a delicious, tightening shudder in the pit of her taut stomach, a rush of emotion, a fire creeping from her belly to the tips of her fingers. He was here.

George Drake put down his ledgers for a moment to muse at his good fortune. He leaned back in his chair with his quill playing at his lips, and idly looked out the window of his study. The shutters were still drawn, and occasionally a lightning flash illuminated the many trees on his property. He had to look twice when there came a flash and he thought he saw someone moving. The second look brought no help, though, because of the darkness, and he was taken utterly by surprise when a dark figure loomed up to slap something against the window glass, then darted away. George stared, transfixed, wondering if he had seen anything or not. But a curious dark patch remained on his window, something had come and left it there. George shook his head and was beginning to rise when the window exploded.

There was something pathetic, even Khordas had to admit, about killing this man. George dropped to the floor like a stunned child, a peaceful man suddenly apprised of a capricious God, as shards of glass flew and melted into his face. The wave of fire that came at him melted his fingers together like a wad of candles, and he never really grasped the situation. Shock. Pathetic.

George lay on the floor and stared at the door of his study and tried to speak and found that he could not, and he saw that the walls of his study were in flames, and he watched in awe and terror as the things that marked his life went away, one by one. Trophies, melting like his fused fingers, prized wine bottles which he thought made rather creative bookends burst and flew apart, sending glass and wine through the study, and George looked at the floor and could not tell where the burgundy ended and his blood began.

It was then, as George Drake watched the books catching fire and tried to think of something to say, as he lay on the ground like the child that he really was, that he felt a boot kick him once in the side. George turned his burnt visage up to see a man standing in the flames, a man standing with his wife. The man had red hair, just like Lauren, and a hard, young face, but his eyes were oddly suited (George thought, for his thoughts were everywhere) to his face and hair. The eyes of the man were black as coal, and large, so large that he barely could make out the whites. The strange man was standing over him, still, his gloved hands folded before him. George was about to call out to Lauren to run, he was sorry, there was nothing he could do, run, but then he realized that it was Lauren who had had the gall to kick him.

The red-haired man, behind whom the fire made a flaming halo, stooped down for a moment near his face, his gloves still clasped. "It seems you have," George heard the man say, "something that belongs to me."

George gasped out: "Whuh . . . what?" which came out "Whuhhhuh?"

"Why, my good man," and with this the fire man stood up again. "Your wife. Of course."

"Khordas," George heard Lauren say, "here, it's ready." She handed him a packet wrapped in what appeared to be a sheet of loosely knit pieces of metal, like chain mail, only larger. George had seen chain mail, once. Must have chafed terribly. The fiery man took the packet and lay it next to George's head, before his eyes, and pressed down the tape that ran along its sides. "Watch this for me, would you," said the man. George only continued to gape, his jaw hanging slack like that of a village idiot. He was losing consciousness, but not fast enough.

George's wife and the strange man who had a halo of fire around him turned now and headed out the doorway, which was burning. He barely heard the man say that since George wouldn't be needing his less cumbersome valuables, they would be taking the liberty of relieving him of a few of them. The red-haired man around whom Lauren seemed to be wrapped dropped a fuse and lit it, and George watched the fuse begin to burn, and now he only prayed to wake up, or to go to sleep.

Khordas and Lauren held hands as they ran down the hallway of George Drake's estate, laughing like children. Lauren was carrying a torch she had made from a chair leg and used it to set the walls aflame as she passed. They had thirty seconds, give or take.

"Did you deposit the goods?" Khordas asked, jumping a settee as they came into the den. He dropped a flare packet, the trigger connected, and the settee burst into flame.

"Safely outside," Lauren said. "Hours ago. Care for a

swim?" Both of the Immortals were covered in a sheen of soot, and the idea sounded marvelous.

Lauren jumped over the body of her double and opened the back door, and she and Khordas made their way into the hallway that adjoined the main house with that of the pool. The Immortals entered the pool house and ran along the stones for a few feet before jumping together in the water.

The two had barely surfaced again when they looked through the glass wall of the pool house at the fire, and counted down together.

"Five," whispered Lauren, as she kissed Khordas and began to tear off his shirt.

The Immortal answered her, spoke "Four," into her hair as he tore her gown away, and buried his face in her breasts, and the splashing water beaded and trailed in the soot that covered their pale skin. Lauren threw back her head, not caring about how cold the water was, feeling Khordas' fiery mouth on her, as she watched the fire of the house and said, "Three."

"Two," said Khordas, as Lauren plunged under water and tore his trousers away, and burst through the surface again, parting the slick of soot.

"One," and Lauren felt Khordas thrust deep into her, fire inside and fire without, as George Drake and his house exploded with a force that mocked the storm, bursting the glass walls of the pool house. Lauren laughed as she and Khordas moved together in the water, and the sky rained glass and wood and soot.

It is not easy to walk in myth and be faced with truth every day. But some people are good at it.

There is in myth much truth, thought Khordas, *and the reverse is also true.* And if there were any one thing of myth and truth that Khordas understood with perfect clarity, that thing was what he liked to call the element of fire. No, not an actual element, that had been agreed upon years hence, but an element of life, yes, always. Fire endured, whether people understood it or not.

Khordas laughed at the pomposity of science. "Here," said the man of science, "fire is thus because oxygen is *thus,* and matter is *thus*." And yet still it burned, still it lay waste to entire cities, still it acted according to its own rules. Mortals hunted explanations as if the explanation made the truth less dangerous.

Khordas knew the myths, all of them: the Christians with their fiery teeth-gnashing hell, the burning bush, the flaming swords of the Zoroastrian angels. The figures of speech: fire in the soul, fire in the heart, fire in the palm of one's hand, if one were a soldier, and it all amounted to the mortals taking the element and trying to answer to it, and use it. Some mortals were cleverer than others: some could tell where it would go and win, and never grew tired of the roll of flame, the way a sailor never grows tired of the sea.

But Khordas was the best, because he did not *use*, could not even conceive *using* fire. He accepted fire, worked with it, nourished and lived with it. Khordas knew the truth. Fire as the breath of the god was *true*. Because Khordas, the Salamander, was the god. And somehow, he would make the mortals understand the power of that truth.

On a cliff at Martha's Vineyard stood Lauren's lighthouse, the one she had so sorely missed in her lucrative married months, where the spinning lantern reamed its constant message through the fog and kept the ships from foundering, and Lauren lived and planned with her love. Khordas himself did not go into the lighthouse much, of course. Child of fire and water that he was, he preferred the grotto.

The grotto was deep below the lighthouse, underneath and nestled against the cliff, and protected by an encircling wall of rocks, a natural gate. The enclosure was accessible in two ways only. From the lighthouse one could descend through a series of connected and hidden passages, which the pair had built during their tenure on these cliffs, or one could swim between the rocks, negotiating a single passage large enough for a two-man boat at best. At the edge of the grotto lay a cave, where Khordas made his home and kept his goods. For now, it was the perfect home for a Salamander. For now. He would be moving on, soon. Already Khordas could feel the change at work. Soon the God would return.

Lauren lay the last sack of goods on the stone floor and

leaned against the table. Her hair was dirty and wet, and hung down across her face, and she pushed it out of the way and drew a cigarette from Khordas' holder.

Khordas was busy pulling a tarpaulin over the rowboat, which he had anchored at the back of the cave. The Salamander stood straight and turned toward Lauren, held up his hand, and smiled as she tossed the cigarette holder through the air. A moment later the match flared and died, and the cigarette began to glow in the low light of torches, shadows on rock face. Khordas held his cigarette before him and studied it for a second—a cigarette would burn down in seven minutes as he rolled them, and he had at times employed them as fuses. The cigarette as seven-minute fuse was an amalgam of all that Khordas found enthralling about the modern world. The capture of fire and the taming of it, setting it on a short pole, delicately held at one's lip. And the seven minutes, the modern separation of the day into hours, minutes, finally seconds. Each moment was complete and separate, although a part of the others, like tendrils of flame, like each tiny ring of paper along the cigarette that burned before the next ring caught. Khordas stared at the seven-minute fuse and said, "I saw MacLeod."

Lauren was toweling off her hair and looked up. "Connor?"

"Duncan."

Lauren put the towel over her shoulders and strode over to Khordas, stood behind him and wrapped her arms around his torso, placing her head against his muscled back. "He was on the ship?"

"Yes. The Highlander was a passenger on the *Andrew*. Apparently he has come to us. Who knew? America!" Khordas smiled, tracing with his mind his own steps across the globe.

"Did you fight him?"

"No," said Khordas, blowing out a stream of smoke. Fidgeting, he threw down the cigarette and crushed it out, instantly regretting it. "It was not the time. But I will see him soon."

Lauren kissed her lover's back slowly, kneading his shoulders. "So important to you . . ."

Khordas pulled away, and knelt down by the docking bay,

and looked at his reflection. He lit another seven-minute fuse and tossed the match into the water, watched it rupture the reflection. "I know it is painful for you to hear, Lauren, but yes, it is *so* important to me. MacLeod will be punished for . . . taking my Nerissa."

"I try, Khordas. I try to understand the Salamander, but he mystifies me."

"The Salamander values your love and support."

"But the Salamander loves another," said Lauren, crouching beside him. "I do as he says, I worship him, but his heart is with one who is dead," she said, slowly. "Indeed, with many who are dead."

Khordas felt a flare of anger and quashed it, for it did not befit the Salamander to be angry with his Companion. Instead, he said, "I see that your mind wanders, Companion, to forbidden questioning. Perhaps it is time for the root of faith." He looked at her and she seemed to consider this, and nodded. Khordas continued:

"You have shown me much about the life of the Immortals, though you are so much younger. But my destiny remains," he said, looking at the water, "although at one time I thought it lost. And the greatest part was lost with her: my Nerissa." He sighed. "She was perfection." Khordas allowed himself a chuckle. "*Her* mind wandered at times, too. She, too, worked to change me, when we learned the 'truth,' when all of the Children of the Salamander were dead. When our language died, replaced by new ones harsh to my tongue. She tried to show me what we could be. But I was Khordas, and I am still. And Duncan MacLeod's was the last crime this Immortality will commit against me."

"You've made her into something she can't be. None of us are angels, Khordas."

"Not angels, my Companion," Khordas said. "Gods. Overseers and rulers. Princes of the universe. Nerissa shined; she was the given goddess, the provided one, the satiator. The Companion. As now are you."

"The Immortals say we are simply Immortals, like them. Is it not so?"

"I wish to speak no more of this, Lauren. Go to the lighthouse. Leave me for now. I am not angry, but I am not well tonight."

Lauren pulled away and turned. "You are the oldest Immortal I have ever met," she said. "You should be proud of what you are."

"I love what I am," Khordas said, and images washed over him and began to soothe him, fires cleansing, water washing sins away. Fire on water, the Salamander's gauntlet.

"Nerissa," said Khordas, as he sank to the floor. All the children were gone. All the truths were gone. "Nerissa. I will still remember you, with the fires I light. And I will avenge you," whispered the dead and living god. "And Duncan MacLeod will pay for his crime."

Chapter 7

Nantucket

Duncan MacLeod owned and more or less ran a boarding house on Nantucket, a two-story, twenty-room house that would more properly be called a hotel, were it not nestled into a private drive. Duncan had approached the house as an exercise in salvation, of sorts. The place had fallen from use in recent years, and looked it, and when the Highlander arrived on the east coast, the house seemed an interesting diversion. It was certainly a far cry from running a newspaper in Washington State. He bought the place outright and set to work revitalizing it. New lives for old.

"This is it, for now," said Gabriela, indicating the several suitcases that now rested in the foyer of Duncan's boarding house. Mrs. Brandeis, Duncan's manager and resident crab, was livid. The house had come with Mrs. Brandeis included, or vice-versa.

"I should hope so," said the widow. Duncan's prize employee turned and glared at him, as usual, with scorn. Duncan suspected it was some primitive form of affection, but he didn't dare pursue the matter. "Did you know this woman was coming?"

"I invited her myself," Duncan smiled, leaning on the bannister. Mrs. Brandeis ran a tight ship, and sometimes seemed on the verge of forgetting that Duncan owned the place. Perhaps it was the hours he kept.

"Well," snapped Mrs. Brandeis, "perhaps you can tell me where you'd like her?"

"I'm sorry?"

Mrs. Brandeis looked at the mound of luggage that Gabriela had sent over from her father's house in Martha's Vineyard. "We're all full on the first floor," she said.

"Put her on the second floor." Duncan shrugged. His room was on the second floor. There were ten unused rooms up there, five on either side, and his room was the one next to the east stairwell.

Mrs. Brandeis shook her head in disgust. "Without warning you bring a guest and you want her in rooms that haven't been touched in years. Took a good month to get *your* room in order, remember?"

Duncan nodded. She had him there. He had honestly forgotten what those rooms must look like. Now he looked at Gabriela, standing there in a muff and yet another smashing hat, considered telling Mrs. Brandeis to move upstairs and let Gabriela have *her* room, but the temptation passed. May as well keep the old woman this side of volcanic. "Let's just take the best one," said Duncan.

Within a minute Mrs. Brandeis led them down the hall and up the west stairs, moving as always like a woman twenty years her junior. She fished out a key and the door swung open. "Here. Two-oh-one. The best there is up here. I warned you, Mr. MacLeod, I said, shouldn't we prepare the upstairs, Mr. MacLeod? 'No, silly Mrs. Brandeis, when's the last time we had more than ten rooms rented. Never.' Well, Mr. MacLeod. Here we are."

Duncan and Gabriela peered into the room and Gabriela expelled something not unlike a yelp. God, what a nightmare. "I call it," said Mrs. Brandeis, who really was a bit smarter than Duncan liked to acknowledge, 'Ode to Dust.'"

As well she should. Duncan watched Gabriela step into

the room and make her way straight to the window. She tore a film of paper away from it and flooded the room with light, and now Duncan could see the place better. The room was large—Duncan had chosen the house partially because of the abundance of large rooms—but there were cobwebs everywhere, that now caught the sunlight brilliantly, practically sparkling, oddly beautiful. The windows were so dirty that it was impossible to see outside, but Duncan managed to say, in an embarrassed voice, "That view should be nice . . . when we clean the windows."

Attacking the window with a handkerchief, Gabriela managed to clean off a spot the size of her hand. Duncan watched the Argentine, her every, delicate motion, trying to gauge her mood. She seemed to be doing well, but what did he know? He had told her little, and the two had hardly spoken a word, since their lifeboat retreat from the sinking *Andrew*.

All night he had cradled her at the hotel where they stayed, avoiding reporters and gawkers. And he had whispered into her silky hair, *you're safe here, you're safe with me*. And when he wanted to give her a better explanation, of the demise of Captain Savedra, she had shushed him: *Let me rest. Tell me I am safe, and let me sleep.* This morning he had looked into a few things in town while Gabriela went back to her house on Martha's Vineyard. Arrangements were made, and now she was here. For how long, he had no idea. It just seemed like a good idea. And right now, he felt like having her around. Gabriela was a strange mourner. Or perhaps simply a silent one.

Gabriela looked out the cleaned spot in the glass. "Oh! I can see the beach from here."

Duncan smiled, looking at Mrs. Brandeis. There was no such view from his room; leave it to this new stranger Gabriela to find beauty wherever it hid. Gabriela now sighed and turned around to survey the barren desert that surrounded her. She walked to the one mentionable set of furniture, a brass bed with a wooden table beside it. She swept a hand and removed an area of cobwebs, ran her hand along the table, and sighed again.

"Really, Gabby, this won't do, I can . . ."

"No, Duncan," she said. "It will. Really, it will."

"But this is terrible."

She shook her head. "Please. I told you I don't want to stay at Martha's right now. And I don't like hotels." She looked around and seemed to be calculating. "I can handle this."

"Are you sure?"

"I actually think I'm going to enjoy it."

Mrs. Brandeis said, "Well then, yet another lunatic out of the asylum. Rent's two dollars a week payable on Sunday."

"Fine."

"Nonsense," said Duncan. "She's a guest." Mrs. Brandeis blanched at this, but Duncan ignored her. It wasn't as if *her* salary was going to be affected.

"I love it," said Gabriela, "I'll take it."

"I'm sure you will," mumbled Mrs. Brandeis, "being free of charge and all."

"Thank you, Mrs. Brandeis," Duncan said. "Don't trouble over the bags, by the way, I'll take care of them."

"Very well," said the old woman, who retreated into the hall mumbling something about her 'never-mind,' whatever that was.

Duncan felt some dust enter his nose and sneezed, then made his way around the ruins of countless spider empires to take a seat on the old bed. "God, I hope you're right."

Gabriela smiled and walked over to the Highlander, and sat down beside him on the bed. She leaned forward, resting her arms on her legs and clasping her hands, looking like someone forming a grand plot. "I think so," she said. "I feel like a project is a good idea. Besides," she smirked, "I think you'll find I have my resourceful moments. And that window will be well worth it. Even though it's winter now . . ." and she trailed off. She had stumbled into what she seemed to consider an off-limits area. Then she said, "I'm sure it's beautiful in the spring."

Duncan stroked her hair. "All things are. A little rebirth can do us all a lot of good."

"Well," she said, "this room is a wonderful place to start. Now. Where are *you?*"

"What?"

"Your room. Where is it?"

"Down the hall. Exact opposite, next to the east stair. *I* don't get a view of the beach."

"I shall let you visit me then," she said, and she was going to kiss him, but she collided with a cobweb on the way to his face and started sneezing instead.

Duncan lay back for a moment but found he wanted to move. "I can hire someone to do the room."

"No. Let me."

"All right," he sighed. "Want to go for a walk?"

Gabriela was looking at the dusty window, and the tiny space that let pure light in. "That would be nice. Where?"

"I was thinking of heading for the shipyards."

"Buzzards Bay? A little information hunting?"

"Yes," Duncan said, instantly feeling guilty for banishing some mood, crushing some brief respite from pain. "If you don't want to come, I under—"

"No," Gabriela said. "Besides, I know the territory. And this means a great deal to me."

"I know. That's why I thought you'd want to help."

"I do," she said, and now she turned to him. "And I want to take this as slowly as I can . . . but I have a lot of questions for you, Duncan."

"What questions?"

"Not here."

"Please," he said, propping himself on his elbows. Duncan felt almost accustomed to the dust now. "You can ask me anything," he lied. Or was it a lie?

"Not here," she said, turning sideways to kiss him on the nose. She put her fingers to his lips and said, "I want this to be a place of peace."

Duncan tried to smile and managed an approximation of one. Somehow, he felt sure, peace was going to elude her.

Gabriela Savedra stood with her hand in her coat, and watched the waves knock against the pilings. Here and there the lip of foam receded, chased by bits of broken wood. How many of those pieces came from the hull of the *Andrew*, she did not know. It was misting, and she did not feel like crying. Not anymore.

"You haven't told me how he died," said Gabriela. Duncan, this stranger from the cruise, was standing behind her on the dock. He was silent. The man said he was from Scotland, but if this were the case he hadn't been there for a long time, because his accent was barely traceable. Gabriela knew well how hard it was to drop an accent. And he had been on the boat just as she had been, but he had seen her father die, and she had not. And for this, and because he seemed to be the only strong thing around, and she was very tired, she had just moved in with him. But there were many questions that must be answered.

"Fast," said Duncan. "I know he didn't . . ."

"Not how quickly," she said, calmly. "How." A song was going through her head, something her mother would sing to her father, whenever they went out on the ship. Her mother would steal the stage from the hired singer. *Por un amor, me desvelo y vivo apasionada* . . . Passionately, Sra. Cuadra de Savedra had lived indeed, and so had her father, even though his was a sad passion in the end. . . .

"He was caught in a blast. There was a bomb in the safe and it went off when he opened it."

Gabriela folded her arms across her stomach, staring at the clash of the black gloves on her red wool coat. She felt suddenly colder. *Breathe.* "Where were you?"

"I was on the other side of the door of the ladder that leads down to the engine room."

Gabriela turned around, leaned against the wet iron rail. She was breathing more calmly now, but somehow this wasn't making sense. None of it did. Why? Duncan was standing still, a perfect cipher. And she wasn't sure if she trusted him or not. "You saw the blast through the window, then. I don't mean this the wrong way, Duncan, but . . . why were you not . . ."

"I was thrown down the ladder by the shock. The engine room was flooding. The water broke my fall."

Gabriela bit her lip, and nodded. "A very lucky man, Mr. MacLeod."

"Gabriela, I . . ."

"No! Don't try to explain. There is nothing you can say, Duncan."

"But . . ."

"I don't want you *dead*, Duncan. That's not what I'm try-ing to say. But my father was all I really had. And somehow it's just eating at me that you came in, and he went out. Just like that."

Duncan had a look that Gabriela couldn't read, either hurt or mad or annoyed, she couldn't tell which. "I didn't have anything to do with it," he said. "I promise that."

"All right. You mentioned a name. Khordas," she said, and this part *did* come out as an accusation. "Who is Khordas?"

Duncan paused. "He is . . . a pirate."

"A *pirate*? In 1897?"

"He's a late bloomer."

"Not funny. Not funny at all. Why did you leave when you did?" God, don't even think it. Duncan had broken away, sent her skipping off to supper, and then . . .

"I . . . something came up." Oh, weak, so weak.

"Something came up and then you go around a corner and then a bomb goes off?" She shook her head. "This looks bad, Duncan. This looks really, really bad. You've got to tell me."

"I don't see what . . ."

"You *knew* it. You *knew it was going to happen!*" And now she was moving without being aware of her movements, she was raising her fists and beating on the tall Scot's mas-sive chest.

Duncan let her pound away for a moment before grabbing her hands and stilling them. He looked into her eyes, and his eyes spoke the truth, but it was a controlled truth, tempered by a lot of things Duncan wasn't being straight about, she knew. "You have my word, Gabriela. I had no idea Khordas was coming. I did not know it was him until the first bomb."

"How do I know you're not making this man up?" She frowned, putting her forehead to his chest, and then looked up at him. "Why should I believe you?"

"Because it's true."

"Oh, that helps a lot."

"I saw him, Gabriela. I'd recognize him anywhere."

"Does he know you?"

Pause. "Yes."

"Why?"

"It's a very long story."

Now she yelled at him. "My father is going to be *dead* for a very *long* time, Duncan MacLeod! You're evading my questions, why? You knew *something*, because you stepped away when you did. You were standing near my father when he was caught in a bomb but you knew better than to get caught in the blast! A lot of why's, Duncan."

"Gabriela . . ."

"Why!" She stabbed his chest with a razor-sharp nail. "What in Hell are you not telling me? Because I want the truth, Duncan. I enjoy your company very much, but this is hard." Duncan looked at her as if to say that it could get harder. "I want to be with you, Duncan. But if you had anything to do with this then there's no way I can get past it; the very thought is ridiculous." She spat out the words, feeling so many emotions she couldn't count them.

Now the tall man put his hands to her jaw and stroked it, and she felt herself calming, hating this power that he had over her, staring into those perfect eyes, that beautiful, peaceful face. "Gabriela," he said, "there is no way I know to make you believe me, but I had nothing to do with the destruction of your father's ship. But now that I have seen this man, I will find him. I have to do this. I need your help, Gabriela, and more than this, I don't want you to go away."

"I'm not going anywhere," she said. "And I want to find him, too."

"Let me help you."

Gabriela nodded. Why did she believe him? She had no idea. Sometimes, she thought, trust came down to a risk. And this was a great risk, but for some reason, so was her trust. It knotted in her stomach and bound her to him, made her feel ill and elated at the same time. *Yes, I do trust you. No, it makes almost no sense at all.* "There's more I want to know, Duncan MacLeod."

"In time."

"You take your time, Duncan, but you have to be straight with me. All right?"

"I will."

Gabriela nodded, slowly. "You never say, 'I promise,' do you?"

Duncan cocked his head. "Well . . ."

"I understand," she said. "The very words of a vow are redundant. 'I promise' in place of 'I will' only suggests that otherwise, you wouldn't."

Duncan pursed his lips and nodded in agreement.

"Which reminds me," she said. The mist was turning to snow, and he put his arms around her, and they kissed, and Father and Khordas and the bits of the *Andrew* were a thousand miles away. When she pulled away she said, "Come on. There's someone on the harbor I want to see."

Gabriela walked fast and talked as they made their way down the docks, past ship after ship. "I take it that this Khordas knew where he was going. He picked the ship."

Duncan nodded. "I'll agree with that."

"There are several ways of finding out about the ship traffic in this water. I find the best way is through the Tariff house."

Duncan smiled. Gabriela seemed to straighten out, taking on an almost military determination, as if her own feet tapping against the boards replenished some lost fuel. "Tariff house?"

"Right," she said. "The ships post their itineraries with the keeper, so that a record may be kept of goods passing through Buzzards Bay."

"To discourage smuggling?"

"Not really to discourage it, but at least to isolate it—the more secretive the ship, the more suspect."

"Who are we going to see?"

"His name is Barney. He will help us."

"How do you know?" Ahead of them, a small house, the boards stained with salt, mementos of unusually high tides.

"Because he likes me," Gabriela. "So he doesn't quite know what to make of me. And because he's a Quaker." She managed a smirk, one she knew to be charming in a guileful sort of way. "They don't make vows either. Do or do not, Duncan. Come along."

Gabriela peeked inside and a bell rang at the top of the door. Duncan followed her in. Barney sat in a rocking chair behind the desk, napping, his chin buried in a mountain of grey cloth. Gabriela had never seen the man without the same grey scarf wrapped completely around his neck and muzzling his chin, connecting his head to the familiar black coat of his people. Barney the Quaker was a smallish man with a few wisps of white hair, and he was not as old as he seemed at first. Until rather recently, Gabriela had believed her father whenever Captain Savedra told her that Barney wore his scarf because, if he took it off, the Quaker's head would roll right out the Tariff house and into the Bay.

Gabriela removed her gloves and hat and stepped to the desk. She put her hand over the bell that sat next to a bound ledger.

"Please don't ring that awful thing, my child," said Barney, as he shifted in his chair and looked up at her. "I have a headache as it is."

"Barney. How good to see you."

"And thee, as usual, Gabriela," the man said, and he rose and stood behind the desk. Barney shook his head. "So sorry, dear heart, so sorry for thy loss."

Gabriela nodded politely. "I assumed you'd heard."

"Aye," said the Quaker. "We dedicated the monthly meeting to the loved ones of the departed, and we are building a fund. If thou hast any needs, please, make them known."

Gabriela smiled, now. The archaic language charmed her. The fact that no Quaker, egalitarian to a fault, would ever stoop to the use of the formal *you* reminded her of Argentineans she knew, although there were few of them around. How like Spanish England could be!

"Our only need is information," Gabriela heard Duncan say.

"Oh?" Barney glanced at Duncan. "We have not been properly introduced, dear. Let me guess." The Quaker looked Duncan over and mused. "We get a lot of God's peoples here. Thou art husky and large, and I am thinking a Briton, and a Scot, at one time, no?"

Duncan bowed, as if trumped. "Duncan MacLeod."

Barney nodded in lieu of extending a hand. "Barney Hale. Hast thou taken on Miss Savedra's affairs?"

"He certainly has not," said Gabriela. "He's providing me with a bit of help."

"Of course, my willful child," said the old man. "How can I be of service? Things are slow today, so I have time." Barney looked around the small house. It was a very homey little place of business, with plenty of books to read during the off hours, and various trinkets given by friends and sailors and people seeking "help." Not far from Barney's chair, a teapot began to whistle. The Quaker turned and went to pour some water into a cup. "Tea?"

"Thank you, no," said Gabriela. "Barney, you have a record of valuables on board a ship, do you not?"

Barney was busying himself with his tea. He set it to steeping, and turned back to them. "Near as can be kept, I'd say."

"Can anyone . . . peruse these records?"

"Well," said Barney, "not the originals, no. But I transfer a list of valuables to this ledger here," he said, indicating the large leather volume, "in case some argument may come up."

"I thought," said Duncan, "that the Tariff house only concerned itself with imported and exported goods on which duties might be owed."

"Well, yes," said Barney, "but we record anything that wants recording."

Gabriela nodded. "What he means is, the Tariff house makes a good neutral place to keep a record of valuables for insurance purposes. I remember my father sending messengers with insuring papers recording the goods deposited on the *Andrew* before they set out." She saw Duncan nod. Captain Savedra would have done so this time, as well.

"You said people couldn't look at the originals. I take it the ledger is easy to get a look at?"

"Well, no," said Barney. "I mean," and now he smiled and shrugged, "one could, I imagine, easier than the originals, but one cannot simply walk in and look the ledger over like a library book."

"No?" said Duncan, and Gabriel was slightly annoyed that Duncan sounded accusative. Even so, she felt the same way.

Barney said, "The ledgers are long and heavily coded. A quick glimpse wouldn't afford a great deal of help to someone who had never looked at it before."

Gabriela leaned in. "Help . . . with what?"

Barney blinked. "Are you sure you wouldn't like some tea?"

"Why would—" she stopped and rephrased. "Has someone had a look at these records recently?"

"Of course not," said Barney, nervously. "Gabriela, thou hast me confounded. I don't understand what thou desirest."

Duncan seized the ledger from the counter and opened it. He was running his eyes down the last page when he stopped abruptly. "It's all right, Gabriela," he said. "We're through here for now." Duncan closed the book as he gasped in a tiny breath, and he gave her a strange look that Gabriela had seen before, on the *Andrew*.

"Thank you, Barney," said Gabriela. "You've been," and she wasn't sure if she were lying or not, "very helpful."

Duncan and Gabriela stepped out into the February cold and Duncan pulled his collar around his chin. "Well," she said, "what do you think?"

"Oh, I think I'll see him again," said Duncan. "But for now . . ." He looked up and down the boardwalk as they began to walk away from the Tariff house. He looked back once more. "There," she heard him whisper.

Gabriela looked down the dock past the Tariff house and saw her. A woman, tall, in expensive boots and a smashing coat, with a full head of long, red hair, was walking towards them. The figure suddenly froze. The woman was staring at Duncan, who shifted his weight and stared back.

"Who—"

"Sh. I don't know."

The woman started walking again, and got closer, and then disappeared into the Tariff house. But before she did so she looked back at Duncan, and Gabriela got a good look at the red-haired woman's face.

"I know who *that* was, Duncan," said Gabriela, "and you are a man with very expensive taste."

"Who was she?" Duncan seemed to notice that Gabriela was walking away and he followed her. Gabriela led them down a flight of steps to the rocks underneath the boardwalk.

"Mrs. Lauren Drake. Quite the socialite, she," said Gabriela. Gabriela leaned against a post and breathed. She knew she was glaring. Now when Duncan came closer she slapped him. "Or should I say, *was*."

Duncan staggered back. "I don't understand," he protested, rubbing his jaw.

"What sort of little idiot do you take me for?"

"What?"

"I want answers. *Now.* This is getting strange, Duncan. And I am not amused."

He seemed to consider smiling, but adopted a blank look instead. "I don't understand."

"You don't read the papers, either. Lauren Drake is *dead.* Or at least she should be. Her body was dug out of the remains of her house yesterday."

Duncan shook his head. "What do I . . . how do you know it's her?"

"I'm a well-kept daughter, Mr. MacLeod. The fact that I slum with sailors doesn't mean I don't know my way around a social registry."

"All right," he said. "All right."

"She wouldn't expect to be seen by anyone who knew her on the docks. But why was she here? And why was she looking at you?"

"I don't know."

"Let's get something straight, Scot," she said. "You lie to me again and I'll turn you in."

"For what?"

"I think you could be up to your ears in this little game, whatever it is."

"I'm not."

"Want to try me, Duncan? Just try."

"No. I believe you."

Gabriela folded her arms and breathed, and watched the steam coming from her mouth. Damn right she was breathing fire. "You know things I want to know. I can't handle secrets, Duncan. You got that look in your eye back there, the same as before, and off we go. You were looking for this woman before we even got out the door. Just like on the *Andrew.* Kindly explain this."

"I cannot," he said.

"Not good enough."

"I'll explain *this,*" Duncan said. "The 'Lauren Drake' part is new to me; I know that woman from somewhere else.

She's Khordas' . . . Companion. Where she is, he's not going to be far behind. Interested in news? This morning I paid a visit to the morgue of the *Nantucket Anchor*. Khordas has been busy. This time last year he hit six ships, at least, if I'm reading the newspaper accounts correctly. Then he lay low. Now he's back."

"Where were you?"

"I was across the country," Duncan said, and the words themselves sounded sad. *What are you hiding, Duncan MacLeod? What is your secret pain?* "But he's getting his information from your Quaker Barney."

"Barney is a friend."

"Need I remind you that your father is *dead,* Gabriela."

Gabriela nodded, slowly. "You're changing the subject, Duncan. I want to know what's going on. How are you connected to these people?"

The waves were lapping cold against the rocks. Duncan looked out at the ocean. "It would be very difficult to explain."

"We have all the time in the world."

The Scot seemed to turn something over in his mind. "Where do I begin?"

"Try the beginning."

"That's too much," he said. "I can tell you this, but only because I suspect it may be important that you know as much as you can. If you doubt what I say, I can do nothing about that."

Gabriela nodded. "All right."

The tall Scot whispered something to himself about *different tactics,* and he was silent for a moment. When he finally opened his mouth again the words poured out like a litany: "I am Duncan MacLeod, of the Clan MacLeod. I was born in 1592 in the Highlands of Scotland. I am Immortal." Duncan turned and looked at her, and Gabriela breathed in, staring. "Should I go on?"

Chapter 8

Lauren sat in a chair at the top of the lighthouse, watching the beam of light cut through the night, glancing off the rocks below the cliff. She was a guide to the lost, and somehow she enjoyed that. All those ships out there, looking for her light, trusting her to warn them of the dangers of the rocks. Lauren played with this role in several ways: On the one hand, she was the savior of the ships. On the other, she was a fiery angel, a beacon warning them to come no closer—a savior only if they chose to follow her warning, a destroyer should they approach. She liked the latter construction more, she decided.

The sound of the scrape of the metal as the light spun around mixed with that of the waves crashing against the rocks far below, and through this rhythmic monotony that she found she had missed so, Lauren heard and felt Khordas coming up the steps. When his head came through the top of the spiral staircase, she said, "Welcome above ground."

Khordas went to Lauren's chair and stood behind her, placing her hands on her shoulders. "I like to have a look at your world on occasion, my love," he said.

"I paid a visit to our friend on the harbor," said Lauren.

"And what did you find?"

"I presented him with the narrow list we'd devised from

the suggestions he'd had, and he helped me whittle it down. I think we have an excellent target."

Khordas licked his lips. "Tell me the name."

"The vessel is called *Gratiano*. Eighteen thousand tons. Six thousand tons of cargo. Diamonds, gold, wheat," Lauren mused, "an excellent sacrifice."

Khordas put his lips to Lauren's ear and whispered, "How many people?"

"Seven hundred, my love." She sighed. "Barney was very helpful. We should pay him better."

"He is being paid as much as he deserves," said Khordas.

"There's more," said Lauren.

"Oh?"

"I saw MacLeod on the docks. I'm not sure, but I think he might have come out of the Tariff house."

"What would he be up to?" Khordas asked himself, aloud. "Do you think Barney has exposed us?"

"I cannot be sure. I don't even know how MacLeod would have been led there. But there is this—he was with a woman."

"So?"

"So I think I've seen her before, and I think she may have recognized me."

"Excellent," said the Salamander. "Soon our plan will come to fruition. Already I feel the godhead manifesting itself. I am well pleased." But then the red-headed god bent low and kissed Lauren behind the ear. "Have no fear, my love. Without worshippers I am but a husk, a cocoon. But soon we will be born anew."

"After the sacrifices?"

"After the sacrifices are done, and after my Nerissa is remembered."

Lauren rose and looked out the window, and raised a hand so that the beam of hard light filtered through her fingers. "Khordas, why do you not play the Game?"

"We have been through this."

"We are Immortals."

"I am the Salamander first, and you my Companion. That is our life. I recognize no Game. If in the end, as they say, there can be only one, then of course it will be me. Of this I am certain. But then I will rule, and the people will worship. It has nothing whatsoever to do with the Game."

Lauren nodded. She had only learned of the Game from other Immortals she met, long after finding Khordas, when he took her in. She did like his way better. But still . . . "What if your myths are not the ones to follow?"

Khordas lit a match, and brought it to his cigarette. "Try this, my Companion. What if the Game is but a myth? A laughable hoax foisted upon a bunch of Immortal beings. It keeps them from declaring war on the mortals by forcing the Immortals to declare war on one another. How are they to know? I play my own Game, Lauren." He approached her, took her by the shoulder, and turned her around. He brought his palm to her square jaw, playing at her lips with his thumb. Lauren smiled and nibbled at it, feeling the bony hand against her lips. Khordas retrieved a cigarette and placed it between her lips. "You prefer it this way, don't you?"

"There is," Lauren said, as Khordas lit her cigarette, "no other way."

Khordas smiled, and then his face took on a serene look. He went to the window and took her into his arms, and spoke into her hair again. "I have seen a vision, my Companion. The time has come for the return of the Salamander, and his Children, and his worship." There was a goblet beside his knee, and this he used to scoop a small amount of water. Khordas ran his hand over the mouth of the goblet and raised it to the Companion. "Drink," he said. "Drink, and all will become clear."

At half past nine o'clock, Barney lay down his book and went to the door of the Tariff house and locked it. It was time to count out, and then he planned to head home and retire early. He did not feel at ease, and he had a toothache besides.

The bell on the hinge jingled a bit as Barney pushed the door to, startling him, and he berated himself for being so jittery. *All over soon,* he thought to himself. *Not very much longer, and then everything goes back to normal.* Barney pulled the curtains, dingy rags that they were, closed, and went back to the cash box. Alone with his only friend, he began to count.

It is difficult to live daily with money that is not one's own. Barney had been particularly fit for the responsibilities of a tariff collector, it had been agreed, because of his almost complete lack of passion. The Quaker neither drank nor swore, had no weakness for women, no land, no desire to trade in slaves or molasses, nothing to fuel a desire for money. And he was plagued by faith, and thus nearly impervious to temptation. Add to that, he was old.

But year in and year out, collecting coins and specie, carefully recording vast accumulations of wealth in transit, a crack had developed, through which seeped a desire to *have* that shamed him greatly, like a boy with a collection of improper books. And that crack had widened when the red-haired man and woman arrived, with a proposition. *Just a bit, Barney, a handsome tip for yourself.* Odd, he had not yet decided what *thing* he would acquire, for no thing really gave him great pleasure. But the *ability to acquire* was a thing enough.

The oil lamp on the counter cast plenty of light for Barney as he sat at his desk and ran his pen down the length of the ledgers. At one point he heard a piece of paper shift on the counter and cursed the rotten Tariff house with its salt erosion and impertinent drafts. Barney glanced up at the counter, saw but did not register a tall, dark figure standing behind it, and glanced back down. He began to look back up when the lamp went out.

A voice, soft, coming from a silhouette behind the counter. "Barney."

The Quaker froze. Now the silhouette began to move to the edge of the counter and around, coming towards Barney's desk. The figure moved as if it were on wheels. "Who's there?"

"We've met, Barney," came the voice again.

"I have seen thee," said the Quaker, timidly. "Thou'rt that Scot that was with Miss Savedra. If you burgle this place, I can identify you."

"I don't intend to steal anything," said the shape, as it stopped at the edge of the desk. "I don't want money. I don't need it." The shape leaned in, and the face became visible in the dark, the haunted, large eyes, the gaunt face. "Do you, Barney?"

"I don't understand."

"Let's talk," said the haunted face, "about ships."

"All . . . all right."

"Valuable cargoes. Let's talk about that."

"I cannot divulge privileged information."

"Oh," said the Scot, "but you *have*, haven't you? You can do the same for me."

"I have done no such thing," said Quaker.

"There are things I need to know, Barney. Simple things, and I know this is not new to you. So tell me and we can be done with it." The figure bent closer. "Or things can get difficult."

"I have nothing to say. What makes thee think that . . ." Now there was a flicker of movement, and the man—MacLeod, that was his name—moved his arm and Barney heard a scrape and now he was turning over a coin he had drawn from the counting box. "I thought thou intended no theft."

"I intended no theft," said MacLeod. "This is a fine coin. Five quid, no? Do they pay you in pounds, or in dollars?" The figure peered at the coin in the dark. "People are dead, Barney, and your hand is in it. You know that, don't you?"

"I don't know what you're talking . . ."

"Please," said MacLeod, "don't get formal on my account. Call me *thou*. I like *thou*."

"Thou? Thou," said Barney, numbly. Suddenly there was a hand at his throat, pinching him behind his jaw. Barney's mouth flew wide open despite his efforts. The dark figure still held the coin in his other hand and now brought it to Barney's lips.

"You'd give . . . information . . . *privileged* information . . . for this coin, wouldn't you," said the soft, vaguely Scottish voice.

"What . . ." Barney mumbled, because he couldn't make his mouth work right.

"What's the next ship, Barney? Tell me. It will be a good

one, won't it, because the end will come soon and then it's lay-low time for the Salamander, isn't it?"

"What . . ."

"Dead people, Barney. Innocent people. Caught in sinking ships. Drowned. Caught in explosions. Burned alive. Here!" Barney felt the coin on his tongue and the left hand shut his mouth. Then the right was over his nose and he began to gag, and suddenly he felt the coin going down his throat. He panicked and pitched, but the dark figure with the soft eyes held him still, and he breathed as the hand came away from his nose. "Root of all evil, Barney. If you don't have a large enough appetite you could choke. I'm glad to see your appetite is large, indeed."

"Please . . ."

"Ships. So many. Which one?"

"Please . . . he'll kill me . . ."

"Tsk, tsk, tsk." The right hand now produced two more coins. "Ten quid. A goodly amount, eh? Hungry?"

Barney raised his hands now, *my god, fight this man, what are you thinking?* and he immediately gave up as the left hand tightened a bit at his throat. Oh, weak.

"I can't remember. . . ."

"Here," two coins now, on the tongue, "maybe this will help."

Tightening, gasping, gagging, god, the scrape of metal against his esophagus.

"Please . . ."

Barney gasped and bent forward, and the Scot forced his head back. "Now?"

"Please . . ."

"I could go on predictably, Barney," said the voice. "Now three, then four. You're a very hungry man, though, so I think we'll skip ahead." Barney heard the scrape of coins in the box, now clacking in the tall man's hand. "Seven is a nice, prime number for this particular pump, hey?"

"He'll kill me . . . I know very little . . . I didn't know he would . . ."

"But you kept giving information even after people died, Barney. A *very* large appetite, indeed." The Scot held the seven coins in his hands, stacked together. "Hm. You'll need to have a gullet for this, I think."

"Mr. MacLeod . . ."

"*Thou.*"

"Thou!"

"Could be interesting to see, in fact. Might tear your throat right up. You won't vomit though," he winked. "I promise. Open wide."

"Please," Barney shook, and now he felt the coins being laid one after the other into his mouth.

"One," said the Scot, "a wee amount." Plunk. "Two . . ."

"Ships," said Barney, in a way that came out "shezz . . ."

"Mm-hmm? Three . . . four?"

"Uh sway uh kand ruhmuhmbuh . . ."

"Keep trying. Five, six . . . seven. That's a full mouth, Barney."

"Shezz . . ."

"Down the hatch," said MacLeod, and he began to manipulate Barney's throat.

"Garshannuhhn! Garshannuhhn!"

"What! I can't understand you. Are you trying to tell me something, or just trying to swallow?"

"Pleez, uhl tuhl yoo . . ." Barney gagged now, and was beginning to choke, and suddenly MacLeod brought his head down and he felt the coins falling out of his mouth, jingling on the floor. Barney was staring at the coins lying on the floor and the Scot crouched, and looked up into his eyes.

"What was that?"

The Quaker spoke in short, panicked breaths. "*Gratiano.* The ship is called the *Gratiano.* She'll be here in three days."

"What's the cargo?"

"Very big ship. Lots of cargo. Everything."

The Scot stood, and fished something out of his pocket that looked like a small pouch, as for tobacco. MacLeod began to walk around the counter and he tossed the pouch on the counter as he opened the door. Over the jingling bell Barney heard the dark figure say, "Something for your troubles. I know how much you like to get paid."

Later, when he dared move, and he was sure the dark Scot was gone, Barney gathered the reward. It was a collection of coins, and on each coin a name had been carved, and a date of death. And although he found it distasteful, Barney pocketed them all, just the same.

"Is there any way I can send a message to a ship?" Duncan asked. He had waited by the front door of the Western Union office until the clerk arrived, bright and early.

"A message? Like a telegram?" Benjamin Stigmore was a wiry man who looked like many of the copy editors Duncan had known in his newspaper days.

"Exactly," said the Highlander. "There's a ship called the *Gratiano* that I'd like to contact."

"Urgent?" Stigmore scratched his head.

"Aye, a bit."

The clerk whistled. "Can't imagine anything that can't wait until she puts into a port. She'll collect her messages then. What office do you want to send to?"

Duncan stared at the counter. At the paper he had more or less relied on the wires. "I thought we could wire ships."

"Yes, it's being worked on, I hear. But just testing on a few ships here and there. What kind of ship is this?"

"Passenger liner."

The clerk shook his head again. "No luck there, I'm afraid."

"You're sure?"

"Yes, son, how many times do I have to say it?"

Duncan was silent for a few seconds, looking over the clerk's shoulders, out the window, where he could see the Bay. Inwardly he shrugged. He had waited long enough for this move, indeed, he had considered doing it in any event. "All right. Then I do have a message to send, but not to a ship. To an office."

"Good then," said Stigmore, happy to be back on the routine. "What city?"

"London."

"Addressee?"

"Care of the Royal Preventive Service," said Duncan, and he began to pour out a message that he hoped would reach its destination in good time.

As he walked out of the office and back into the shipyards

he saw the hurried movements of the men of the sea, carrying bundles on and off all manner of ships. He had to have information, and more, transportation.

The wind picked up a bit and Duncan pulled his cap over his ears. He walked past a sailor, in foul-weather gear smoking a pipe, who appeared to be waiting for something. The sailor was looking out to the ocean, and he stood at the gangway of a merchant ship. As Duncan passed, he heard the sailor say, with a shrug, "Red sky."

"Pardon?"

"Red sky this morning."

Duncan nodded. "Sailor take warning."

Duncan arrived at the boarding house near noontime. He had made his rounds among the company men, and had finally laid hands upon the plans that he wanted. They had cost him some pretty money and a bottle of cognac, to boot.

Moreover, Duncan had been forced to give up a goodly amount of money on a yacht, called the *Spanish Lady*. He had taken the *Lady* out around the Bay for an hour or so, testing the steam engines, the strength of the wheel and the top speeds, and found that, as the owner promised, she could easily reach twenty knots. Duncan had considered renting the vessel but knew better than that. A quick trip to the bank and he was ready to buy, and within three hours of his first sight of the *Spanish Lady*, she was his, and he took her back to Nantucket and docked her there.

Duncan rushed into the boarding house and straight up to the room he had given to Gabriela, avoiding, or at least trying to avoid, Mrs. Brandeis, who was eager to discuss the latest winter boarders with him. Duncan saw the woman coming and made great drama of an invented hangover, telling her they could discuss business tomorrow. Then he bounded up the stairs and reached the door of Gabriela's room. When the door opened, the effect was not unlike that of milk entering one's mouth when one has reached for what one thought was a glass of rotgut. The empty room had been a wreck, he remembered it well, dust deep enough for insects to swim in, cobwebs galore, and a window so dirty that Duncan feared he'd have to take a hatchet to it to see through it.

But now, he blinked, and the strands of cobwebs he expected congealed into something different, fishnet, hung at seemingly random intervals from the ceiling. At the far end, the ugly cast-iron bed seemed to have been polished, actually *polished,* and on it someone had placed a lovely set of scarlet bedclothes, complete with frilled throw pillows. An oriental rug that nearly filled the whole room left only a bit of the hardwood floor visible, and this glistened, as if someone had actually had the time to wax. Something else caught the light that Duncan noticed was streaming so brilliantly through the cleaned windows: there were mementos on the wall, an anchor here, a quadrant there.

And in the midst of this unexpected sight, sitting in a burgundy-draped rocking chair next to a polished cherry lamp table was the lovely Gabriela, reading a book. The captain's daughter wore a dark nightshirt and a pair of almost homely slippers, and she only casually looked up as Duncan entered the room.

My God, my God, what have I done. "What in Hell came through here?"

Gabriela smiled and laid her book aside, and Duncan noted that the bookmark, too, was burgundy. "You've been gone since yesterday afternoon. You should know your Mrs. Brandeis wants to speak to you rather badly."

"She intercepted me at the door," said Duncan. "You really are the most intriguing creature." He shook his head in disbelief. Even for the Gay Nineties, this girl was forward. Or was that the word? The word was more likely *forthright.* Forthcoming. Bold as hell. Whatever. "I'll ask it again, because it's worth it, what happened—"

"To your fabulous wreck of a room?" Gabriela stood and padded over to him, and Duncan could smell the rosewater on her neck as she put her arms around his waist. "I thought I'd put some of my mad money to good use. If I'm to have a room, it might as well be a splendid one. Like the sea motif?"

"Splendid," agreed Duncan. Visions of decorating the whole house were dancing in his head. And then it struck him: she was really here. This was a bold statement she had just swathed in burgundy. And here she stood, her olive flesh covered by the slightest downy shirt, smelling of rosewater, and he accepted the statement without hesitation. Then he blinked from his reverie and said, "I have information."

"I thought you might."

Duncan nodded and went to the table, and picked up Gabriela's book. He laid it in her chair—nice chair, too—and unrolled the set of large papers he had under his arm.

"Here she is," said Duncan, indicating the plans. "The *Gratiano*."

Gabriela put her hand on his shoulder and looked the paper over. Her trained eye scoured the plans for a second before she shook her head a bit and let out a slow whistle. "Are you sure she's the right one?"

"Pretty sure," Duncan said, as he ran a hand along the plans, "and Khordas is getting brave."

"Aye to that," she said.

"The *Gratiano* is seven hundred feet long. Her displacement is eighteen thousand tons. Top speed, twelve knots."

"How much cargo?" Gabriela was looking at the plan of the hull.

"Hull is divided into ten watertight compartments, patterned after the *Great Britain* subdivision method. She can carry, and will be carrying, six thousand tons of cargo."

"Passengers?"

"About two hundred in first class cabins," Duncan paused for a moment, "but counting steerage, there could be anywhere up to," he breathed out, "six hundred. Plus a crew of about a hundred."

"Seven hundred people?"

Duncan nodded. "She's an older ship. Now the boats are getting smaller again, but the *Gratiano* is a holdover from the days of the giant steamers."

Gabriela nodded again, and Duncan reminded himself that he didn't have to give Gabriela Savedra a lecture on ships. She knew them as well as he did, if not better. She said, "And why is she attractive to Khordas?"

"Good question," said Duncan. "It's not for her bulk. But among that six thousand tons of cargo should be a good lot of the kind of baubles he likes. He can carry an expensive amount in a gunny sack."

"There's something I don't understand, Duncan," said the Argentine. "Isn't there something overblown in all of this?"

"How so?"

Gabriela picked up her book and sat down. She crossed her legs and clasped her hands about her knees. "Couldn't he just rob a bank? Or a mine? That ship has an iron hull, what's the point of going to all the trouble . . . And this ship is *huge,* this isn't like blowing up another *Andrew.*" Duncan was smiling, and she stopped. "What?"

"Khordas is an Immortal. After a few thousand years you develop a penchant for drama. But I think that ships represent something."

"Something that robbing a bank would not?"

Duncan nodded his affirmation. Now he sat on the bed and pushed his hair away from his eyes, and began to massage his temples. He knew he looked terrible after being up all night, and he felt a slight headache coming on. Pains and aches and love, layer upon layer. "The ship is due in Buzzards Bay tomorrow night. I expect to meet Khordas on the water."

"I see," she said. "And I take it you'll chop his head off."

"That's usually how it works."

"Or he yours."

"Right." Duncan rubbed his neck. He needed sleep. Then he heard the words coming out of his mouth, they had to be said, rotten, rotten Game. "Gabriela, this could get dangerous. Perhaps . . ."

Gabriela sighed deeply and shook her head. "I must be going insane. Are you telling me to leave?"

"I know it's all very difficult to grasp."

"Are you referring to Khordas, or the matter of your being 'Immortal?' " Gabriela placed her hand under her delicate chin.

"The whole thing."

"Yes it is," she said. "It is very difficult to *grasp.*" Gabriela rose and came to the bed, and climbed up, placing her knees on either side of Duncan's legs. She put her hands to his face and Duncan watched those hands, so throbbing with blood and youth.

Gabriela was unbuttoning his shirt, now, and speaking into

his chest, and Duncan was watching the thin wool sliding along her thighs. "But do you know what, Duncan MacLeod? This may be very difficult for *you* to grasp, but you seem to have caught me at just the right time. I am twenty-seven years old and unmarried. I have spent my life watching my father sail ships and making a nuisance of myself. My father followed some sort of dream *he* could never explain, either. If he had explained it, it would have seemed crazy, I think, and so he did not. You have explained your dream, or your destiny, or whatever it is, and I have almost no interest in understanding it. For all I know, it could be a lie." The shirt was free now, and Duncan sat wearily, allowing her to remove it for him as she went on.

"And maybe it is not a lie," she said, as she pushed him back and began to play at his belt. "I don't care. Right now, I am glad that you have come into my life as another who was dear to me went out. I need no more. Can you handle that?"

"I don't understand what you're . . ."

"You seem to think that you have to spare me, Duncan. That this great secret destiny of yours is so vast that it will kill me, one of your enemies will do me in, or you'll *God forbid* fall in love and then I'll wither away and die, is that it?" She had the belt away and was making quick work of removing Duncan's trousers. "I don't care. So you can spare me that."

"But . . ."

"Duncan" she said, as she removed her shirt and climbed up to bring her lips to his face, "*callaté*. Shut up."

And maybe she thought she was insane for believing him, or maybe she thought he was insane, or just a good liar. Or maybe, Duncan thought, mortals and Immortals alike can be aware that life is short.

And oh, it was . . .

Chapter 9

Seven nautical miles south of Iceland

Captain David Carruthers was in his quarters aboard the whaler *Dido*, reading a book he had picked up in London the last time he had gone ashore. Edmond Rostand's *Cyrano de Bergerac* had sat waiting at his table and the captain had not had the time to give it a glance: old Davy had been unhappy with them ever since they crept out of port and had been throwing storms at them for near half a month. Carruthers had been as busy trying to keep the ship from turning over as he was trying to keep the crew from going on a Jonah hunt.

If anyone were the bringer of bad luck, mused Carruthers, it had to be he. After all, he had chosen a circuitous route through treacherous waters to avoid the Preventives, who were constantly combing the seas for contraband: assuming his pursuers would sail due east from the channel headed for North America, Carruthers had ordered the ship north, slicing along the choppy waters south of Iceland, before turning southeast again. The *Dido* had been paying for this. But at least they had legitimized themselves a bit—they had managed an actual whale or two.

Now, after two days of good weather, the captain had finally set aside time to read, and he was falling asleep. Maybe it was the rocking of the ship, or the way the candle at his table swung slowly, like an inverted pendulum, its flame always perpendicular to the surface of the water. Perhaps it was the tired singing of the sailors' crude songs, like a lullaby to him. Cyrano was going on about his notion of the afterlife, an afterlife of the mind where one sat about gabbing with Socrates and Galileo for eternity. Carruthers shook his head and closed the book. The Vikings had Valhalla. Now *that* was an afterlife. So perhaps it was a quibble with the book.

The captain looked up as a bell rang at his door. His first mate was standing there and waiting to be received. "What is it, Rooke?"

"Preventive ship, Captain."

Carruthers grimaced. "Where?"

"Two hundred yards off starboard," said Rooke. "They're signaling. They want to come aboard."

Captain Carruthers put down his book and stood up behind his table. He removed his cigarillo case from his vest and retrieved a French cigarette, and lit it with the candle. Hell, he didn't feel like reading, anyway. "Are the whales in place?"

"Aye, Captain."

"Then bring them on." Rooke nodded and disappeared. Smuggling was getting more difficult by the year, and afforded much less profit than it once did, Carruthers reflected. This would be the third time in the past two months they would be boarded by British preventives, trying to sniff out smuggled goods.

Perhaps, thought the captain, as he made his way up to the deck to get a look at their visitors, it was time for a change. At this point he had no intention of going aground, oh, no. He had properties to go to, but Carruthers got enough appreciation of the land watching his crew run down the plank every time they put in, the bundlemen taking provisions to near-forgotten wives and children. All the cities were falling apart, dirty with soot and politics and ever-sillier wars. Even his own ship was fitted with steam engines. The fact made him cringe, but they needed the speed. The ships were uglier now, too, but at least they were ships. And at least at sea he had fewer reminders of how the world was changing. For the sea was like the desert: man could travel across it, but he had not yet figured out how to destroy it.

Carruthers strode to the forecastle deck and looked out. Sure enough, there was a smallish, sleek steamship moving steadily towards them. About twelve men stood on the deck, proper limeys all, and Carruthers took a drag on his cigarette and raised an arm as a greeting. When they were within hearing range he cried out, "Ho! What news?"

A man in foul-weather gear looks like any other, but one of the men hoisted a megaphone and spoke into it. "Captain Jacob Devereaux, Preventive Ship *Gregorian* coming alongside!"

Carruthers raised an eyebrow. *Devereaux?* "Nothing but blubber to see here, and not much o' that," he shouted back.

"Just the same, Captain," replied Devereaux. "We all have our duties."

Heh. Whether we like it or not, eh? "Then we're always happy for visitors. Come alongside."

A quarter hour later, Captain Carruthers was leading Captain Devereaux into the main hold. He noticed the blanched faces of the crewmen, and he nodded at each one, silently reminding them with his eyes that they'd pull through this one, too.

"Having any luck this time of year?" asked Devereaux.

"Some," said Carruthers, who opened an oil lamp and revealed the bloody skins that formed a great mountain of flesh in the hold. "It's been a good season, in fact."

Devereaux nodded. "This is it? Just whale meat?"

"We are a whaler, after all."

"So I've heard." Devereaux smiled.

A man in British foul gear, one of Devereaux's crew, came jogging down into the hold. The sailor slipped in the whale's blood on the floor of the hold but caught his balance before hitting the deck. He stood with an embarrassed look.

Devereaux rolled his eyes at his young crewman. "Yes?"

"Everything in the other hold seems aboveboard. No sign of contraband." The sailor looked past Devereaux at the mountain of whale flesh. "That's quite a haul," he said.

The captain of the *Gregorian* looked at Carruthers. "Yes, the captain was just telling me what a fine season they've had, eh, Carruthers?"

Carruthers half-smiled. "Aye."

Devereaux continued, "Tell the party to return to the *Gregorian*; I'm satisfied."

The sailor was still staring at the wall of meat and blood. "But . . ."

"Butts are for scuttle, sailor. Look alive!"

"Aye, aye, Captain!" The sailor snapped a salute and disappeared as quickly as he could without slipping.

When the sailor was gone Devereaux looked around to make sure there were no more crewmen coming down, and sat down on a provisions barrel. Carruthers took out a couple of cigarettes and handed the captain one, and Devereaux lit his with the lantern. Then he said, "He wanted to look under the meat, old chum."

Carruthers shrugged and blew out a stream of blue smoke. "I can't imagine why."

Devereaux gave a short laugh. "Righto. But I'm sure you wouldn't go to the trouble of covering contraband with a bloody mess of whale."

"What a novel idea," said Carruthers.

The Preventive Officer looked around, ran a finger along a dusty plank, and studied the results idly. "The northeast route was a grand idea."

"How many know we're out this way?"

"It was suspected, but I got the charge, so you're free and clear from here on, I think."

Carruthers tilted his head. "Then why bother finding me? You could have just looked and missed us by a few miles."

"Yes, but then I couldn't have given you this," said Devereaux, and he reached into his coat. "Someone knows a great deal more than one would expect. Haven't been giving away too many secrets, have you?" Devereaux smiled politely, but he was serious. He handed Carruthers a small tin.

"I wouldn't be concerned," said Carruthers, evenly. He

took the tin and dropped it in his pocket. Then he threw down his cigarette and mashed it out with his boot. Then he fished an envelope out of his coat and handed it to Devereaux. "The usual amount."

Devereaux finished his own cigarette and crushed it as he took the envelope from Carruthers. "Of course," said Devereaux, as he stashed his pay. "Pleasure doing business with you, old chum," he said.

"Right," answered Carruthers. "Fair winds, Captain."

"And following seas," said Devereaux, and he was gone.

By the light of the oil lamp Carruthers retrieved the tin that Devereaux had given him and sat down on the barrel. He unscrewed the lid and withdrew a rolled sheet of paper, and unfolded what appeared to be a telegram.

To: Captain Jacob Devereaux, Preventive Service
For Captain David Carruthers, Vessel *Dido*
From: Duncan MacLeod

HARD NEWS ON NANTUCKET.
TOO MANY SALAMANDERS.

End.

The man who had once been known as Connor MacLeod looked up from his old student's note. He had to move quickly.

There was Hell to pay.

Six hours before Duncan MacLeod reached the hulking *Gratiano*, the ship received another visitor. The man who introduced himself as Commander James Brimstone, USN, had arrived at 1500 hours in a small naval scout vessel. He had signaled that he was alone, and begged to be allowed to board, saying he had an urgent message. Captain Bertrand Lewis of the Crescent Line Ship *Gratiano* escorted the officer to his own private dining hall after the scout was attached by tow line to the *Gratiano*. At 1530, Brimstone had settled into his seat and grimly delivered his message.

The message, if urgent, was not good. It was laughable.

"Do you mean to tell me," said Captain Lewis, "that you think we are going to be boarded and attacked by a *pirate*?" The captain's dining hall was quiet except for the white-gloved stewards, who hovered about Lewis and his visitor like flies. Lewis liked his dining hall; it protected him from the odd requests that wealthy passengers tended to throw at a ship's captain.

"That's right, Captain," said Brimstone. "I know it sounds incredible, but we've had trouble with this particular fellow before . . ."

"I fail to see how *we* could be under any sort of threat." Lewis smiled. He had been running this route for eight years, and this whole conversation seemed just a pleasant diversion. He held up a hand and one of the stewards came over. Lewis glanced back at the visitor. "Would you care for some tea?"

"No, thank you."

"Coffee?"

"Fine. Black," said Commander Brimstone. Brimstone was an odd one, but even if he hadn't shown up in the scout, Lewis would have been sure he was Navy by the way he held himself. Naval officers tended to fall to extremes, and Brimstone was clearly on the tight, serious end. Brimstone had red hair, cut short, and a solid, if gaunt, frame. It was difficult to tell how old he might be. Most pleasing to Lewis, the Commander wore his ceremonial sword. Lewis called out the orders to the waiter and looked back at Brimstone, who was talking again.

"I'm not saying for certain, Captain Lewis, that you would be under a real threat. But this man is insane. He's sabotaged a number of ships of late in the New England shipyards, and we think he's headed for you."

"Why?"

"People talk. He thinks you have a valuable cargo."

"That we do," said Lewis. Lewis was trying to trace Brimstone's accent. There was something strange to it. Brimstone's voice was not old, but it was well-controlled and almost artificial; if he were American, the man probably had foreign parents. "But we also have an iron hull compartmentalized into ten holds. This isn't the kind of ship you just set fire to."

"Of course not," said Brimstone, gravely.

"So what do you want us to do?"

"If this man arrives, let him board. I have orders to arrest him."

"I can let you have a few men."

"That would be very helpful. Let me confront him first—there's no telling; he may come easily. I hope so, Captain, I truly do. Then—do you have a holding pen?"

"Of course. Sometimes the passengers can get rowdy," said Lewis, by which he meant the drunks who got a little over friendly with the ladies. He leaned in with a smirk, as if to share a confidence, "And then, so can the crew, eh?"

Brimstone had no perceptible sense of humor. "Fine. Let me confront him first, and then we'll see if we can get him into the brig. When we get back to port I'll escort him to shore, where he'll stand trial, in time."

"What charges?"

"Murder."

Lewis leaned back and touched his chin. The waiter arrived with the coffee and tea and the captain took a sip. "Why are you alone?" he asked. "Isn't that a bit ill-advised for the capture of a dangerous suspect?"

Brimstone dropped his guard a bit and looked a bit embarrassed. "This has been a . . . delicate situation, sir. This man has caused a lot of trouble, and the Navy doesn't want to draw attention to itself chasing down one man who should have been arrested a long time ago. We think he'll come easily."

Lewis nodded, envisioning the scenario. This "pirate" was probably a Navy man, too. "I understand. When do you expect this visit?"

"He works at night. Until then, I should very much like a tour of this most impressive ship."

"Of course," shrugged the captain. "She is a sight, at that." Captain Lewis put down his tea and rose, and the Commander followed his cue. As they exited the dining hall Lewis asked Brimstone, "So what's his name?"

"The suspect's name is Duncan MacLeod," said Commander Brimstone. "And I want you to let me handle him. I'm not very worried," he said, with a sigh, "but there's no telling what he might try to do."

Chapter 10

Lauren the Companion of the Salamander waited until the naval scout was successfully tethered and her love was away before she boarded the *Gratiano* on her own. At 1520 hours, after shimmying up the tether line, she hopped over the side, and quickly changed into the sort of outfit that a passenger on a Crescent Line ship would wear.

She went over the plans of the *Gratiano* in her mind as she made her way down the promenade. The ship had three kitchens, the most difficult of which to access would be that of the captain's private dining hall. It would not pose a serious problem.

As Lauren passed a bevy of shuffleboard players she saw a two-sided placard on the deck, proclaiming the schedule of the day. Dinner would be served promptly at 1900. Three hours, almost. Not a problem at all. From a pocket near her breast the red-headed woman drew a fan and flicked it open. Each stem of the fan glistened with opaque brilliance, the mercury-like substance inside the crystal stems churning with the motion of her arm.

The substance in the spines of the fan had been developed at considerable time and expense to the Salamander, but in essence it amounted to a derivative of the same root that the Children of the Salamander once ingested at the Time of the Return of the God. As the steerage dining hall loomed ahead of her, Lauren laughed inwardly at Khordas' brilliance, and Duncan MacLeod's apparent idiocy. There was more to the Salamander than piracy. Such a ship as this must tithe, of course. But it was so much better if one had worshippers to do it.

The Salamander, her lover, nay, her God, had said so.

Lauren was one of four sisters from Wales, and by Lauren's twenty-fifth year, the sisters had turned out thus: one was the wife of a cooper in Southampton, and had three children. One was a court maid and rumored to be a mistress of the king. One was the wife of a blacksmith and known to be a mistress of the parish priest. But Lauren, an adoption, a case of good Christian charity, remained ever the outcast, and inevitably the outlaw. By the time her courtesan sister was dallying for mother and England, Lauren was a highwaywoman in Scotland.

In 1737, at the age of thirty, fairly well-known as the feminine scourge of the Highlands, Lauren was caught up to and surrounded by a group of villagers who had tired of her constant waylaying of visiting cousins. She was run through with a sword, shot seven times, posthumously declared a witch, and buried in a shallow grave there, where she had died, at the crossroads. That was October the sixth.

On October the seventh Lauren awoke to the sound of hooves pounding the earth over her head. She gasped, and began to gag on the dirt that filled her throat. She lay still, blind, and waited. After a moment she tried to breathe and found that air was coming into her nose.

Calm down. Calm down. You've been buried alive, but not very deep.

Then, as she tried to move her muscles, and felt the earth falling away from her, as her lungs exploded with fresh air and she wiped dirt from her mouth, Lauren began to scream. Each bullet, she saw, remembering now, flying through the air—*that's the one with my number on it, no, that one*— seven in all, the holy number, and she felt the sword once again, thrust into her, breaking ribs and puncturing lungs, her heart palpitating wildly as she crashed to the earth she was *dead. Dead!* Images, now, angels in paintings and sculpture, all the things of the church, all the men she had killed, all the men who had killed her, little by little, before the band of avengers finally brought her down, horses' hooves pounding and Lauren, Highwaywoman, buried under the crossroads, dying. *Dead!* No Heaven! No Hell, thank God, thank God, no thrashing and wailing and gnashing of teeth and Lauren was horrified by the joke that she had fought so long and hard for her punishment and now *where is it? Where is this Heaven, this Hell? And what is to become of me?*

Senses, now, *new* senses, blinding her with deeper colors than she had ever known, vision clearer than even her eagle eyes had afforded, the specks of the sun brilliant in the dirty strands of her red hair, the wind howling. And now Lauren simply had to move, she was frightened and elated at once, and she jumped from her shallow grave and looked down the road when she heard, at a distance, another approaching horse.

Lauren knew she must look ghastly, and she felt at her blouse where the sword had torn it and her, and there was the tear, but no wound. Lauren stood by the side of the road, drunk on her new senses, violently needing action, needing to move, and now the horseman came around the trees and she saw the rider.

The man on the horse slowed as he drew near the crossroads. Lauren looked him over and saw that he was paunchy, but he had an expensive pistol—so he must have a good purse, as well. The horse was good. The man brought the horse closer and said something to make it slow, and he looked at her.

"My lady, are you injured?" The man shifted in the saddle and tipped his cap. "Is there anywhere I can take you?"

Lauren walked slowly to the horse, feeling the grains of earth in her boots so clearly she could count them, feeling the very soul of the steed the man rode. She was silent, and now she took on a pleading demeanor and reached up, and touched the man on the chest. The stranger smiled, as if a bit confused but not very, and before he could say another word Lauren jerked on his collar and dragged him quickly to the earth. The man landed on his shoulder and Lauren heard a crack, and she jumped on his back, reached for his head, and gave it a sharp twist.

Now she had a horse, and a pistol, and some money. And now she began to ride, furiously, because whatever euphoria had taken hold of her was beginning to cede to sheer confusion and panic.

Lauren rode for days, southward, not even paying attention to the fact that she drove the horse to death. She left the carcass behind, wandering madly, now into the swamps near of Loch Rannoch, slogging through the mud, and it was after she had slogged on for half a day that she realized she was being drawn by something, something with *answers*.

And then on the eleventh of October Lauren reached a mound of earth, and as she stepped past a patch of dark ground she felt it. Or, more correctly, Him.

A vision, now, of herself, as outside herself, dropping to her knees, scratching at the earth, now drawing her dagger and beginning to dig. Hours upon hours, days passing, blood running from her fingernails and the wounds healing. Her brain rocked with the presence that poured through the mud as a wall of clay broke inward, and she found a tunnel leading towards the *broch*, the tunnel itself filled with hard clay.

I know you, already, I who have served nothing, who is alone, I sense the violence within you, the hatred, the loneliness, it calls out to me, aye, and I will resurrect you.

And I will serve.

Teach me, for I have come to serve.

Lauren found a lump of clay, like the first man according to the Judeo-Christians, a lump of clay that contained a presence, that was curled like a babe with a lump in its arms that gave off no presence, and now she was taking her dagger, slicing away the hardened clay and seeing blood flow freely, tearing the clay away from the man's nose and the mouth.

The clay man, bleeding from his wounds, began to move, to rasp with a voice unheard for near a century, and his darkly covered arms came away from the prize he clung to and reached up, hardened earth falling away from his limbs, and the clay man brought his hands to his face and ripped the clay away from his eyes, and he screamed with the new light.

And the clay man lay staring for a long time at the creature before him, and Lauren knew, somehow, she had found her purpose.

And finally the clay man reached up a hand and touched her on the shoulder. "I am weak, my Nerissa. My companion."

"My name is Lauren."

"Lauren, then. Lauren the Companion." The face would be comic were it not so strange and fierce, the swath of white skin showing through the clay on the flesh of the man's face, surrounding his great, burning eyes. The clay man breathed as if unaccustomed to the task, his voice slicing through the air and taking her soul. "I am Khordas. The Salamander. The God."

Aboard the *Gratiano*, Lauren finished scattering a handful of the powdered root of faith into the water tanks, her last stop after the three kitchens. Over her head, she heard crewmen walking along iron catwalks. Lauren closed her eyes, and now she felt the edge of Khordas' presence elsewhere on the ship. Khordas would now be taking a tour, guided by the captain, after delivering his warning about the mad pirate.

Lauren made her way up to the main deck and began to walk along it, feeling the breeze against her face. So this was to be Khordas' new home, the site of the new civilization, the place of the Rebirth.

Something in the back of Lauren's mind flashed a signal, like a glowing buoy, bobbing on the horizon. *You are mistaken. Leave, now. This is not the way. There is the Game to play, Lauren.*

But Khordas needed his Companion. And Lauren reached into a pocket and drew out a small capsule of gelatin, containing a dose of the Root of Faith. Lauren put the capsule to her mouth and swallowed, and soon, all became clear. There was much work to be done.

After an hour, Lauren saw the crew filing into and out of their early supper, and the results were already becoming apparent. Lauren strode down the deck and spotted a trio of sailors standing limply on the deck as if hung from a clothesline. Lauren smiled. They were emptied, emptied of the world, and ready to be filled.

"You," she touched one of the sailors on the shoulder. "Go stand guard and await my instructions. Look for an approaching vessel. Children," said Lauren turning to the other two staring sailors, feeling in herself the root that made the instructions and the wisdom of Khordas so clear. "The first thing we have to do, is make a lot of mud."

Duncan felt the cold sea air bite against his face as he sped along what he had planned as a collision course with the *Gratiano*. He grimaced into the mist, seeing no farther ahead than a quarter mile. The sea was dark.

The *Spanish Lady* hit twenty knots and Duncan ducked under the canopy. He consulted his maps to confirm that he was on a course to match the *Gratiano*; now all he had to do was look for her. Not that he could miss a ship of that size. And at about nine in the evening, her vast stacks popped over the horizon, clearly visible against the clouds.

Duncan went back to choke off the engine a bit. Naturally, the *Lady* ran on steam, and like most private yachts she was fairly efficient in her use of coal, which no gentleman liked to spend much time in shovelling.

The vast hulk of the *Gratiano* loomed as he drew close to it, and when Duncan came within a mile he realized that the ship was not moving. The *Gratiano* had dropped anchor. Duncan drew a pair of field glasses from the canopy and peered through them, and he could make out the shapes of men on the deck, keeping watch.

And now he heard something else, strange, vibrating through the air. Drums. Duncan pulled his coat closer to him and walked out to the prow of the *Lady*, and began to crank the alarm horn.

As he began to crank the horn, Duncan immediately doubted the wisdom of the warning, and wondered if he should approach in silence. But the *Gratiano* was not on fire. The boat was still, but there; people were walking along the well-lit deck. And he would have been completely at ease were it not for the steady drone of those drums, rhythmic and foreign. He was coming up on a ship built in the late nineteenth century. But the drums defied the exterior, a strange, tiny, odd detail that threw the whole picture off balance. He felt as if he were entering another time.

Duncan's vision went blazing white as a search light turned on him and he heard the sound of voices shouting orders to one another. When he pulled the *Lady* alongside, he looked up the hull and saw that the men were dropping him a rope ladder, and Duncan scaled it until he reached the rail.

Once on deck, Duncan finished pulling the rope ladder after him, saying, "Can't leave this down, gentlemen—I should like to speak with your Capt—"

Duncan looked at the sailors who surrounded him and noticed, for the first time, the curiously dull eyes of the men. Duncan stepped to one side and the eyes followed, but the crewmen made no move to stop him. They stared at him without taking any real interest in him, it seemed. Then one said, "You will come with us."

"I understand your concern," said Duncan, slowly. *My god, have you been drugged?* "It's not often a chap just hops aboard in mid-cruise, eh?"

"No," came a voice from behind Duncan, "no, it isn't."

Duncan reached into his coat and through the carefully concealed pocket there, and he felt the handle of his katana slip into his hand as he pivoted on his right foot to meet the voice.

He was met by a man with a deep-blue face, a stylized, ancient salamander face, one that Duncan had held in his own hands, once. Khordas' velvet voice was altered by the mask, it expanded within the funnel and became as a god's. Duncan eyed the tall, gaunt red-head, wearing a robe like the one he had worn so long ago, and the katana came forward with his arm, as of its own power, the coat flying out of the way. "Khordas. That costume proves what I've known all along."

Khordas stood still, hands serenely beside him. "Proves what, MacLeod?"

"You're out of time," said Duncan.

"Aren't we all?"

"Let's go."

"What is it, Duncan? In search of a Quickening? You just don't understand the elements, do you?"

"What else is there, Khordas? Money, love, power, and the Game. The *Game!*" Duncan said, "On guard, Salamander. I won't give you another chance."

And Khordas only smiled, and when Duncan felt a second presence, coming up fast, he turned his head. But something that was probably the hilt of a rapier smashed him in the back of the skull before he got the Companion—for who else could it be—in sight. Khordas whispered, in a way that boomed and hissed at the same time from the mask, "Oh, MacLeod, I think you will at that."

And as he lost consciousness, Duncan heard something about the brig, and "making preparations."

When the *Gratiano* was first built, the Grand Ballroom was the most ambitious undertaking of its kind, a dream come true for its architects. It was three hundred feet long, one hundred feet wide, thirty-six feet high, the most space ever afforded to a room that would make no profit, save that for the eye. The predominantly white walls were set off by tapestries brought from the Far East, with silver-oxidized ornamental ironwork complementing the gilt decor in a way that the *Times* had referred to as "somehow avoiding, if narrowly, the gaudy." And at midnight, February the ninth, 1897, it looked almost nothing at all like its designers' dream.

At the far end of the ballroom stood a massive fireplace, an orifice eight feet tall, and now inside this hellish mouth had been placed a giant cauldron from the kitchen. In the cauldron, heated by the hot coals, bubbled a bath of mud. And in the mud, as at the beginning, curled and waited the god.

Lauren strode through the ballroom and observed the progress of the evening. The mud they had made from earth brought on the absconded naval scout, bucket after bucket, had been thrown across the walls, covering them, so that in the still-burning chandeliers' light, the ballroom was no longer a ballroom, but a cave. The walls dripped steadily, and the sludgy mud fell in dollops upon the wood floors and Asian rugs. Lauren walked along the walls, reaching into her bag, and out of it she drew a handful of something dust-like, and this glittered darkly as she threw it onto the walls and it adhered to the mud, some of it raining down on the heads of the gathered.

And Lauren the Companion reached the front of the ballroom and stood with her back to the great fire, surveying the Children of the Salamander.

Six hundred people in all, groaning, swaying on their knees, men, women, children, people of all the classes of the mortal world. Lauren vaguely remembered she had been from a lesser class once; that was when she inhabited the old world, before she found Khordas.

In the front kneeled the former captain of the ship, Lewis, and he simply stared forward, like a marionette, his jaw hanging open.

Lauren the Companion stood before the cauldron that bubbled with hot mud. It was time for the Return of the God.

"My Children," said Lauren the Companion, now Lauren the High Priestess, "you have been betrayed by your fellow men, you have not known the nature of this world. You have worshipped the wrong gods or none at all, you have served yourself and destroyed yourself without compunction. You have wielded power without understanding it.

"The season has been a long one, Children, and the crops have withered, and you have lost your spirits, and though the longing has been buried, you have longed for the guiding force, the force of destruction, the force of cleansing."

No words from the Children, simply blank staring, waiting, blank slates taking in the new message, clay waiting to be sculpted, like the clay that held the god, but not for long.

"In time, my Children, you will understand, you will know your parts, you will serve your master. But now you are Children indeed, and it is time to learn. Wretched, indeed, is the world of men, that has forgotten its part in the cyclical drama, and the Return of the God."

Lauren clapped her hands together, red hair swaying with every move, and now the chemical packets in her palms flashed and burned and she felt the joy of burning. She thrust her hands out, sending the dripping flames to either wall, and now the glittering walls sparked, and ignited, and the mud walls of the Grand Ballroom exploded in flame. Now the

Children began to sway more fiercely, the potion within them causing them to see the god in the fire, and in Lauren, and they moaned, waiting for the instructions of the Companion.

Hands thrust high, smoke filling the air, blackening Lauren's face as she called out: "You are the Children of the Salamander! Rise, and pay tribute! Hear my words and make them your own!"

Now the Children of the Salamander rose to their feet, and Lauren the Companion began the ritual. And she felt as the Children: alive, Immortal, and content in her calling.

Khordas, we have come to please you . . .

Light filtered into Duncan's eyes as he awoke, and he was greeted by grey plaster. He saw immediately that he was in a holding pen, on the deck, his back resting against the iron bars of the cell. His head was pounding from the Companion's blow, and he found himself absently reaching up to his neck, as if to prove that indeed his head was still attached to his shoulders. Duncan vaguely heard a sound, like voices chanting.

Khordas, we have come to serve . . .

Duncan rose and looked out through the bars of the cell. The area outside the cell, the chair where there should have been a guard, was empty. And the chanting continued, far off, a slow, murmuring sound, one voice, answered at intervals by a horde of others that echoed down through the bowels of the ship. *Khordas, what are you doing?*

There was a reason Duncan was still alive, any idiot could see that. Khordas had a plan for him, and it couldn't possibly be agreeable. The Highlander groaned and felt the headache passing, and he surveyed the cell for a method of escape. As he stood he reached into his coat, slipping his hand through the lining, and was shocked to feel the ivory handle of the katana in its specially constructed scabbard. Odd. Khordas had not taken his sword. What, did he want a fair fight yet?

At the end of the cell, a small window looked out on the ocean itself. He was above surface, that was good. The window was inset by six inches or so, and could not be more than a foot or so in diameter. Duncan bit his lip. That would be embarrassing indeed, to get stuck in a window and hang half in and half out the ship, just waiting for Khordas to come by and chop his head off. For that matter, a loose cable might do it. "And if your head comes away from your shoulders, it's over."

There would be no breaking through the steel bars that comprised the cell door. But the lock was of the standard key-hole variety, and all that experience with similar scrapes would not to go to waste. Duncan now reached for the back of his head and found that Khordas had absconded with his hairpin, too. *Of all the thieving . . .*

Duncan sat down on the edge of the folding cot that hung from the wall, and removed his right boot. He grimaced at the stench, for he had been sweating, but lifted the boot to his mouth and used his teeth to tear at the stitching that bound the leather. Duncan heard a tiny ripping sound as the stitching gave, and then used his hands to yank the pieces of leather apart. A flash of silver glinted in the dim light. There, nestled in a pocket inside the leather lining, was Duncan's own small set of tools.

Duncan had been in a rather raucous prison in Turkey with that chaotic thieving Immortal Amanda, and although Duncan knew she could be trusted no farther than she could be thrown, the lovely criminal had taught the Highlander a thing or two about escapes. The woman kept more tools on her person than seemed humanly possible, and Duncan had adopted this habit along the way to fit his own needs. Similar pockets could be found in his coat—next to the hidden scabbard—and in his trousers, and especially in his belt (which, also, Khordas had taken). Generally, all of this had proved a wasted effort, it being much easier to simply avoid arrest. But after three hundred years, it paid to be prepared.

Duncan withdrew from the pocket a lockpick, resealed the boot as best he could, and put it back on. Now he went to the lock and proceeded to jimmy it. Within twenty seconds he was making his way down the passageway.

Khordas heard the chanting from outside the pit and his meditation ebbed into full wakefulness. The new world awaited; the new Children were calling for him. Khordas felt the heat of the mud, reddening his skin to match his hair, and he began to rise.

Khordas, we have come to please you,
Khordas, we have come to serve,
Khordas, protect us from ourselves, and make us
strong . . .

The mud parted as Khordas' head emerged, the deep blue mask attaching itself, molding itself to his face as the mud slithered across it, and Khordas opened his eyes and looked out on the six hundred Children.

Khordas, hear our prayer!

"I hear, my Children, and am glad, at last."

Khordas rose, and the mud dolloped off of him as his body slipped from the glove-like vat, and Khordas called out to his Children. Before them all stood Lauren, his Companion. She had taught the Children well. But then, the Root of Faith always helped. Lauren was smiling, proud of her god, and Khordas knew that at last, the season of the Return of the God had come. Khordas threw back his head, clapping his hands together, and the chemicals he had been taught to use so, so long ago flared, and fire burst forward from his hands as he spoke: "I am the Salamander, Khordas! I hold the power of the earth in my hands!"

We are not puny, like our babes,
Nor weak, like our enemies across the hills—
We are your Children, Khordas,
And because we fear you, we are to be feared!

Khordas was pleased. "And what tribute do you pay, my Children, that I might not destroy, but will be pleased?"

Khordas, we beg your mercy,
Khordas, we wish to please . . .
We give you these baubles, poor though they are, but to
us, they are great things.

And now Lauren stepped aside with a bow, and the Children began to come forward, some with furs of great value, some with baubles indeed. Some with diamonds, some with gold. Then the Child who once was called Captain Lewis stepped forward and said, "This and much more we can offer you, Khordas, for below your feet are vast spaces, and these hold more treasure than any man can carry."

Lewis bowed and stepped back, and returned to the congregation of the Children, where he knelt and bowed.

Khordas smiled, and bits of mud fell from his face as he did so. "I am well pleased, my Children. Great things will become of you . . ." and Khordas paused, for a feeling had struck him in the gut, a feeling he knew well. One of the false gods was coming. Ah, good. MacLeod. "Great things indeed. But that I might know your love, I beg another bauble of you."

Lewis cried out, "What can we give to appease the god?"

"I have my Companion, and need no other of that kind. But your good wishes for a babe, to join him in the hot pit, a babe to become as Khordas, the Salamander, fearing no flame, succumbing to no water."

Lauren now began to stride among the six hundred, and presently she found a child, silent and listless, moaning. "This girl is a fitting one," said Lauren, as she knelt by the child. The girl had red hair, like Khordas and Lauren. Lauren now spoke to the Child beside the child, and said, "You are the earthly guardian of this babe, do you give her to the god?"

The woman stared ahead, quivering, Somewhere, sedated, she was an American named Pamela Devon, but this was nothing, a trifle, for she was now a Child of the Salamander. Pamela quivered, and Khordas felt sure for a moment that she would deny the god, but then she spoke: "This babe I give to the god."

Lauren took the girl by the hand, and the child rose, and walked with the Companion.

"She has a new mother," said Khordas. "And I am her new father. She is a child of the god, praise her!"

Praise we give to the child of the god, as we do to the god himself. Khordas, we come to serve . . .

Lauren came to the cauldron now, the girl walking slowly before her, and they stopped and waited at the cauldron where Khordas stood. And Khordas knew that there was a difference between himself and the babe, knew that although he could withstand a scalding bath of mud, she could not, but it was part of the ritual, and must be done. Lauren offered up the child, and Khordas seized her by the waist and held her high over his head.

Praise we give to the child! Go, now, and become as Khordas and the Companion!

And the babe looked into Khordas' eyes and her green eyes reflected only dully the fire of his own, for what was she but a mortal? And would there not be truth in the myth, would some sort of transformation not take place?

Khordas now began to lower the child towards the bubbling mud that surrounded his own legs. ("Khordas!" he heard someone yell, and he knew who *that* was, as the door at the back of the ballroom slammed), and the girl's shoes began to dip into the pit.

"Khordas! No!"

The Highlander was moving through the crowd now, and Khordas cried, "Children of the Salamander! Vanquish this wearisome foe!"

And Khordas watched out of the corner of his eye as Duncan MacLeod was set upon by the Children of the Salamander, and he was kicking and pushing his way through, but not fast enough, he was afraid . . .

The babe's dull eyes grew wide and the child shuddered, freezing in fear, if it could be called that, or exaltation, perhaps, and her legs entered the mud and Khordas heard a slight sizzling sound.

Deafening, the roar of the Highlander, beneath a mountain of Children, pounding him, tearing at him, biting him, and Khordas took a breath and prepared to plunge the babe into the hot mud when something snatched the girl from his arms.

"I reject this child!" came a voice. "Take her away, for she cannot serve, I see weakness in her bones!"

Khordas looked up, enraged. "Lauren! Dare you defy the wishes of the Salamander!"

But Lauren was backing away, not herself, and she nuzzled the child in her arms. Presently she set the child down before her. "She is not fit!" Lauren cried, loudly.

Khordas bared his teeth, now. "You will pay for your insolence, Companion. You will pay dearly!"

The girl seemed to come to her senses as her feet touched the floor. She screamed, feeling at her burnt legs, and now she began to run.

Khordas surveyed the ballroom, the great cave of mud and

fire, and saw that MacLeod had fought his way out of the onslaught of Children.

Khordas called out, "The God has returned, MacLeod! You are too late!"

"Khordas . . . Khordas . . . *you* . . . are . . . deluded." The Highlander was staggering, and he pointed at Khordas, then seemed as if he were about to rush Khordas himself.

Khordas raised a hand and returned MacLeod's gesture. "No further, Highlander! Look around you! This room is sacred, MacLeod. Holy Ground!"

MacLeod roared, incredulous. "By *your* edict?"

"This is the Church of the Salamander," Khordas swept his arms out, indicating the torchlit bog, "and these are his many worshippers!" Khordas' silken voice hissed through the mask. *At last you know. You will all know.* "And you are not welcome here."

MacLeod was a sight, standing still, the only movement the rise and fall of his massive chest. Khordas knew that MacLeod would not break the taboo against fighting on holy ground, no matter how angry he might be. MacLeod seemed to consider it, and then he took notice of the only human-sounding voice in the whole place, the screaming, burnt child who was running madly through the ballroom. Duncan MacLeod snatched up the girl and ran, out of the cave of fire and mud, out into the light.

Khordas felt the presence of the Highlander recede. He had to smile, even though the Highlander had taken the girl.

"Lauren," said the Salamander, "let us speak in private." Khordas looked at her and felt her withering under his stare. She, like the mortals, would come back under his control. All these things would be dealt with.

And now, even MacLeod knew there was no hope.

Chapter 11

Duncan fired up the engine on the *Spanish Lady* and sped away in the night. The child's burns needed tending to, and he wasn't the one to do it. "What is your name?" Duncan asked the child, glancing over his shoulder and shouting down into his own bunk. "Hello?" Duncan looked back behind the *Lady,* to confirm that they were not being followed, and stepped down to the bunk.

The girl's green eyes were no longer dull, but now they reminded Duncan of Christmas tree decorations, so bloodshot they were. The child was exhausted. "Genevieve," Duncan heard the girl say.

"Well, sit tight, Genevieve, everything is going to be fine," Duncan said, knowing this to be a patently offensive and insulting lie. Duncan slowed down and went to Genevieve, and knelt down to talk to her. "Your mother, was she on board the ship?"

Genevieve was trembling, very slightly, but she was fighting to remain calm. It obviously counted for a great deal that Duncan had spirited her away from that ship. She swallowed, and spoke, with a calm that defied her years. "Yes."

"And your father?"

Genevieve shook her head. Duncan grimaced and said, "No father?"

Another shake of the head. Then, the child grabbed him by

the collar, and Genevieve pressed her nose against his and her bloodshot green eyes met Duncan's. "You have to go back. You have to go back for my mother."

"Genevieve, I . . ."

"You have to! That . . . man . . ."

Duncan cupped his hands around the child's face and said, "I will, Genevieve. I promise you, I will. But right now you must trust me that you are safe."

Now the child stared ahead, humming something, something she had just learned, and if the eyes reflected the mind, Duncan knew he would have seen walls of mud and fire, and the Salamander. "Khordas, I have come to please you, Khordas, I have come to serve . . ."

Duncan lay the child back down and checked her bandages. She had suffered minor burns on her calves, but she should suffer no permanent damage.

Duncan returned to the main deck of the *Lady* and looked back in the direction of the anchored ship that had become a world all its own.

Duncan slammed his fist against the rail, his mind racing with possibilities and scenarios. He had underestimated the Salamander. He had not taken the Immortal's ravings seriously, choosing instead to believe that all dark-leaning Immortals were alike, thieves and murderers. He had not wished to admit that Khordas was different. Duncan had been mistaken. And that was the last mistake Khordas would allow.

"Lauren," spoke the voice of the god. Lauren looked around the room that had been the captain's quarters. The walls had been covered over with mud, and the fine, sparkling substance covered them, so that the walls of mud sparkled like the night sky. She was sitting on a stool of clay, her feet and hands encased in some dark, hard substance. "Lauren."

Lauren stared ahead. Like Dante's vision of Lucifer, Khordas was in a cauldron, smaller than the ceremonial pit in the ballroom, up to his chest in mud. Her eyes burned like fire from sockets that were encased in mud. "Yes, my Lord."

Khordas rose from his resting place, and seemed to step out of the cauldron so smoothly that he appeared to simply float out of it and set himself before her. "I want you to explain to me why you did . . . what you did."

Lauren felt her head quivering, and she wanted to spill out a thousand lightning thoughts from deep in her mind, *Khordas, you've changed, what are you?* "The child . . ." She stopped, searching for the words.

"Was a sacrifice! From my worshippers, a sacred gesture!"

"Khordas . . . the child," she bit her lip, and fell back to her statement, "was unworthy. Infirm."

"What?" The voice of the god boomed through the cave, for it was a cave, now, the whole ship was a series of caves, wasn't it?

"She was weak. Her faith faltered, did it not?"

Silence.

"Did it not?"

Khordas held out his hand, and a pool of orange liquid had collected in his mud-covered palm. "And who are *you*," he said, brushing his thumb past the liquid, and now there was fire in his hand, "to decide the fitness of the gifts of the Children of the Salamander?"

"I am the Companion."

The fireball in Khordas' hand flared, and he brought the flaming hand close to her face. Lauren felt her skin heating and stared, trying to look past the fire. "Do you have, now, the wisdom of the god?"

Lauren managed to shake her head. "No. My Lord."

Flare. Blinding. "The strength . . . of the god?"

"No." Lauren blinked, and when she opened her eyes the light had drawn away, and now she blinked again and it was next to her cheek, and her eyes would not tear away from the flame, so beautiful, the element of fire, the gift of the god. "No, my Lord."

"I think *your* faith begins to falter, Companion. Does it?"

Fire. Fire in her eyes, please, god, what dangerous beauty.

"Does it?"

"No. No. No. Khordas, please . . ."

"You are the Companion!" Khordas slung his hand to his side and the flame burst from his palm and hit the walls, and now the walls flared around him, orange and blue flame surrounding them, heating the room, and now they were at the dawn of time, and Khordas walked the earth breathing fire, giving life to the mud. "You are my love, the symbol of my eternal love for the Children of the Salamander!"

"And always I shall be so," said Lauren, as she had said a thousand times, and now echoes of the past were moving through her, Khordas, lying awake at night and telling her of his godhood, and she had worshipped him, and did still, but Khordas, *what are you . . .*

"You were *given* to me!" Khordas cried. "A gift, pitiful though it was, the *best* the Children of the Salamander could offer their god."

No, no, I remember, I found you, I did not know what I was, but I was no gift! Lauren shook away the thoughts, and the good thoughts came, *yes, a gift, destined to find you, to help you, to be your Companion, like she who came before.*

"I . . . have had difficulty . . . with your . . . transformation . . . my Lord."

"Transformation?" roared the god.

"You are . . ." *Say it. What can he do, kill you?* ". . . different."

"I am the Salamander! Have you forgotten, my Companion? Are you delirious?"

"Khordas, please," Lauren said again. "I don't know you. I have done what you told me, but . . ." What could she say? *I didn't think you would take it all so seriously? Having second thoughts, madame?*

Now Khordas swiped his hand again, and Lauren saw a blue flame fly to the wall, and all the burning points flared in a chain reaction, and just as suddenly went out, snuffed by the power of the god. And Lauren was in total darkness. Darkness, as at the beginning. And the Salamander was there.

"I am disturbed by your loss of faith. Perhaps it is time again for you to partake of the Root of Faith."

No, I am Lauren of Wales, I was a highway robber, I had three sisters, I am not some god's little mistress! "Yes. My Lord."

"Good," said Khordas. "When I created man from the

mud . . ." Khordas' hand was caressing her neck, the mud sliding along her jaw.

You? You? Do you really believe that now? Do you believe and at the same time know it's not true?

". . . And *gave* man the fire of life, I knew that at times they would doubt me, for their doubting would make them stronger. As you will become stronger, Lauren."

The velvet, funneled, slithering, hypnotic voice, the nimble fingers, massaging her neck, the smell of sulphur on his hands, it was true, all of it, yes, Khordas, yes, Salamander, Salamander, I come to serve you . . . "Yes. My Lord."

"Then let us drink of the Root, and refresh ourselves, and renew our strength," said Khordas, and his voice was velvet fire. "For we have work to do, and infidels to punish."

And Lauren partook of the Root of Faith, and her mind washed over in orange and red, and she was the Companion, given by the Children to satiate the hungry, lonely god.

A few hours later, Barney sat in the Tariff house, counting out. When the sound came, a whistle in the door, a shape moving soundlessly through the room, he did not look up. *Stay calm.*

"Barney?" It was a woman's voice, sweet and languorous, and the Quaker felt a tingle of excitement and looked up. His fear fell away like a shell. In the dim light she was a silhouette, curving magnificently, and the red hair caught the light just so that he almost regretted charging her. Almost. "More information, dear? I've missed thee."

"You spoke to MacLeod, Barney," said Lauren.

"MacLeod?" The Quaker froze. "MacLeod?" *Idiot.*

"Idiot. What sort of fool do you take me for?" The woman was drawing something from her pouch, raising it up, something that shone in the light, steel, blazing clean, like a new coin.

"What hast thou," Barney said, trying to remain calm. He mustered a smile. "Is this a dagger I see before me?" Its point moved with her hand, seeming to float before her, moving in that dark, muscled, woman's arm.

"This is a dagger indeed."

". . . Which was not so before," he whispered, knowing

what was coming but not believing it, *you knew, you knew this would happen* . . .

"No," she said, "it was not so before." The point came to his chin, and scraped against the faint growth of beard. "For you had not betrayed me before."

"He made me tell," said Barney, "I didn't want to, I . . ."

"Liar!" The point dug into Barney's chin a bit more, and he felt it nip at him, knowing it drew the slightest amount of blood. "Liar. He *paid* you, didn't he?"

"Yes, but . . ."

Lauren raised an eyebrow, "'Yes, madame, he paid me, but I begged him not to,' is that it?"

"No! I swear."

"Liar still!" she cried, and the dagger came down, and Barney felt a sharp pain and looked down to see his own hand impaled on his desk. He moved his hand by reflex and felt raw nerves scream out, and he trembled, and each tremble brought new pain.

The flowing figure of the Companion moved, and twisting a knob, caused the oil lamp on the counter to open up and flare, and her face and hair were clear, burning bright, red as Hell. Hell awaited.

"Don't reach for it, Barney. Really. Do you know something, Barney?" said the husky voice. Lauren now rested against the counter and put her hand to her face, and her head began to move quickly up and down, and soon it became audibly apparent that the woman was laughing.

"Madame . . ."

"We all play our parts, Barney. You're an educated man, yes? 'All the world's a stage,' and all that?"

"Yes," the Quaker said, timidly. She was going to let him go. She was in a good mood. She had driven a dagger through his hand and yes, *by God* he had learned his lesson. *Please go away. Please.*

"The Messiah knew that Judas would turn, did he not?" Lauren was still laughing, and she spoke to him over her shoulder, toying with the oil lamp.

"Cor . . . correct."

"Wouldn't have been possible without him, I should think—Judas, I mean."

"Madame?"

"Whence the crucifixion if Judas did not play his part?" Lauren opened the lamp more, and the light increased, and her reddish form glistened, for she was wet with sweat from the lamp that was so near to her face. She seemed to study the flame for awhile, mesmerized by it, before looking back at him. "Without the sorrowful greed of Judas, whence the triumph of the god?"

Barney nodded swiftly. He had heard as much in Meeting, but . . .

"All the parts we play—Khordas, so many of them—and I am happy to report that yours was played most satisfactorily. For you delivered MacLeod to us." She tilted her head, lost in the flames again. "He has since left, but he will be back. He, too, plays a part. As do I."

"And . . . my part . . . now . . ."

"That's an interesting question, Barney, and it's perceptive of you to ask it."

"I thank . . . thee," Barney whispered. *Please go away. Please go away. I just wanted a little extra.*

Slowly, the lamp tipped over, and the glass cracked, and Barney watched the papers, and all the ledgers there, begin to catch, and Lauren turned to him, lit up from behind by a rising curtain of flame.

"We did our best to help you along, Barney. We knew you would betray us, but I like to think there was a part of us that rather hoped you wouldn't. Ah, well. All in the script."

"Please, I . . . he tortured me! Tortured!"

Lauren glibly clicked her tongue. "Doesn't really make that much of a difference now, does it?"

Lauren reached into a pouch that was slung low on her hip and withdrew a small packet, and began to unroll a cord from it. She laid it on the desk in front of Barney, and the Quaker stared at it, and back at the red-headed goddess. A match flared and the end of the cord began to sparkle and hiss, and she patted the packet, as if it were a pet. "Marvelous thing, this. My love has something of a talent for these things. Watch it for me."

"What . . ." Barney moved his hand again and gasped at the pain.

"Don't move, Barney. Still life, I want to remember you just this way." Lauren drew a watch from her pouch and consulted it, and said, "I have my own part to play, so I must be going. Still life, Barney."

Barney reached with his other hand for the packet and suddenly, so fast he didn't see it, another dagger was piercing through his hand and he was stuck to his desk, a fly in a child's collection.

She was moving away, now, around the growing wall of flame on the counter, and the cord was still hissing at him, moving steadily down towards the packet.

From behind the wall of flame he heard the bell of the door ring, and Lauren said, "I thank you, Barney. Somehow I feel better about my own part, now. But as for yours . . . well . . . ten," the door closed, and outside he heard her lilting, lovely, terrible voice, "nine . . ."

Barney stared at the spreading fire and the shrinking fuse.

Two. One.

Curtains.

Chapter 12

"Who did this to her?" Gabriela asked, after she was sure that Genevieve was asleep. Duncan had called her at five o'clock in the morning, Mrs. Brandeis beating on her door and telling her she had a *telephone call* as if this were some sort of crime. When Duncan said that he was at the area hospital with an injured child, and would she bring some blankets, she was off. Gabriela met Duncan as he was carrying the child off the ferry to Nantucket, and she already had the surrey cab waiting. Now, all was quiet outside the surrey, save for the horse's hooves.

"Who else?" Duncan answered, staring out the curtained window. It was six o'clock in the morning, and the sun was coming up.

"How did these injuries occur?" All Gabriela knew was that the girl had received second-degree burns to her lower legs, that thankfully she had been shod at the time of the burns. Gabriela lifted the blanket to peer at the white gauze.

"It looked like Khordas was bloody well going to boil her in mud," said the Highlander. "But I cannot be sure. I had a small army of unarmed passengers on me at the time."

"The passengers of the *Gratiano* attacked you?"

"The passengers of the *Gratiano*," repeated Duncan, "seem to be thoroughly under Khordas' control. They've been drugged, I think. Mesmerized, as well."

"But you got to her in time."

"Her name is Genevieve," Duncan said. "And no." He turned to her and put his fist to his chin. "That's the odd part. Lauren Drake interfered. The Companion stopped the sacrifice."

Gabriela shook her head. "I cannot believe any of this. Human sacrifice on a cruise ship, three hundred year old men . . ."

"And women," corrected Duncan. "And *I'm* three hundred; there's no telling how old Khordas is."

Gabriela ran her hand along the sleeping girl's face, and said, "*Pobrecita niña.* What's to become of her, does she have a mother?"

"Aye," said Duncan. "And her mother is a captive of our friend the Salamander. You should have seen this ship. He's converted it into some sort of replica of his own myth, and the people are his worshippers."

"What is he going to do?"

"I have no idea. Right now he's just sitting there on the water, miles off. This much is true, though: when that ship fails to put into port, someone's going to notice."

"Is that what he wants? To be noticed?"

"That's too simple," said Duncan. "And too easy."

They heard the driver shout, "Twenty-two Roderick Lane," and the surrey began to slow. As they got out and Duncan turned to pay the driver he said, "I would very much appreciate it if . . ."

"She can stay with me," said Gabriela, with the slightest of smiles. This would be entertaining. "I'm just gaining all sorts of loved ones, aren't I?"

"Don't worry," said Duncan. "Her mother is on board that ship. And we'll get them all back."

"What are you going to do?"

"I'm going to think," said Duncan. "He's been knocking about for a long time for me not to have a proper angle on him."

"I do not understand this man," said Gabriela, as she lifted the girl from the surrey and they began to walk in the dawn light to the front of the boarding house.

"He's an Immortal," Duncan said flatly. "And I'll deal with him as an Immortal. He's just made it more difficult."

That night, Duncan drifted in and out of sleep, and vaguely heard the curtains lifting in the breeze. Then the curtains spoke to him, reciting something.

"The very Salamander lives in's eye," Duncan heard a familiar voice sing, "to mock the eager violence of fire."

The Highlander awoke to the sound, wherever it came from, and the presence flooded his mind. *Here?*

The candle at his bedside fluttered a bit, and Duncan saw that the window was open. His hand flew to the dragonhead katana where it rested on the wall, and he rose with it before him, and peered out the window. When he looked down through the billowing curtains, into the yard of the boarding house, he saw a dark figure in a hooded coat. There was no mistaking it, even if he'd stopped the serenade. "Khordas."

The figure's arms raised and came to the lip of the hood and lifted it back, revealing the blue-painted mask of the Salamander. Now the god in the raincoat stood still, and then, as if satisfied that he had Duncan's attention, the Salamander reached his right hand into his coat as if to draw a weapon. After a moment he retrieved what looked to be a pocket watch, and Duncan saw the moonlight glint off the silver casing and reflect in the Salamander's face. In the night Duncan swore he heard the watch click open, and Khordas turn his dark mask towards the watch's face, look at it, and nod. And then he looked up at Duncan.

Something below, on the first floor, blew, and Duncan felt the house shake as flaming boards flew out across the yard. Duncan leaned across the window sill and tried to see—the explosion seemed to have come from the foyer. Duncan looked back and Khordas was gone.

Gabriela. Duncan jumped into a pair of trousers and threw on his coat and went to the door into the hallway. Gabriela's room was at the other end of the hall. Now Duncan began to hear the screams of the handful of boarders, people rushing along the lower floor. The sound of breaking glass mixed with that of groaning wood.

Oh, Christ. Duncan threw open the door and stepped into

the hall. The top floor was quiet, save for the echoes of terror downstairs. It was a strange feeling, to hear so many panicked below, muted by plaster and wood. It was like seeing someone die a mile away. Muted, the sound of impotence.

"Count yourself lucky," somebody shouted, somewhere in the noise, "should you see the creature the Salamander. For he is myth, alive in the world, despite all we know. Myth and the world: the Salamander knows the difference. Rare, my son, rare indeed."

Ignore that. There was no one on the upper floor to worry over save Gabriela and the girl, for only Duncan's and Gabriela's rooms were occupied. But why were they silent, had they not heard the explosion? The cacophany below continued as Duncan ran down the hall towards Gabriela's room. A flash of hope crossed his mind that they had indeed heard the blast and had retreated down the far stairwell near Gabriela's door, gone now, they would be safely outside by now *near Khordas.*

A crash of glass, from Gabriela's room, and an Immortal presence hit him in the gut.

Duncan heard something else, now, and instantly deemed it too strange—no, that was it, someone was playing a phonograph in Gabriela's room. Duncan would know the piece anywhere, and now the sound of flames and cracking wood and the cries of terror far below were met by the distinct sound coming from the end of the hall, from Gabriela's room, of Mozart's *Requiem.*

And Duncan found himself choreographed to the dreadful sound, seconds stretched out into hours, and someone was on the far stairwell, stepping around the corner. Duncan had reached the halfway point of the hall, and he heard himself call Gabriela's name.

The presence swelled with the *Requiem,* now, as the Immortal Khordas stepped out into the hallway, standing next to Gabriela's door, and still no sound came from within that door save that of the chorus. The shadows danced across the blue mask to Mozart, and Khordas was walking, but he flowed like a bird, or a salamander.

And now the god was walking toward him, fast, surely, but still everything was slowed to the most minute degree, dreamlike. Khordas' coat flew open and he drew out a container, a glass vessel, and the vessel flared as the gloved hand drew back and then came forward. Suddenly Duncan saw it tumbling through the air at him, glassy and flaming. The Highlander ducked as it struck the wall behind him.

"This is petrol, MacLeod. The latest thing."

A wave of heat and flame caught Duncan in the back as the glass bottle burst, and Duncan felt glass fragments slice past his neck. The wallpaper was on fire, now, and he kept moving toward Khordas. He had to get past Khordas to reach the room. "Gabriela! Gabriela!"

And now, Duncan heard a scream from within Gabriela's room, joined by another, the cry of a child. Duncan glanced past Khordas at the door and back at his foe in time to see another flaming jar coming at his face. Duncan cursed himself even as he reacted, wrongly, swiping out with his sword, and the bomb burst before him, glass flying through the hallway, and Duncan cried out in pain and he knew that he was on fire. But now, at least, he and Khordas had met.

Duncan gritted his teeth and lunged, and Khordas parried him, bringing the rapier up, and back down, and Duncan was distracted by the feel of his own flesh searing to his coat, and he felt the metal of the rapier slice through him.

Now, a voice somewhere, a new voice, but a very old one, *Don't get distracted. If you find yourself surprised, become new. Rebuild. Always, again and again, you must rebuild.*

The chorus was singing mournfully and the flames were racing back and forth and dripping down with the paste in the wallpaper, and Duncan looked at Khordas and in his mind he allowed himself to step back. On purpose, now, half a second stretched out into a minute, and Duncan breathed, ignoring the pain in his face, his arms, his body, ignoring the flames, knowing who he was and where he stood.

There is no surprise. I stand in the home that I have made, with the faculties that I have earned, and now I am set upon. Set upon, I yet suffer no surprise. Attacked, I yet suffer no loss. Burned, I yet suffer no pain. And wounded, I will suffer no defeat.

Duncan dropped a bit and kicked out, landing his right

boot in Khordas' stomach, and Khordas had to retreat a few steps.

"Good, lad, a bit of fire in you yet."

Duncan brought his katana down, hard, in an arc from right to left, meeting Khordas' blade and glancing past it, and he did not stop, but brought the sword back across from left to right.

Out of the corner of his eye Duncan saw that the hallway was an inferno, now, a true home of Khordas, and the sound of the *Requiem* was gone, and so were the cries of Gabriela and the child. And so loud were the flames and the sizzling wallpaper, that he could not tell if he would have heard these things, had they still been there at all.

"This Game is over, Khordas."

"Oh," said Khordas, as he stepped back and lunged at Duncan, expertly sidestepping the blow, "you haven't understood me, Highlander. You're the one playing the Game. And you cannot conquer that which you cannot understand." Duncan felt the rapier slice into his arm. *No pain.*

"I understand perfectly."

"No. Mawkish, impudent youth. You understand *nothing!*"

Duncan dove, now getting close to Khordas, and came up and butted his head against Khordas' chest. The Salamander only seemed amused by this and stepped back, and came again, and Duncan circled around him, and they moved farther down the hall. "Again and again you come at me, MacLeod, but if there is any Game, it is only the Game of the cat and the mouse. I laugh at your attempts, Highlander. I have no intention of killing you," he said, as the rapier contacted with Duncan's thigh. "You? You and all of your foolish Immortals, like the mortals you were. You deny me my destiny and I scorn you, and for this you will be punished."

At the end of the hall, not fifteen feet away, Duncan heard a new sound, a woman screaming and beating on Gabriela's door, pounding at it. "Please! Please!"

Duncan looked over his shoulder and felt himself moving against his own instinct, running for the door, and when he reached the door he reared back to kick at it and heard Khordas' voice.

Down the hall, slowly moving back, Khordas was surrounded by flames. And whatever substance coated his clothing kept him free from harm, and so he stood like a god in the fire. "Wouldn't do that it I were you," and now the screams increased, unseen fists pounding more fiercely at the other side of the door. "You never did understand my elements."

Duncan kicked at the door, his foot contacting with the wood at the lock, and the door swung open. Khordas was gone, now, but he was laughing, Duncan was sure of it, and as the door opened he saw the shape of a woman and a child, orange silhouettes against a yellow and red field that flared and grew. And all at once the wave of orange hit him, and the silhouettes disappeared as the full force of the flame burst through the doorway, gasping for air, smashing into the Highlander, bursting the door's frame, knocking him straight back. And Duncan felt boards crack and give way as he flew against them, fire searing his face, and by the time his back smashed into the window of the room behind him, all the orange and yellow and red faded to a merciless black.

Chapter 13

"Coming around finally, are you?" came a voice, and Duncan's vision began to clear and he saw a blurred figure standing over him. "I had to carry you back in a sack. A bloody mess. I hope you appreciate that."

Duncan blinked, and the blur began to abstract itself, an angular, tanned face, and oh-so-familiar, small, piercing, Immortal eyes. "Connor?" Duncan felt queasy, as if the room were moving. He focused his eyes and saw that in fact, the room *was* moving, back and forth. He was on a boat. "You got . . ." he rubbed his head. It hurt to talk. Duncan touched his face and immediately pulled his fingers away, because something about his forehead felt . . . odd. "You got my message."

The captain of the *Dido* nodded. Duncan looked around and saw that he was lying on a cot in a small room. Nearby was a table scattered with maps and ledgers.

"Christ," said Duncan, as he rose, feeling his joints burning. "Where am I?"

"You're on board the *Dido*," said Connor. "And I'd take it easy there. You took quite a spill."

"God, I hurt all over."

"Some healings are tougher than others. Think of them as re-growing pains."

Duncan expelled a short laugh and his lungs fought back valiantly. "How do I look?"

"You look," said Connor, as he expelled a stream of air from his cigarette, "like hell."

"Well. I'll live."

"Yes," Connor chuckled, "you will. But not for lack of trying. You should know that your house is rather gone. And whatever blast you walked into damn near tore your head off. Your face has been putting itself back together again for the last twelve hours or so. Don't worry, though, you're still pretty."

"Always jealous, teacher." Duncan grimaced. God, the pain. "How bad was I?"

Connor shrugged. "Bad, but you were always a quick healer. The gift manifests itself in different ways. At any rate, you were lucky—your spine didn't break. *That* would take some serious time. But this?" Connor waved, as if Duncan had fallen and scraped his knee. "This is just so much tissue."

Duncan sat up, gasping, "Oh, my God—Gabriela."

"Who?"

"Damn it all, Connor." Duncan forgot about the pain, or perhaps it was just going away. "She was under my protection. She and a child."

"Where . . ."

"Gone. Right before my eyes," he said.

Connor crushed out his cigarette and sat down next to Duncan on the cot. "How did he find your house?"

Duncan stared at the deck. Connor had dressed him in a sailor's uniform, and the boots were rather tight. But he was glad to feel his own feet. The little things; they all matter. "My house? How should I know? He sensed me."

Connor shook his head. "Followed you?"

"No."

"Then let me tell you how he found your house. Or let me guess. What name are you using now? Hm?"

"Name?"

"Right. Hello, I'm Captain Carruthers, who are you?"

"Duncan MacLeod."

Connor sighed. "Of all the . . . are you really still using that old name?"

"Are you really still using Ramirez's old katana? Of course I am."

"Mistake," said Connor. "And a grave one."

"Connor, we've been over this a thousand . . ."

"And I'll tell it to you a thousand times more until you get it into that tenuously attached head of yours. You have to *blend,* Duncan."

Duncan grimaced inwardly. Less than five waking minutes with Connor and he'd fallen into his old role. And he just couldn't help playing it. "I blend."

"Like hell. I've seen you. The bits of cloth I peeled out of your wounds looked rather expensive."

"Aye. Pajamas. It was good material, but I've seen better stitching . . ."

"Peacockery!" Connor shook his head before calmly asking, "Have you learned nothing? Oh, I've heard of your exploits, all right. Training with every great teacher around. But every time I see you the Highlander is dressed to the nines, like you're three-hundred years old and have money to burn."

"What does that have to do with . . ."

"An Immortal should pass through a crowd of mortals without as much as attracting a glance. There is the Game to think of. You advertise yourself, Duncan. Using your old name—no wonder he got to you."

"Connor," Duncan said, coolly, "this is entirely unfair. Just because I'm Immortal doesn't mean I have to forget everything else that I am. Duncan MacLeod is my name. I am *proud* of that name."

"Forget? Never. Adapt? Always. I don't care how proud you are of your name, you keep *that,*" he said, tapping at his chest, "in here. But this is not about you getting to be Duncan MacLeod, Immortal roustabout. It's not about *fun,* Duncan. And it damn well isn't about pride."

"I don't need this." Duncan reached up to his throbbing temples and found the flesh more normal now, accepting the right amount of pressure from his fingers. He was coming along. But Gabriela wasn't, was she? Genevieve wasn't. *Congratulations on a job well done.*

"Oh, I think you do," said Connor. "I come all the way out here and find you reforming under a pile of broken wood, and you tell me you lost mortals who trusted you. I think you need this very much."

"Gad, Connor, no wonder you travel alone . . ."

Connor jabbed his finger at Duncan's sternum. "What the hell do you think you're doing?"

"Living, Connor. It's what we do." *But not Gabriela. But not the girl. But not Amber Lynn.*

"Wrong. Again. You're going to get yourself killed, Duncan. You're so good a swordsman you forget to watch your back. The Game is played for *keeps*," Connor spat. "*That* is what you're supposed to be doing. *Playing the Game.* We will battle down to the last, and if you don't take it seriously enough, the last will not be you. And if it's an evil player, Duncan, the consequences will be catastrophic."

"I know."

"Never forget it, Duncan." Connor cursed and fished out his cigarette case and held the metal in his hands. He seemed to study his own reflection in the case and peered up at Duncan, shaking his head. "I knew it was a mistake to stand there and watch you go into hiding for ten years the way you did. 'Oh, I'm so depressed, because my mortal family has been killed; Oh, I'm so tired of fighting; Oh, I think I'll retreat to holy ground and meditate.' Meditate on *this*, Duncan. While you were under, lots of others were still playing." His voice dropped now, to near a whisper. "We're whittling down, now, did you know that? I don't know how many more centuries this can go on."

"You've always said that." Duncan bit his lip. Connor was glibly recalling some of the most difficult years of his life.

Connor nodded, slowly. "It's more true every time. What you must remember, Duncan MacLeod, is that despite what you may think, and despite what some of the more chaotic Immortals like Amanda may tell you, you are not in this Game for *yourself*."

Something flashed in Duncan's brain and he sat up,

quickly. "Tell me. Please. Was there another Immortal there?"

"At your house? No. Everyone was gone by the time I arrived. There was an old lady being interviewed by the police; I had to get around them to get to you. Khordas was gone."

"No, not . . ." Duncan shook his head. "Forget it. I was . . . confused." *But I felt sure . . . could I have been wrong?*

Connor nodded, and seemed to be studying Duncan's face. He clicked open the steel cigarette case from his coat and extracted two cigarettes. He offered one to Duncan, and Duncan shook his head with an almost queasy look.

"When did you pick that up?" Duncan grimaced.

Connor shrugged, and finished lighting his cigarette before speaking again. "It's all the rage in Paris."

"Ah."

Duncan girded himself for another round before Connor said, "I think you're finished, now."

"What?"

"Your face. It looks normal, now. How do you feel?"

Duncan rubbed his neck and stretched. He felt back for his hair, and found it had reached its normal length. Eyebrows. Good. "All in one piece."

"Good, then," said Connor. "Enough teaching. Let's go onto shore for a drink, and you can tell me what happened with the Salamander."

Duncan felt like a man sticking his head out the window after a storm. All clear. He breathed deeply, feeling the burn of Connor's smoke in his nostrils, and said, "All right. One thing I can tell you is, he's not playing normally."

"He never did," said Connor.

"Oh," remarked Duncan. "I think you'll be gravely disappointed in *his* respect for the Game."

Half an hour later, Duncan and Connor MacLeod sat at a table near the front window of a pub called the Ratter, from which they watched the sailors moving constantly up and down planks, swarming like ants about the shipyards.

Connor downed his Glenmorangie and lit another cigarette. "So he's out there, eh?"

Duncan nodded. "Aye." He was trying to get used to Connor. When was the last time? Would that have been '72, after the massacre? Less than thirty years. It seemed much longer, Duncan decided. He could not get over how much, and at the same time how little, Connor had changed over the years. The Scots accent was gone, now, entirely erased, so that Connor could have been from almost anywhere in Europe. He had passed into another phase. Duncan wondered if Connor even particularly cared about his old home anymore. They were really less than a hundred years apart, and yet Connor always seemed so much *older.* Or perhaps, Duncan allowed himself, the mentor/pupil relationship simply lent itself to the feeling. Connor was near four hundred years old now, but Duncan could remember the Elder Highlander when he hadn't yet hit the century mark, and the Elder Highlander had *always* been this intense. And, if Duncan dared think it, a bit paranoid. And often, tiresomely, right.

"So he raided this ship, the *Gratiano* . . ."

Duncan shook his head. "That's the odd part. Khordas has moved into a different area, it seems."

"How so?"

"I expected he'd be his usual self; that's what it had been leading up to. He wrecked seven ships and seems to have gotten away with a fortune in the past few months. Another fortune in jewelry, silver and gold from a wealthy man named Drake, who died with his wife in a mysterious explosion about a week ago. His wife was declared dead too, but we know different."

"The woman from the *Rosemary,*" said Connor, remembering the death of Amber Lynn. "So he's been stockpiling a lot of money."

"Right. But he reaches the *Gratiano,* and suddenly we've got a different Khordas on our hands. Incredible. He's converted the whole Grand Ballroom into a giant cave—literally, complete with mud all over the walls and phosphorous flaming substances. The ship itself is a floating, gigantic version of the mud house. He's made his own little world out there, Connor."

"What about the people?"

"Six hundred passengers."

Connor swore under his breath. "Wonderful."

"It gets worse. The people have been drugged, and Khordas seems to have transformed them into . . . what did he call it . . . the Children of the Salamander."

Connor nodded, taking it all in. "Curious Khordas."

"It makes no sense at all."

"Why?" asked Connor. "Because he's not just running around chopping off heads?"

"Partly that. Khordas hardly tried to take my head. He said as much. Connor, this man could be thousands of years old, and he acts like the Game doesn't exist."

"And there's our problem. Khordas isn't just cheating, he has no interest in the Game at all. He has his own agenda."

"All very well. I want to know what he's going to do with that ship."

"I'm very curious about that myself," said Connor. "What I'm suggesting, is that Khordas, somehow never learned the Game, and no one was around to teach him."

"Doesn't help that he was already a local god."

"Remember the mud house? We said Khordas adapted. Now I'm not so sure that he has, all that much." Connor chewed on his lip, then took a drag on his cigarette. "Think of it. There you are, your people think you're a god, and then you never die—maybe one day you take a fall and crack your head, you wake up—no one around to tell you you've died and come back. So you live forever. You have a belief system that makes perfect sense to you, why abandon it? But then your people, all of *that* lot die. And the world changes. And sooner or later, you start to run into others like yourself. And the mortals are not very appreciative of you."

"A crisis of identity," said Duncan. "But why did no one find him? Why did he never hear of the Game?"

"He heard, but too late. Maybe at that time there weren't many of us around. Maybe he was the only Immortal in Scotland. But it's not as if he never had the chance. Remember Nerissa? She seemed to understand the Game. So maybe he simply refuses to play. Who can say?"

Duncan had to smile. God, it was good to have Connor

around for a while. With a protracted sigh he said, "What now?"

"We start by fighting the evil," said Connor. "And I have an idea where that evil is going to make his next move."

Chapter 14

—————

While the two had been sitting in the Ratter, Connor noticed a seaman enter the pub, speak briefly with the bartender, and nail a poster to the wall next to the door. When he was gone, Connor rose and read the notice, discreetly removed it, and brought it to Duncan.

"What odds will you lay," asked Connor, "that Khordas knows about *this*?"

Duncan took the poster from Connor, setting his drink down. " 'Valentine's Day . . . guests in our waters, tours and entertainment?' "

"The *Troilus* and the *Cressida*. Right here."

"How big are these ships?"

Connor whistled. "Big. These are gunships, mate. Flotilla leaders both. How wonderful that in peacetime such sister ships have time to host the day of universal love, no? As it says, 'Come one, come all.' "

"Come the Salamander," said Duncan, slowly. "This is no coincidence. Of all the ports, he picks this one to terrorize. He knew this was going to happen, that's why he set up here."

"Guaranteed."

Duncan was mulling over the possibilities, going over the poster. "Naval ships. Christ, Connor, that's a lot of power in one port in peacetime. People swarming the docks . . ." Duncan had a vision of cotton candy and fire, and melting things. "Could he want to blow them up?"

"Or take them over?" Connor murmured. "Light a fire on Nerissa's birthday."

"Wh—oh. God, yes, of course." Duncan remembered it now, the mud *broch* and the burning arrow. Nerissa was the first Companion of Khordas. "I killed her."

"Yes you did," acknowledged Connor, "and quite well, I recall."

"He blames me for that."

"Rather correctly, I should think."

"Is her birthday—was her birthday—Valentine's?"

"Hm." Connor was staring into space. All those dates, over the years. "Three hundred years is a long time, Duncan. When was it, when we saw them at Aberdeen . . ." Duncan thought he could see the images flashing through Connor's brain, like a long painting on rollers, scrolling across his forehead.

"1624."

"No. '25. Carmichael . . ."

"Had a feast," said Duncan. "After St. Valentine's Mass?"

"Yes. You were still losing to me, then. We went to mass after practice, and then to the feast."

"Right," said Duncan. "Right. And we saw Carmichael off on his ship. And it blew up."

"Right there in the harbor," Connor intoned, and it was clear he was seeing it all perfectly now.

Duncan remembered the stick figure evaporating in fire, and Connor, wading into freezing water, as if he could do anything. Connor was young then, but Duncan had no idea how young . . .

Duncan nodded, repeating. "Right there in the harbor."

"Valentine's Day. 1625."

Duncan and Connor's eyes met, both of them staring at the calendar in their brains. "That's two days from now, Connor." Duncan felt the air thick in his lungs, as if it had solidified around them and neither wanted to move. They were sitting on a bomb. "We have to warn the Navy."

Connor nodded minutely, his eyes distant and scurrying,

as if reviewing a thousand options. "You make it sound so easy."

"You're saying they won't believe us?"

"I'm saying," said Connor, "that I doubt there's time. The nearest base is at Newport, Rhode Island. What do you suggest we do, send them a telegram: 'No explanations, but an Immortal pirate is going to attack your flotilla'?"

"Something like that," said Duncan, although he knew there was no way. "We could go in the *Dido*."

"Sorry," said Connor, "but I'm not taking *Dido* anywhere near a naval base. I've been dodging preventives all along, and I don't want that kind of attention."

"Connor," the younger Immortal said, "you're a privateer, but you're not still gunrunning, are you?"

Connor simply smiled what amounted to, for him, a sheepish grin. "There's gunrunning and there's gunrunning. Look, Duncan, some of the men are wanted. Some of them are deserters. I don't ask questions," he said, "but I owe them as much as not handing them over."

Duncan nodded. "Then it's . . ." This was insane. No way.

Connor's eyes met his. "It's up to us," said the Immortal. "We have to move."

Bertrand Lewis picked up a bucket of mud and carried it along the passageway until he reached the stateroom. His boots sloshed through the mud that ran across the deck in the passageway, and when he opened the door to the stateroom his eyes were blinded by the cleanliness of the room, the white of the walls and the pure color of the fibers in the oriental carpets. Something slithered past his foot, a salamander, and it flopped around on the carpet, horrified by the dryness of the garish fibers. Khordas would be displeased if his domain remained in such a state. He reached into the bucket with a brush and began to paint the walls.

Across the wire system, the band was playing something ancient, the bandmembers chanting out the words the Companion had taught them, chanting out the praises of the Salamander. Mud sloshed out of the bucket and onto the carpet, and the salamander at Lewis' feet was pleased, and seemed to breathe more easily. The creature looked up at him and

Lewis was sure it smiled, and Lewis felt that Khordas looked through those tiny eyes.

Somewhere, Lewis knew something was not right. But the thought was a clean one, pristine and modern, and as the mud sloshed down and along the wall, it obscured the evil thought. The world of the Salamander was near complete.

Lewis heard a sound, someone thrashing and crying out, and he looked through the door and saw several figures moving down the passageway towards him.

It was the Salamander himself. Khordas was accompanied by two Children of the Salamander. One, a woman, the god himself had by one arm, her other held by a servant. In the arms of another servant, whom Lewis vaguely recognized as one of his own sailors, squirmed a child Lewis recognized as the sacrifice that Lauren the Companion had found unfit. The Companion had sent the ill gift away, after which Khordas had sent the Companion away. Khordas had then closed the ceremony after sacrificing a better gift, one he found more acceptable. He had sacrificed two, in fact.

The woman had been dipped in the mud and had screamed, Lewis knew, in appreciation of the power of the god, and when she and the child were removed alive, Khordas had ushered them away to whatever reward awaited them. Lewis knew that he, too, would make an excellent sacrifice. Something clean and modern at the base of his skull cried out impiously against the thought and Lewis applied more mud. Khordas had warned them that such thoughts might intrude, and to only look forward to the feeding of the Children, which would come again soon.

*　*　*

Newport, Rhode Island

Jacob Devereaux of the Royal Preventive Service strode down the passageway toward the brig, sifting through the file in his hands as he did so. Next to him, the arresting officer, who identified himself as Commander Steven Glenn, was spewing his debriefing.

"His name's Crabbe," said Commander Glenn.

"When did you pick him up?"

"Yesterday. An informant turned him over."

Devereaux snapped the folder in his hands closed and handed it to Glenn as they reached the brig. The Preventive Officer sighed and opened the door to the interrogation room. Inside, a squat, dirty man wearing a prisoner's uniform sat chained to the table. Devereaux sat down across the table from Crabbe as Glenn took his place by the door.

"Crabbe, is it?" Devereaux did not need to ask this—he knew this man. Just another smuggler on the list.

The man looked up. "Do you have a cigarette?"

"That I do," said Devereaux. The Brit reached into his coat and gave it to Crabbe, then lit it. "You stole some very big guns, Crabbe."

"What big guns?"

"Who did you sell them to?"

"I don't remember."

Devereaux snarled, then relaxed. "I have all the time in the world, Crabbe. Soon you and I will be going home to London, and I will go back to my lovely wife and my luxurious bed and you will get to know the many luxuries of Hastings. How does that sound to you?"

Crabbe cocked his head and smiled. "Doesn't make a lot of difference, does it, now? I'm going to Hastings either way."

"Perhaps life can be easier. You picked up a load of armaments here in Newport and then sold them somewhere farther north. Who did you sell your cargo to?"

"Sorry, Captain."

Devereaux leaned back in his chair and stared at the ceiling for a moment. Oh, these boys, they were all alike. In his career Devereaux had almost come to view the smugglers as something like an extended family. Really, who cared if they tried to buck tariffs on whiskey, when there was a cooled palm to be had? But there were limits. Whiskey was one thing, guns entirely another matter.

"Let me be straight with you, Crabbe. You can't just unload a thirty foot gun and expect that I'll treat it as if you've been selling schnapps to wayward New Zealanders. I said Hastings and I meant—"

"Two months, tops," sneered Crabbe. "You know the score."

"Yes," Devereaux leaned in, "I do know the score, and I don't think we're clear, here. You're not going in as a privateer, laddy. You're going down as a full-fledged cannontrader. Do you know what that means? Hastings isn't a threat, it's an offer. I can *leave* you here to be prosecuted by the Yanks."

"So?"

"So they harbor a great deal of resentment against us." Devereaux smiled at the Naval Officer behind him. "Something about burning down Washington, DC a while back. And if I leave you here, you'll hang."

"Go on," Crabbe smirked.

"Hang!" Devereaux slapped his palm against the table. "For Christ's sake, Crabbe. You're one of my boys. Let's go nicely back to Hastings. Just tell me what we want to know. Or I'll leave you here," he said. "And it'll be a short internment, indeed."

Over Devereaux's shoulder, Commander Glenn said, "He's right, pal. We'd love to prosecute you, but Devereaux here has first dibs. Tell us what we want to know."

"A right smart deal," said Devereaux. "Death or Hastings. Information."

Crabbe crushed out his cigarette and cleared his throat. Pause. "What was the question, again?"

"Who," said Devereaux, "did you unload your cargo to?"

Crabbe leaned back and scratched his chin, the front legs of the chair coming off the deck. *A name, Crabbe, that's all we need.*

"All right," said Crabbe.

"All right."

Crabbe leaned forward again and the chair slapped against the tiles. "I sold them to Carruthers."

The Preventive Officer felt his jaw dropping. "You're having me on, Crabbe, think harder."

"No. No," said Crabbe. "The *Dido*'s been around Massachusetts."

Devereaux nodded. He knew that, but Carruthers wasn't into big guns. Then again, could he be sure? He couldn't, could he?

"I unloaded my cargo to the *Dido*," said Crabbe. "What happened to it after that I have no idea."

Devereaux frowned, shaking his head. "If you're not being straight, Crabbe . . ."

"Straight up," said the prisoner.

Jacob Devereaux took out a cigarette and lit it. True as gold, he had no choice but to pursue this. This was too big to be smoothed over with the petty bribes he'd been taking from Carruthers. Now the telegram he had read but not understood ran through his head. "Carruthers. Glenn?"

"Aye, Captain?"

"Do you have any ships headed for Massachusetts in the next couple of days?"

"I can check."

"I'm on it," said Devereaux. "And as for you, Crabbe," he exhaled a stream. "Thank you very much."

Devereaux sat at the table while Crabbe was unchained and ushered back to his cell. Carruthers had some explaining to do. Most likely, Crabbe had picked a name out of the air. David Carruthers knew better than to deal in cannons. But Crabbe was right—Carruthers was here. The telegram, the one with the curious "salamander" comment, had been an urgent one.

Carruthers was definitely in the area. And that was too much of a coincidence.

Connor ushered Duncan back onto the *Dido* and immediately called the crew together. "Gentlemen," he said, as everybody gathered at the mast, "I know how fond most of you are of the United States Navy."

There was a general murmur of discontent, and a few

harsh laughs. Duncan took a seat on a barrel and watched Connor with his men. He had never seen the Elder Highlander so at home.

"What's the problem, Captain?" called Thomas Rooke, loudly. Rooke was slightly drunk, as were the rest of the crew, this being the first time they had put in to port in quite a while. Rooke, Connor had said, was a former Navy man himself, and would be still if not for an embarrassing incident involving an unyielding and dangerous superior. People may die because of an officer's orders, but assaulting one is a federal offense, he had come to find. Rooke had found a home on the *Dido*, bucking preventives and avoiding his old comrades quite well, indeed. Most of the *Dido*'s men had similar *vitae*, it turned out.

"It seems," said Captain Carruthers, as he was known to them, "that the squids have gotten themselves into a spot of trouble." The captain looked at Duncan and said, "This is Duncan MacLeod. He has served with me before. I trust him with my life and I expect the same from each of you. He will explain."

Duncan looked up, now, and stood, and suddenly felt glad that Connor had lent him a dingy suit of clothes. He cleared his throat. "There are two ships, of similar design, coming into Buzzards Bay on Valentine's Day. They are called *Troilus* and *Cressida*, and they will be fully armed, iron-hulled, steam-propelled battleships. These ships are in trouble."

Rooke scratched his head. "How do you know?"

"There is a dangerous man called Khordas," said Duncan, "and though it seems incredible, we know he intends to attack the Bay. With those ships and all that weaponry floating about, we think our man will be drawn to the Bay like a moth to flame. He's been preparing for it. There will be a multitude of citizens on the piers, gentlemen, and they will be in grave danger. Khordas has a ship as well, a steamer of eighteen thousand tons. He may have armed it by now, but what we know is that this man has single-handedly destroyed numerous ships, and with a full crew he will wield tremendous destructive power." Duncan paused. "And be assured, he is completely and thoroughly insane."

"What can he do against iron hulls?"

"I'm not eager to find out," Captain Carruthers spoke up. "This man destroyed a ship of mine, mates. It's time to pay him back. And I hope you will help me."

Rooke looked around at the others, all of whom had fallen quiet. "What do you expect us to be able to do?"

"We are a small ship," said Carruthers. "But we have speed. We've outrun many a fast preventive, and we can give as good as we get. The *Dido* is going to rendezvous with the *Troilus* and *Cressida* before they reach the Bay."

Duncan spoke up. "If they do not listen, we will return to port ahead of them." He frowned. The sister ships would be so gunhappy it was unlikely they'd listen to wild tales of danger. "I have a yacht called the *Spanish Lady*. She may be used to keep an eye out for Khordas's ship, the *Gratiano*." They had wandered the docks today, and there was an undefinable edginess in the air about the Bay. The Tariff house had blown up, Duncan noticed. And people were deeply worried about the cruise ship that had yet to arrive. A broadside being distributed advertised that the Daughters of the American Revolution would be praying for the safe return of the ship, and all along Duncan knew its whereabouts—thirty miles off, in the hands of a god. Or rather, a madman.

"We?" Rooke looked at Duncan. "Are you coming with us?"

"Aye," said Carruthers, "he is. Duncan has been on this man for some time, and I want to provide him with all the help he needs. This is catch-as-catch-can, gentlemen. Only we know the destructive power of this Khordas, and only we know how much he needs to be stopped."

The men began to murmur now, and Duncan felt as if he were reading a play. It was true, what they said in the stage directions. *Crowd murmurs.* "This is serious, mates," Carruthers continued. "I may be asking you to lay down your lives. But there are many more lives at stake. And those lives will not have been spent half as well as I know ours have."

Carruthers smiled slightly. Rooke nodded and said, "Then I'm with the captain. Bring him on." The mate looked around, and the men seemed generally agreeable. But Rooke was still watching his captain, and it was clear that he would demand a fuller explanation soon.

Connor turned to Duncan. "You heard him. Bring him on."

"Great," said Duncan. "What now?"

"Now," said Connor, "we wait a few hours, and then we go visit our friends in Uncle Sam's Navy. On the water, where we thrive, of course."

"Do you think they'll listen?"

Connor shrugged. "If they don't try to destroy us first. I'm afraid some governments have found this vessel rather unpopular."

Chapter 15

"Leave us," Gabriela heard the man in the mask say. "I wish to speak with the infidels." Genevieve was crying at her feet, her legs still bandaged. What was to become of Genevieve. *What is to become of me?*

The light from a few candles flickered and cast serpentine shadows across the room, and Gabriela got a sense of growing, solid shadows, creeping past her feet in the form of mud. She found herself seated in a chair at a large, ornate wooden table. At her feet, an oriental rug was halfway covered in mud, and now the man pouring mud along the floor looked up as the two sailors who had dragged her in here let go and quickly exited the room. The mudlayer looked at the masked man, who said, "The room may be completed later, my Child."

"I wait on your honor," replied the man. The mudlayer was an older man, and Gabriela recognized the uniform of a captain of a cruise ship in this line. There was a brass name plate on his breast, engraved "Capt. B. Lewis." This must be the captain of the *Gratiano.*

The masked man said, "I will have new duties for you shortly. Please go to the main deck. The boats should be arriving now, with special cargo. Await me there."

"Yes, my Lord." Lewis bowed, and exited the room.

Khordas went to the table and lifted a bottle of wine and

poured two glasses. He held one out for Gabriela. "Drink," he said. "It will calm you."

Gabriela stared at the rug, which like the room itself seemed one-half steeped in mud, as if a new world were creeping across the old one, covering it over. She put her hand on Genevieve's shoulder and looked up at her captor. "You are Khordas."

"Yes," said the man in the mask. "Tell me your name."

"Find it out for yourself," she spat.

The mask nodded, as if amused. The nose of the mask seemed to grow and shrink in length with the flickering candlelight. "Tell me your name," said Khordas. "Or the child dies. I say this simply, so that you may see the truth of it." He still held the glass in one hand, but the other hand flicked at the wrist, and Gabriela saw the glint of a steel razor. "Tell me, or many will die, and I will burn each one alive and ask each one as he dies whether or not he knows your name."

"You won't get it that way." *This is ridiculous, she wanted to say, I am nobody, what on earth could move you . . .*

"Try me," said the masked god. "Tell me your name."

Silence. Then, "Gabriela Maria Cuadra de Savedra."

The mask tilted. "Quite a name. And you are the Companion of Duncan MacLeod?"

"I know him."

Khordas slowly circled the chair in which Gabriela sat, and ran a hand along her cheek. "What did he tell you about me, hm?"

"Only the truth," she said. "That you are a murderer. A thief. A *ladronito*. A two-bit bandit."

Air sucked in through the funnel in the mask and Khordas' head quivered slightly. "I like a woman of fire," he said. "Your insults please me, because they have little force."

"Give me a chance, Khordas." She wanted to move, to rip the mask away, to scratch out his eyes, but she knew that would be ill-advised. The sword at his side told her so, as did the fact that, according to Duncan, tearing out his eyes would probably not do a great deal of damage.

"And has he told you we are alike, you and I?" Khordas gave up for a moment on the wine and set Gabriela's glass down. He took a sip from his own goblet.

Gabriela stared ahead. The girl, Genevieve, was sobbing at her knee. The girl had not spoken a word since her arrival at Duncan's boarding house; now she seemed to drift from vague shock to abject fear. She shook, and Gabriela bent low to comfort her. "Shh," she whispered to the girl. "We will find your mother soon."

"You know," said Khordas, bending close to her ear, "that doesn't seem likely."

Gabriela looked up at the mask, and her eyes asked, *what do you mean. Don't say it, please* . . .

"The woman who provided this child as a gift came in quite handy, I'm afraid."

Gabriela's mind raced. She had awakened to the sound of glass breaking at Duncan's boarding house. A trio of men dressed as sailors had come in the window, seizing her and the girl, who slept at her side. They had been thrown into a coach and whisked away.

But through the window of the coach she had seen the men torching the house, and something else, two more figures, another woman and another child, being dragged screaming into the room and left there. *To die in her place.*

"Why have you done this?" she whispered. "Such destruction, what do you hope to gain? My father died in the fire on the *Andrew.* Why have you spared *me*? What do you want from me now?"

"Fate is an interesting thing," mused Khordas. "Duncan MacLeod on the *Andrew,* that was fortuitous indeed. And a new Companion of his, as well." Gabriela shot him a look that betrayed her ignorance. "Oh . . . oh, you don't know, do you?"

"Know what, Khordas?" Gabriela was tired of this. "I know all I need to know about you."

"Ah, yes," he said, touching her face again, and she moved away in disgust. "But you do not know all there is to know about *you,* do you? MacLeod has been unwise. He has told you nothing."

"I don't know what you are talking about."

"Your friend Mr. MacLeod is a very old man, Gabriela, did you know that?"

"I know."

"Tell me what you feel as you sit near me, Gabriela."

She shook her head. He was insane. Answer his questions, ingratiate herself with him, and she might buy time. "I don't understand."

"Does your blood," the mask drew near her, "curdle? I'm sure whatever you've heard about me has been less than flattering." Khordas sighed.

"When the Children of the Salamander walked the earth I found for the first time that I was not alone in the world, when I found my Companion. Her name was Nerissa. She is dead now. Your Duncan MacLeod, the Highlander, laid waste to her at my home, now two hundred years ago. It is now almost her birthday."

"He . . . he killed her?"

"Yes," said Khordas, "yes, my dear. Lopped off her head. Took her soul. But let me tell you of a happier time.

"I do not know the year I was born, for we had no years, as we speak of them now. I was the god, Khordas, educated as such as made so, and finally I became so. Understand this. I am Khordas, the Salamander. No one else may claim this.

"And every year the Children sacrificed to me a Companion, named according to ancient truth Nerissa. And every Nerissa I would draw into my pit after the sacrifice, and I would hold to her tightly. I would feel her pitch and moan under the hot mud, feel her heart beating madly, the mud rippling around her limbs as she fought, I would hear her cries under the mud as she tried to become Companion of the god.

"But every year the Nerissa was only a symbol, not a truth, like myself. And every year the Companion's mouth filled with hot mud and I held to her, demanding life from her, and I prayed to myself over her as I felt her finally end her struggle and lie dead, in the mud, a hollow reflection of the Companion of truth."

Gabriela shifted in her chair. He was talking more rapidly now, pouring out his tale of a people long, long gone. And each syllable was cast godlike from the funnel mouth of the mask, reverberating through her body, and she found herself swaying to it as if it were music, and she stroked the hair of the child and listened as the velvet voice of the god went on:

"But one day a miracle occurred, Gabriela. At the Time of

the Return of the God, I rose from the pit and demanded sacrifice, and after the gifts of valuables were given, the Companion was thrust forward, and I felt something in my gut. Not strong, mind you, but different, a feeling that at last my Companion had come. She was a vision, unique entirely, with white hair and reddish eyes and pale skin. I believe she would now be referred to as albino.

"I took this Companion in my arms, *this* Nerissa for *this* Return of the God, and drew her with me into the hot mud. Down into the pit went she with me, and I held to her as the thrashing began, and I prayed to myself, and felt her heart beating strong against the mud, her limbs flailing, her mouth opening, her screams lost in the hot mud, that pale mouth filling with mud. And again, against all my hopes, Gabriela, she stopped. The heart ceased to beat, the mouth to scream. And I clutched her in my arms and cried in the mud, tortured by the thought that it would be hundreds of Returns more, as it had been already, before the true Nerissa would come.

"And in the morning, she awoke."

Gabriela was stroking the hair of the child at her knee. "Awoke?"

"Yes!" cried the Salamander, "I had left her in the pit, to be disposed of later, and had gone down to the lake to meditate. And then, as I contemplated my greatness and my loneliness, I felt a presence, strong and fearsome, striking me deep in the belly and sending my head reeling. I turned my head to see the figure of a woman, white as snow and covered in mud, walking slowly down the hill to where I sat. She was the *true* Companion. The *true* Nerissa."

"And it was this Nerissa, the true one, that MacLeod stole?"

"Yes," said Khordas. "And one day I received a visit from another, whom I thought would be my Companion. This is only one hundred years ago, now, more or less. That Companion was Lauren, and she has tried to serve me well."

Oh, god. Oh, no. Gabriela trembled. "But Lauren no longer serves you?"

"Lauren is not the true Companion. The Companion must be a sacrifice; I must *make* her of my own will. Do you understand? I think if you asked the Highlander, he would understand."

"MacLeod is not here," said Gabriela. "I can ask him nothing."

"He has told you so little, Miss Savedra. You are so much more than you know. MacLeod has been unjust to both of us, but from this injustice we will find great fortune. You are an unblemished stone, perfect clay, like the clay I breathed life into in my true form, to make man. Untarnished by the false truths about the Immortals. The perfect Companion. Here," Khordas said, lifting her glass. "Drink with me. We are to be together."

"Why me?" she asked, slowly, but she knew, didn't she? And Duncan had known, he had known all along . . . She took the glass, shaking, what kind of fool had she been played for? Gabriela took a sip.

"Why you?" Khordas chuckled softly through the mask, and now he removed it, showing his face for the first time. And it was beautiful, the red hair shining, the eyes burning brightly, godlike indeed. "Because it is the time of sacrifice, **my Companion, my new Nerissa, my Gabriela.**" His voice . . .

Now Khordas took her and raised her up, and she looked into his eyes, losing herself in them. She felt him draw her to his breast, the candlelight flickering, casting their shadows on the walls, the god and the Companion. And in the flicker of candlelight she saw the glint of steel, and felt it enter her breast, pushing through, sliding serpentlike between ribs and slicing through her heart.

And Gabriela's eyes fluttered and she felt herself falling against him, her head against his breast. And then someone turned the lights out on the world.

But only for a little while.

Captain Jacob Devereaux of the Royal Preventive Service tapped Captain Daniel Hendricks, USN, of the *Troilus*, on the shoulder and pointed. A sailing vessel had just come over the horizon and he had recognized it.

"Is that him?"

"Aye, Captain," said Devereaux. "As I said. This smuggler Carruthers has been dodging us for a good while. If possible, I want him captured."

Hendricks nodded. "Do you think he's carrying guns this time?"

"I wouldn't put it past him," said Devereaux. "I received a tip that he would be in and around New England. It looks like we've just run into him, headed back to England."

"Well, then," said Hendricks. "Let's see if we can get his attention."

At the launching of the *Dido,* the first thing Duncan noticed was that she was travelling under sail. "I thought this was a steamship," he said, as he joined Connor.

"Oh, yes," said Connor, with that bizarre, staccato laugh of his. Connor was a dark wire of a figure against the ocean, a face floating atop a foul-weather coat. "But I prefer to keep that under wraps, shall we say?" By this he meant, as he showed his student, that Connor preferred to keep his steam engine for emergencies, the paddlewheel stowed under a great hood, disguised as a lifeboat and a series of badly stowed nets. "Part of strength is in the hiding," said Connor, with a wink.

"But where's the smokestack?"

"Smokestack?"

"For your exhaust," said Duncan. Connor shrugged with a coy smile.

The *Dido* left Buzzards Bay under Captain Carruthers at 1400 hours on the thirteenth of February. She travelled thirty miles out before moving southward, scanning the area for her quarry. Duncan stepped aside when Thomas Rooke approached. The sailor glanced at Duncan and made it clear that he wanted to speak to Connor alone. Connor and the First Mate stepped a few feet away and whispered.

"Captain," said Rooke, who Connor sensed was disturbed to even speak directly to him, "the men are concerned."

Connor scanned the horizon, a pair of field glasses held before his eyes. He brought them down for a second and said, "Oh?"

"It's just that, going up and engaging a naval vessel . . ."

"We're not engaging them," said Connor. "We're just

going to give them a message." He smiled. "Don't worry, our holds are empty, we unloaded everything."

"Aye," said Rooke. "But . . . we just wanted to voice our concern."

"Tell the men I understand," nodded Connor. "Tell them I appreciate their honesty, and their loyalty."

"Their loyalty is unquestionable," said Rooke. "It's just that we've turned around so quickly, and all this strange business with the Navy—it's *him*." Rooke tilted his head towards Duncan, lowering his voice still further, but naturally not to the point that Duncan, a very skilled listener indeed, could not hear it. "Are you certain he can be trusted?"

"Yes, Rooke," said Connor. "As I said, I would trust him with my life."

"I hope so," said Rooke. "Because we are trusting you with ours."

As the *Dido* travelled south, a number of ships appeared, and each time the sailor at the topmast cried out, and each one Connor inspected at a distance. And finally, at 1800 hours, as the sun was going down, a pair of shapes topped the horizon, twins, gigantic in size.

Connor ran to the rail and inspected the ships, which now seemed to pick up speed. He climbed the ladder on the mast about ten rungs and peered through the glasses again. Even in the failing light the shapes were unmistakable: the low-slung decks, looking more like a monitor than a seagoing ship, the guns at ready. Oh, the twins were going to put on quite a show. "That's them!" cried Connor, as he dropped to the deck of the *Dido*.

Duncan ran to the alarm horn and began to crank the handle as the three ships flew towards one another. "Go to their starboard side," cried Connor, "nice and easy."

The *Troilus* moved steadily north as the *Dido* changed course, and soon the battleship was flanking them, separated by two hundred yards of water. The twin ships looked like a pair of horses before a carriage, the *Cressida* barely visible behind her sister.

Duncan heard a distant sound, an oscillating whine. "What . . . ?"

Rooke ran up to Connor with a megaphone. "They're

sounding their own alarm," he said evenly. The alarm died out and Connor signalled for Duncan to cease the *Dido*'s call as well.

"What does that mean?"

"I don't know," said Connor, as he held the funnel to his mouth. "Ahoy! *Troilus!* This is David Carruthers, vessel *Dido!*"

Someone on the deck of the *Troilus* returned an amplified greeting, but the response was lost on the misting waves. Connor lowered his megaphone and called over his shoulder, "Close thirty yards!" The sun was down now, and the lights of the battleship were burning brightly. Duncan could make out three or four men gathered together at the starboard rail.

The sails of the *Dido* shifted now, sailors moving to catch the wind correctly, and several minutes passed until Connor held up his hand, "Steady," and looked at Duncan, "Let's try again, gentlemen. Ahoy! *Troilus!* This is vessel *Dido*, Captain David Carruthers!"

The call was met by silence, except for a distant cranking sound that Duncan did not recognize, but he noticed Connor stiffen slightly. Connor was raising the megaphone to his lips again when suddenly a brilliant light erupted from the *Troilus*, blazing hot and white across the water. Duncan raised his hand and tried to peer between his fingers.

"Steady, steady," said Connor, then, lower, "Oh, Christ, they've been expecting us."

"No cause for alarm?"

"*Tremendous* cause for alarm, Duncan, but I'm trying to pretend it's not, thank you." Connor spoke into the megaphone, again, using his own hand to shield his eyes. "We have . . ."

"*Dido!*" came a great cry from the *Troilus*. Connor looked at Duncan for a moment.

"That's a Briton," said Connor.

"*Dido!*" came the voice again, "prepare to be boarded!"

Connor muttered, "Devereaux."

"Who?"

"Preventive," snapped Connor.

"Captain Carruthers, you and your crew and your vessel are under arrest by order of the Royal Preventive Service and the United States Navy on charges of gunrunning and piracy!"

"That sounds pretty official," said Connor.

Duncan folded his arms. "Wonderful."

Connor barked over his shoulder, "Rooke! Uncover the wheel! Benjamin! Haskell! To the boilers, quick! Furl those sails, and be ready!" Connor turned back to the blinding light and cried, "No time to chat now, Devereaux! I have a message for the sister ships! You are in danger of attack!"

Silence. Then, "Are you threatening me, Carruthers?"

Connor shouted to his own men, "Let's go." Even as he said so, the sails were being wrapped by teams of eight men each, binding cords and taking positions. He turned back to the rail and answered "No! You are the targets of a plot . . ."

Someone far across the sea shouted a command that Duncan could not make out, followed by an odd whistling sound, but when a large pocket of water near the port hull of the *Dido* exploded, sending water spray onto the ship, he knew well enough what the order had been. Duncan was frowning at his teacher.

Connor saw his look and said, "You know, and here I thought I could trust him . . ." The Elder Highlander shouted through the megaphone once more. "You have been warned, *Troilus*! Damn it, Devereaux, they're riding into an attack!"

Another explosion, and the two Immortals were doused in water. Connor sighed, "We're under attack." The captain turned. "Men!" he cried to his crew, "let's show these squids what we can do. Move off! Reinhold! Vents, if you please!" A sailor yelped, "Aye, aye, Captain," ran to the bulkhead and began to turn a crank.

Now the entire body of the *Dido* began to shudder and move, and Duncan felt her picking up speed as the water wheel slapped loudly against the waves. Another shell ripped into the water and Duncan held to the rail as the *Dido* pitched.

"Fear not, oh ye of little faith," said the Elder Highlander. "You're not actually worried, are you?" Duncan saw the gleam in his teacher's eye, and then blinked, because his own eyes were full of smoke. A wave of smoke buried Connor for an instant and Duncan saw that the deck had filled with it. He looked across the deck of the *Dido,* and could barely make out a series of opening wooden vents about half a foot across, scattered throughout the deck. They were moving, opening further, spewing black smoke that filled the air and blackened Duncan's clothes. The vents locked into place. Even the floodlight from the *Troilus* was drowned out by the black cloud that surrounded the *Dido.*

Duncan coughed. "This can't be healthy," he murmured, when somebody tapped him on the shoulder and thrust a paper mask into his face. Duncan took the mask and put it on as the sailor disappeared again.

"Don't be ridiculous," said Connor. "We think of everything."

The *Dido* hurtled back to Buzzards Bay in record time, and after a while Connor had the crew douse the cloud and kill the engines. By the time she put back into port, the *Dido* was a sailing vessel again.

"You don't think of everything," said Duncan, as the ship reached the docks. "You didn't know you'd been ratted out."

"Touché," said Connor. "All in a day's work, I guess. You just can't bribe some people."

As sailors hopped onto the dock and began throwing lines to one another, Duncan said, "What now?" He looked at Connor, who now resembled, as he was sure he did too, a chimneysweep.

The chimneysweep Immortal fished a cigarette from his case and lit it. "Now we go to plan B," he said.

"And that is?"

"Get cleaned up," Connor exhaled a stream of smoke. "And get dirty again tomorrow."

Khordas adjusted the mask on his face and actually considered taking it off for a moment, but the moment passed without his doing so. The mask was here to stay, so long as there remained mortals who refused to recognize him. Above him, a system of pulleys and ropes could be heard, cranking away, as his outfitting of the *Gratiano* neared completion.

Khordas was supervising the placement of the guns. All those diamonds and gold stolen over the years had bought weapons of many kinds, and now, the Children who were most able with a boat were ferrying his own small craft back and forth between the anchored *Gratiano* and the lagoon he and the Companion had called home for the past year. The nine small guns were already in place around the main deck of the *Gratiano,* and even now, the final touch was being placed.

"Excellent," said Khordas, as he climbed the ladder. Captain Lewis was supervising the placement of the *pièce de résistance.* The gun he had bought from Crabbe, using George Drake's money, was huge, jutting thirty feet from its base, an eighteen-inch bore gaping wide. And plenty of ammunition. Plenty. The smuggler Crabbe had been happy to provide everything he could get his hands on. Ah, what fires there would be.

Khordas pulled Captain Lewis aside and put his hand on the man's shoulder. "I have a special task for you."

"Yes, my Lord."

"How many lifeboats does this ship have?"

Lewis thought for a moment, and Khordas suspected he was struggling with the confusing thought that this was *his* ship, else how would he know? The Root of Faith would take care of that. Lewis answered, "Eleven."

"Then I want you to choose ten small crews, led by the most able sailors among you. Can you do this?"

Lewis stared forward and answered, "Yes. What will the men be needed for?"

"Fireboats," said the Salamander. "I need crews for when our lifeboats become fireboats. Which is, of course, only fitting."

"Yes, my Lord."

Chapter 16

Valentine's Day

"Ten o'clock," said Connor, "and all's well." Connor and Duncan MacLeod stood at the prow of Duncan's *Spanish Lady*. The *Dido* was safely moored at the docks, fishnet and fake barnacles covering her every marking. By the time the *Troilus* and the *Cressida* had arrived, there were so many craft in the Bay that the *Dido* was impossible to spot. On that vessel, the crew awaited the return of its captain. On the *Spanish Lady*, the two Immortals had little idea what they were awaiting.

"Could it be we were wrong?" Duncan chewed on his lip.

"No chance. He'll come. He's as much a creature of habit as you or I. It is, after all, Nerissa's birthday."

Aboard the *Gratiano*, six hundred men and women moved at a steady clip to the beat of the drums. Along the length of the hull, on either side, Khordas' specially ordered preparations were being completed on the fireboats.

"Fireboats?" Lauren had asked the Salamander.

"Yes," he smiled. "Used to great effect against the Spanish Armada, you will recall. Small boats were sent out with a team on each, with orders to lash their boat to their target. The fireboats were full to the brim with explosives." Khordas indicated the fireboat lashed to the hull. A line of Children passed packet after packet of explosives and missiles—nails, shredded metal, a potpourri of impending chaos. "Even an armored hull won't withstand that," said the Salamander. "Not when we're right on them."

"We?"

"Aye. Oh, Lauren, it will be grand, indeed. A sacrifice the likes of which these infidels have never seen."

Lauren stared at him and her vision blurred for a moment. Her mind snagged on a detail and boiled on it. All of a sudden it infuriated her that he was still wearing that mask.

"Khordas, my love," whispered Lauren, as she nuzzled against him and touched his mask. She reached under the mask and brushed against his chin, the reddish stubble underneath. "Khordas, won't you take off the mask for me?"

The eyes within the wooden slits turned to her, and they neither blazed nor scowled, but simply smoldered, like dry ice. "I will not remove my visage."

"Mask," she said, shaking her head. "Khordas, have you gone thoroughly . . ."

"Do not ask me to be less than what I am, Companion."

"But . . ."

"Enough!" spat the god. "We have important matters to which to attend." Khordas' masked head looked down at the fireboat near his feet. "I have a special assignment for you. It is very important that we make no mistake. You have been with me for the entirety of my second life, and I trust you more than any other to accomplish this mission."

Lauren nodded. "Of course."

"Duncan MacLeod has been cavorting with his former mentor. They are aboard a ship called *Dido*. It is a wooden-hulled sailing vessel, a whaler. I want you to lead the fireboat against that vessel."

"Lead . . . a fireboat?"

"Aye."

"But," Lauren blinked. *Was he really asking her to . . .* "do you not need me with you here on the *Gratiano?*"

"I *need* you," snarled the velvet voice behind the mask of the Salamander, "where I *wish* you to be."

Khordas, I have come to please you. Khordas, I have come to serve. "Of course. As you wish." Lauren looked down at the Children preparing the fireboat and pulled away from Khordas, and walked to her quarters, for she felt sure she must partake of the Root.

And as she passed a ladder, she felt sure that she sensed something, for a moment. Something like a presence, faint and distant, buried, somehow. But the moment, and the presence, passed.

The Child of the Salamander called Genevieve waited where she was told to, and jumped rope, chanting.

Genevieve held the handle of the muddy jumprope as the rope flew in great arcs over her tiny body. With every beat it sliced under her feet, mud flying into her hair and over her dress.

Down at the pond, I caught a salamander,
Put it in my pocket, and soon it died . . .

Hollow echoes throughout the muddy room, the sound of her tiny chant dripping off the walls and ceiling in mud, dripping hollow against the cauldron. In the cauldron baked a surprise, and she waited, chanting.

Down at the pond, I caught a little skink,
Put it in my pocket, and all the girls cried . . .

Genevieve thought she heard a sound and increased the intensity of her chant, doubling her speed on the rope as she did so, whipping it twice under her legs as she soared and splatted against the mud, the mud that flew against the iron cauldron, sizzling on the flame underneath, mud from which rose the Salamander, *Khordas, I have come to serve . . .*

Down at the pond, under the mud,
Tell me, O tell me, what a good girl am I!

Faster now, and a sound, mud sloshing against the inside of the cauldron, bubbling against the lid, and Genevieve's tiny mind arced in the way that only children and the child-like make sense of things.

Down at the pond, under the mud,
Salamander, in the fire,
Skink smells blood . . .

Something moving in the cauldron, mud slinging off the rope and flying through the air, mud in Genevieve's eyes, and now she lets go the handles and the muddy rope slices through the air and sticks to the walls, sliding down, slowly, like a salamander. *And the worms crawl in, and the worms crawl out . . .*

Alive! Alive! Genevieve looked around the room. A heavy wooden candlestick lay tipped upon the mud-strewn table. She seized it, wax sliding between her fingers, and began to swing it in a wide arc, clanging it against the cauldron.

Gabriela!

You are the new Companion, like no other before you, great will be your life. You are so much more than you have known.

Gabriela Savedra opened her eyes and saw nothing. She was curled in a fetal ball, hands clasped around her calves, and there was something thick surrounding her head and her body. She moved and felt as if she were swimming, but swimming through . . . finally it came to her: *mud*. Drums pounded outside the darkness, somewhere, and Gabriela's eyes closed again, and reopened, and she felt the sting of mud against her eyeballs. *Alive.*

Suddenly Gabriela gasped and mud filled her mouth as she threw out her arms. She felt her fists collide with something hard and metallic, something that surrounded her, like a dark womb. Her arms went up, flowing through the mud, up above her head and she struck metal yet again. And still, vibrating through the mud, the sound of drums, and still, snaking through her mind, the voice of the Salamander, *You are so much more. We were meant to be together, you and I . . .*

Gabriela stopped squirming, and let herself go limp for a moment, feeling the vibrations in the mud and the pounding drums moving through her. She thought for a moment, let herself think, as she rested and drifted in the mud, that the shock of sound was the throb of her heartbeat against the womb. She was about to be born. *Gabriela,* a new voice called, in time with the vibration of the drums.

"Gabriela! Gabriela!" came the voice again, and now she realized that there was another set of vibrations besides her heart, detached from the muffled, distant drums, something solid pounding against the walls. Gabriela listened intently and felt drunk on the new sounds in her ears, the new *types* of sounds, deeper, fuller, like she had never heard before. Her eyes saw only darkness and mud, but the darkness and mud were *full.* Oh, what a wondrous gift!

"Gabriela!" called the voice again, and now Gabriela noticed that the voice was small and high, and still the creature that called to her from the other side of the womb beat frantically against the walls. These vibrations weren't in time with the drums at *all,* she now perceived. Someone was beating on the walls and calling her name!

Now, slowly, things began to come back together, as she lay in the mud and heard the pounding outside. The Salamander had reincarnated her, rescued her from a life of mortality, had told her not to fear, that he was giving her new life in exchange for the old. And waiting for her, calling for her now, was another servant, a Child of the Salamander.

"Genevieve," Gabriela spoke, and the mud sucked into her mouth, and the voice continued to call, tiny and surely exhausted fists beating against the walls of the womb. Gabriela reached up once again and began to push against the ceiling.

No movement from the hard surface. The Immortal Argentine lay back, now, a wave of mud displacing and flowing around her as she settled to the floor. She winced in the slightest pain, for the floor was very hot against her back, as if there were a fire on the other side. She curled her bare legs above her and placed her feet against the ceiling and pushed.

Something gave, slightly, and there was a sucking sound as mud escaped through what must have been a seam, the outer edge of what was not a ceiling, but a lid. She was in . . . what, a stew pot? A cauldron? Gabriela grunted under the mud and pushed with all her might, the muscles in her legs straining, and she heard something scrape as more mud from above the lid flowed around the edge. The lid was rising, and Gabriela pushed with her feet until she had raised the lid half a foot, and now a sound, air sucking and displacing, as the lid raised above the surface.

Gabriela heard a violent clang as the lid fell to the floor and she brought her legs under her and began to stand. *Well. Time to re-enter the world of the living.*

Gabriela Maria Cuadra de Savedra stood in the cauldron and blinked her eyes. There was something new in her brain, new thoughts, new sensations. Something in her blood, leaving her open, something that had seeped into her pores and exposed her mind, so that she wanted to be filled with knowledge. And who would give that knowledge? She looked out on a dark room lit with hundreds of tiny fires, each candle anchored by a small mound of mud. And before her stood the child, staring up at her.

"The Salamander instructed me to wait for you, and to wake you, if I could," she said. The tiny girl was pleased, clearly, and Gabriela stepped from the cauldron and slowly lowered herself to the girl's level.

"Do you know who I am?" asked Gabriela. "Do you remember me?"

"Yes," said the girl. "You are Gabriela, the Companion, the true. You are Immortal, like unto the god."

Alive! Alive! Alive! The Root of Faith in her blood, reinforcing, *why are you alive? Because Khordas has made you so!*

"Yes," said Gabriela, as she embraced the third member of Khordas' new family, "yes."

As the sun went down, the *Gratiano* began to move, and the masked god stood at the foredeck and addressed the six hundred Children. "Now, my family. We go to the reckoning place."

"There she is," said Connor. He handed Duncan his glasses and Duncan peered across the sea, out of the grotto where the *Spanish Lady* lay nestled.

"What now?"

"Wait," said Connor. Duncan turned towards the Bay, and looked through the field glasses again. He saw perhaps thousands of people still walking along the pier, lines of them shuttling on and off the *Troilus* and *Cressida*, where glib tours were being given to the cotton-candy crowd.

The *Gratiano* was decked out in mud. "Incredible," said Duncan, as he turned back to survey Khordas' adopted city on the sea.

"Aye," said Connor. "That's no cruise ship. That is a Salamander." The vessel was moving at full steam towards the mouth of the Bay, but now it slowed. Within minutes, the vessel had ceased to move once again. The dark mass simply lay there, rocking in the waves just outside the Bay. "Hm," said Connor. "Full stop. Hand me those," he said, and Connor took the glasses and held them up. "Our Salamander has a bite," he said.

"Guns?"

"Big guns."

Duncan looked back at the dark Bay. "What time is it?"

Connor pulled out his watch and clicked it open, glanced at it, snapped it shut and replaced it in his foul-weather coat. "Twenty-two hundred hours," he said. "Ten o'clock."

"This is strange," said Duncan. "The day is nearly gone."

"Aye. And I don't like it." They watched the silent hulk for half an hour before Connor called to the stern of the *Spanish Lady.* "Rooke, you there?"

"Aye, captain." Thomas Rooke stuck his head up from below.

"Let's head back. We're of no use here," he said, and Rooke began to fire the small steam engine. "Back to the *Dido.*"

At a quarter past eleven, back on the deck of the *Dido,* Connor and Duncan crawled up to the crow's nest and looked out again. "Still there?" Duncan asked.

"Still there."

Duncan rested against the wooden, circular rail of the crow's nest while Connor watched the silent *Gratiano.* "I don't understand it."

"Neither do I," said Connor. The Elder Highlander put down his glasses and proceeded to light a cigarette.

"We're missing something."

"We are at that."

Duncan folded his arms in front of him and stared at his boots. "Valentine's Day. Here we are. Lots of people, worshippers not worshipping and waiting to be punished. Here they are, all of them. What is he waiting for?"

Connor blew out a stream and said, "Waiting until the right time."

"But he's missing it. The people will be gone soon."

Connor looked out on the docks. The crowd showed no sign of letting up yet. On one pier not a quarter mile from the *Dido,* a band was playing *Columbia, the Gem of the Ocean.* The song droned on, warped by its travel over the waves. Next came *Onward, Christian Soldiers.* "Saint Valentine's Day, we went to mass," Duncan said.

"And then to Carmichael's feast."

"Right."

Duncan was thinking back, *what are we missing?* He saw again the vision of the cloud of dust around Carmichael and his ship, and the man disappearing in flame. "What time is it?"

Click. "Eleven-thirty." Snap.

. . . marching as to war, with the cross of Jesus . . .

"Why are the people still here?"

Connor slowly turned. "There's a fireworks display at midnight."

Duncan stiffened and Connor met his gaze. "It wasn't . . ."

"After Carmichael's feast," said Connor, "we didn't see him off until . . ."

"We went to sleep, Connor, you were bloody well pissed, and so was I . . ."

"Right," said Connor. "And when we saw Carmichael off it was—God, near three hundred years, it just runs together, it was—"

"The fifteenth," said Duncan. "Nerissa's birthday is the fifteenth!"

"Yes," said Connor. "Yes!" He brought up the glasses again and looked. "No movement from the *Gratiano.*"

Duncan stared out across the bay with his naked eyes and saw the dark ship in the distance. The tiny boats shuttling visitors around the bay were barely visible save for the lamps they carried. He saw the lights of the temporary, floating pier near the *Troilus,* and there were several men setting up what looked to be a mound of sticks. Two at a time they placed these sticks into canisters, stopping occasionally to chat. "There's the display."

"But what . . ." Connor stopped, then said, "Wait. Look at this."

Duncan peered through the glasses and looked out to the *Gratiano.* "Still no movement."

"Not *her,*" said Connor. "Look at the lights on the water near her."

Duncan focused the glasses a bit, and now he made out a number of tiny boats, each carrying a lamp, rowing by team into the bay. "Lifeboats?"

"I don't think so," said Connor.

Lewis put down his field glasses at the bridge of the *Gratiano.* "The fireboats are away, my Lord," he said.

Khordas strode the deck and watched the ten boats, the men furiously rowing, and he heard them chanting his praises on the water, mixing with the distant sound of the band on the docks. *We are not weak, like our enemies . . . marching as to war . . .*

"Excellent," said the Salamander. "Release our little gift."

"She's moving," said Connor. "The *Gratiano* is pulling out. And she's . . . spewing something." Connor touched his fingers to his lips and held it into the air. "What does that look like to you?"

Duncan looked out. The distant hulk was indeed moving, now, and something besides smoke was pouring from her stack. A dark, shimmering cloud flowed out of the smokestack and into the Bay, and every vessel in the harbor began to shimmer as it drifted toward the shore. Within minutes the stuff was upon them, and Duncan felt it on his face and he suppressed the urge to sneeze. Connor snuffed out his cigarette with his fingers and cursed audibly. Duncan wiped some of the stuff off his cheek, brought his finger to his nose and sniffed. "That smells like . . ."

"Sulfur," said Connor. "Remember?"

Duncan's eye was on the floating pier. "The fireworks."

Connor looked at his watch. "They're going to be on time."

"I'm afraid so," said Duncan.

"Christ," said Connor. "I think we're safe with a few sparks here and there. But one little rocket and this whole Bay is going up."

"What about the boats?"

"We have to stop them." Behind him, the band played on the docks, and the cotton-candy crowd still walked the boards, awaiting the fireworks. *Oh, no. Oh, no.* "Those are manned mines, Duncan."

Duncan nodded. "Fireboats?"

Now the sound of rowers came to his ears, someone chanting that infernal praise to the mad Immortal. A lifeboat full of ten men and women was moving through the shimmering cloud, chanting. One of the sailors knelt at the stern of the tiny boat with a rope in his hands. "That one's headed for the dock."

Connor swept the area with his glasses and said, "Plenty more where that came from."

"I'm for the docks."

"Fine," said Connor. "I'll take the floating pier." Connor turned and shouted out, "Fire the engines, men!" Then, as if in afterthought, "And try not to light any cigarettes!"

As the *Dido* began to move, Duncan tore off his jacket and dove into the Bay.

Chapter 17

On the Bay, Lauren the Companion stood at the prow of her fireboat, scanning the harbor with her field glasses. There were explosives at her feet, knocking against one another, and she saw her target a hundred yards away. The *Dido* had just made its appearance, pulling out from a line of docked ships. On the docks, there were children playing, people pointing, wiping the glistening sulfur out of their hair in confusion. Cotton candy, pink and brilliant, in the hands of mortals who did not recognize the god, and she thought about Khordas' struggle up from the pit and something within her cried out, *No.*

I am an Immortal, born in 1705. I had three sisters, and I rode like a man and robbed like the best of men. All these things, I did before Khordas. Before Khordas . . .

Khordas strode to the prow of the *Gratiano* and surveyed the scene. Lewis was standing at the rail with a pair of field glasses, and Khordas turned to him. "Report." There was a presence approaching, coming up behind him, and Khordas had to smile.

"The fireboats are nearing their targets," Lewis replied.

"Excellent," said Khordas, and he put his hand on Lewis' shoulder. "My Children do me great service."

"Yes, my Lord," said Lewis.

A voice spoke from behind the Salamander, "Khordas?"

The Salamander turned and saw a woman, covered from head to toe in mud, and the glistening substance mixed with the mud and shimmered brilliantly. Energy, fire, seemed to emanate from her and Khordas recognized her as kindred. At her side she held the hand of his new child. "Gabriela?"

The dark brown hair sparkled in the night with fire dust, and she reminded him, somehow, of Nerissa, the first Companion, whom Duncan MacLeod had taken. She stood straight and said, "We are ready."

"We are indeed," replied Khordas.

Duncan MacLeod tried to keep the sulfurous water out of his nose as he swam for the first boat he had seen. The rowers were coming towards him, headed for the dock, which lay some twenty-five yards away.

Duncan considered his options and decided to take the direct route. Swimming before the rushing boat, he waved his arms. "Stop!"

No answer. Duncan caught the eye of the leader of the tiny vessel, and saw the look in the sailor's eye. There was nothing there, just a blank stare and a moving, chanting mouth. The leader held a grappling hook in one hand and a rope in the other, ready to latch on to the docks. "Please!" Duncan cried again. Behind him, people were pointing, some of them laughing, odd, detached laughter, the kind that fills a crowd for no reason other than that people have no sense to know they're going to die.

The fireboat picked up speed, the oars slapping against the water, and Duncan saw the keel of the small boat closing in on him. Duncan grabbed the prow of the fireboat and felt himself swept under by the force of the waves as he clung to the rim.

Lauren looked ahead and saw the dock, the banners, men and women and children wandering aimlessly, men shooting at plastic ducks and throwing rings at milk bottles, and they were going to explode, because they did not know the god ... And moving toward her, her own target, the *Dido*, and now a presence grew, the familiar sick feeling filling her stomach. Connor MacLeod was standing at the prow, and she knew that he saw her.

"Go, my Children!" cried the Salamander, his voice deep and resonating through the air from the funnel inside his mask. Lauren looked back again and saw him standing there, Khordas in his Salamander mask, and the thoughts came again, overlapping, the thoughts that hurt her brain and curdled her stomach: *I dug you up! I was alone, and needed guidance, and over a century I have wasted this way!*

And then Lauren's face clouded with a new thought, a resolution, and she knew what she must do. She leaned on the side of the fireboat with one hand. Lauren drew back and punched herself in the stomach, curdling as it was with the poison of the Salamander, causing her vision to cloud and shimmer like the cloud that flowed across the bay. It was still in her stomach, from her last feeding, and it must be *purged.* Now she reached into her pouch and retrieved a tiny pinch of gunpowder, and this she mixed with salt water, and swallowed. And Lauren leaned over the side of the fireboat, seeing the dock closing in, the people who would die, and she thought of the Salamander and she retched.

"Stop the boat," she gurgled to her men, turning up her bloodshot eyes to them, and the rowing stopped.

For a moment they drifted, there on the black water. Lauren was watching her reflection in the water of Buzzards Bay. How many years could one waste following the wrong truth? How does a killer recognize how much killing is too much? How can the closest thing to a god on earth recognize that calling oneself a god is going too far?

Lauren reached down, still weak from the emptying of her stomach, and touched her reflection in the water. Already, with no supply of the poison Root of Faith in her stomach, the rest of her system was repairing itself, her mind becoming clear. *My allegiance to you is purged, Khordas. Good riddance.*

Lauren sat straight and called out, "Pilot! Change course."

"Aye, Captain."

"Dead astern, pilot."

Lauren worked the rudder as the men rowed, and within a

minute they were headed in the direction whence they came, the direction of the *Gratiano*.

"My Lord?"

Khordas strode over to Lewis. "What is it?"

Lewis lowered his field glasses and looked at the Salamander. "The Companion. She's turned around."

Lauren shouted to her men, "Keep rowing!" The *Gratiano* was getting closer, now, she could feel the presence of her love and her god looming large.

No, not a god, an Immortal, yes, but just an Immortal, like yourself, like Duncan, and like . . .

A glint of light reflected off a pair of field glasses at the prow. *You see my course, don't you, my love? Too long. Too long have I followed you. I was wrong. You are wrong.*

Lauren heard a muffled scream, and she looked off the port side and saw a section of the pier exploding, smoke and fire flying outward and splashing into the water. It was truly beginning. And it was going to end.

On the floating pier, not far from the majestic *Troilus* and *Cressida*, Alderman Brian Forsythe, who had been placed in charge of setting off the fireworks display, was struggling with a pack of matches. He lit yet another match and cursed good-naturedly as the head rubbed clean against the sulfur, without so much as a spark. He looked up at his aide, Carter, with a sarcastic smile. "Any day now, I know."

Carter coughed slightly, and made a vague comment about the air. "Exhaust," said Forsythe. Forsythe had been to London, and considered high quantities of exhaust to be a mark of extremely high culture. He tried to light another match, and looked out at the docks. Funny. A lot of boats running around. Everyone wanted to get a good view. The match seemed to be sludgy, for some reason, and he proceeded to pull out a new box, hopefully one with matches not so grimy.

Duncan felt his body slam against the underside of the fireboat and began to move along the rim, until he reached an oar. He looked up at the wooden oar and the rower attached. He thought for a moment that the sailor would see him, but no. *You have very specific instructions, don't you? Row this way. Tie yourself to a pier. Simon says.* Duncan grabbed for the oar and felt it slap him in the chest and he tugged on it, now grabbing the metal loop through which the oar travelled, holding it in place.

Using the force of the waves travelling under him, Duncan pulled on the metal ring and let his legs come up, and they collided with the next oar. He scrambled to get into the boat and landed with a thud in the rower's lap. The sailor stared at him blankly and Duncan suddenly realized that the crew had stopped its chanting. The leader of the boat leaned forward now, an automaton, ready with the grappling hook.

Duncan grabbed the sailor beside him and made short work of tossing him into the water, and then looked over his shoulder. They were closing in on the docks.

"Stop," said Duncan, to the sailors. "Stop rowing!"

No answer. Obviously, they recognized no authority other than Khordas.

Now the sound of waves lapping against the posts of the boardwalk became clear. Duncan looked around the fireboat. At his feet rolled canister after glass canister of metal and fluid and powder. "Where's the device? What sets it off?"

The prow of the boat collided with a *thunk* against the dock and Duncan felt himself thrown backwards and into the front man, who shrugged Duncan off and proceeded to rear back and throw the grappling hook. The hook caught on a beam overhead. Duncan looked up and saw shapes—the travelling feet of bystanders—visible between the boards of the pier.

The leader tugged on the rope, as if judging its strength, and then threw a second hook to another beam, and the fireboat became steady.

Duncan got next to the drone and said, "What now, brother?"

"Now?" spoke the sailor, quietly. "Now we wait."

Duncan stared at him, and then back at the other rowers, all of whom had fallen into what he regarded as almost a state of sleep. All were covered in the same shimmering substance that smelled of sulfur and burned his nose, and Duncan studied the sailors and saw that their clothes were bulky, bulging here and there. Explosives. These people were catalysts for the fireboat.

And there *was* no incendiary device. Khordas was going to use the air for that.

Duncan drew his katana and sliced through the ropes, and the boat began to drift as he began to reach into the bottom of the boat and throw the canisters into the water. And now the Children truly noticed he was with them, and set upon him.

Alderman Forsythe cried, "Finally!" as his match flared and he held it towards the waiting fuse.

"No!" came a voice, and Forsythe looked up. "Eh?"

A whaling vessel was barreling down upon the floating pier, and a man stood at the front of it with a megaphone. "Do not set off your rockets. Hold fire!"

Carter swore. "Who the Hell is that?"

"Got me," said Forsythe, "but we're running late. I see no reason to . . ."

The vessel banked hard starboard and came round, and the waves kicked up and made the floating pier pitch. "Don't do it!" came the voice again. "This is treacherous air! Don't fire your rockets!"

Forsythe stood straight. "See here," he said, "I am an Alderman, and I am supposed to . . ." the man at the front of the vessel raised his arm and pointed what looked to be a large gun at him.

"Don't do it, or you'll be a dead Alderman, friend."

Pause. "I begin to see your point."

A fist collided with Duncan's nose and he felt blood flow and mix with the sulfur in his nostrils as he kicked viciously and sent the last man into the water. They would be no threat to anyone there. Ten mindless drones began to tread the water, staring up at him and groping for the side of the boat.

Duncan began to row away from the dock when he heard someone speaking through a megaphone from the floating pier. "Ladies and gentlemen, there appears to be some cause for delay . . ."

Duncan smiled. Connor had reached them in time.

* * *

Khordas slammed his fist into the rail. "What?" Someone was shouting something from the pier but the Salamander had no time to listen.

"The Companion, my Lord. She's turned around."

"Ridiculous!" Khordas spat. The damn fool faulty unauthentic self-made Companion was trying to *kill* him. What, was she insane? He was being betrayed!

The Salamander strode quickly to the bridge and shouted down to the fore gunners. "Children! Take aim on that fireboat which approaches there."

The gun cranked down, thirty feet of metal turning in the direction of the woman who had dug him up all those years ago. After all he had done for her, she was trying to *destroy* him.

"Children," cried the Salamander, "blow that damned woman out of the water!"

Connor called down to Alderman Forsythe. "I appreciate your help, Alderman. Now, please tell the crowd, if you would, to go home."

"Home? But—"

"Alderman, this air is dangerous. Just to be on the safe side . . ." As he spoke, Connor looked over at the *Troilus,* and gestured to Rooke, who began to flash his own floodlight, the shortest message to get the point across.

Short. Long. Long. Long. *Dit-dah-dah-dah. Dit-dah-dah-dah.*

Fire. Danger. Hit the deck. Get clear.

Someone at the *Troilus* was shouting down at a strange crew of sailors on a small vessel that had just attached itself to them, and now they began to return their own signal.

Dit-dah-dah-dah.

Twelve grappling hooks from six fireboats tugged at various beams along the docks, the crews waiting for the light. Another boat had just now slammed against the armored hull of the *Troilus,* yet another against the *Cressida.* Leaving two—Lauren's, and the boat that Duncan MacLeod was rowing back into the Bay.

All together now, as Duncan and Connor and the rest of the Bay heard a sharp crack from a gun, a large gun, and a puff of smoke.

Duncan looked over his shoulder and saw the missile fly, in slow motion, through the air, a red streak following the ball where the sulfurous mist heated and wisped.

All at once, the messages from the *Troilus* and *Dido* relayed to the shore, captains across the Bay, shouting at the people on the docks, people in the band trampling chairs and instruments, "Get back! Get clear!"

All at once, the shell from the cruise ship *Gratiano* flew through the air towards the fireboat led by Lauren, the Companion. The Companion was standing in her fireboat and Connor saw the missile fly through her breast and slam into the pile of incendiary matter in the boat.

All at once, chaos. Cotton candy. And fire. Spectators on the pier began to stampede back onto the streets, away from the flaming wave that began to flow across the water.

A cloud of sulfur ignited and the flame ripped across the bay, and the fire seared Duncan's nose and caught the docks. The water itself was flaming and Duncan rowed with all his might towards the *Gratiano*.

Gabriela, standing on the deck of the *Gratiano*, saw this:

The *Troilus* was moving off as the fireboat attached to her hull exploded, ripping a chunk from her side. Alarm bells began to ring now, loud and clear, but these were not as loud as the screams of horror from the people at the docks. Duncan saw the crowds, still moving away onto land, but there were many still on the docks, too close to the fires, pushing past one another in panic and confusion. He saw some that seemed like Carmichael, caught in the wave of fire, matchstick silhouettes going up. Now another sound began to grow, fire sirens, and Duncan saw carriages arriving at the docks, gigantic tanks of water painted red atop them. The sirens roared, joining the alarm wails of the ships.

Aboard the *Cressida*, the crew had gotten the message from the *Troilus* in time to be ready, at least somewhat. The moment the air went up, they had hoses running, drowning the fireboat in dousing chemicals. That fireboat did not explode, and the *Cressida* received no breach. But Gabriela gasped at the sight of the *Troilus*, which was listing badly.

Now a wave of fire swept the deck of the *Gratiano*, burning like a fuse as incendiary dust puffed and spewed sparks. The air around Gabriela crackled and flared and Gabriela pulled her cloak around her, swatting out the fires on her body as the particles in the mud ignited.

The ship pitched, gulping the fiery waves, and Gabriela clutched her stomach, seeing the *Andrew* on fire in her mind, seeing the image, described by Duncan, of Captain Savedra evaporating in a cloud of red mist. Over the velvet voice of Khordas she heard the songs of her mother, and the voice of her father, and something snapped. She ran for the floodlights and began to signal to the *Cressida*. She was tempted to begin with a surrender, but she took a look at Khordas, who stood with his arms held up as panicking and burnt Children ran across the deck, and she called instead for aid.

Dit-dit-dit-dah. Dit-dit-dit-dah.

Evacuate us. Render assistance. Help.

Gabriela stopped signalling for a moment to check Genevieve, who huddled close to her, protected by a tarp that the new Immortal had thrown on her. The rest of the Children did not appear so lucky. Flames licked across the deck of the *Gratiano*, and everywhere the children of the Salamander ran for cover, finding little or none.

And amid the conflagration, the Immortal called Khordas looked out on Buzzards Bay at the great sorrow he had caused and felt the hot air slicing past him, and laughed.

"Why do you falter! What sacrifice we have made! What havoc we have caused! Are we not strong?"

Gabriela hit the signals again, but the beam of light was intermittently swallowed by the flaming waves. She coughed. She would not die, but these *people* . . .

It was then, as Gabriela Savedra signalled for the lives of the Children, that the walls of flame on either side of the *Gratiano* opened like curtains as a great horn cried out across the water, louder than the many screams. Something welled up, deep inside her, so that she almost swooned, a presence unknown to her, coming through the fire.

Parting flames licked and stood aside. Something Gabriela recognized as an Immortal at the prow of a speeding wooden vessel plunged through and flanked the *Gratiano*. The figure at the foredeck cried out, "Children of the Salamander! We grant you asylum!"

Flames everywhere, and Gabriela heard a splash as the anchors dropped into the water, and now she looked to the other side as the great horn sounded again and the *Cressida* burst through the flames as well.

Gabriela picked up Genevieve and began to run, her bare, mud-covered feet pounding against the fiery deck. Down the ladder she ran and across the deck, to where someone had laid out a plank. A man had jumped across, now, and he was guiding people onto the plank and over to the vessel she had no idea was called *Dido*.

Gabriela ran towards the plank and stopped suddenly, feeling the presence grow stronger.

The stranger seemed to study her for a moment, and Gabriela felt ridiculous, standing in the burning, sulfur-drenched mud with a child in her arms, and no sword. Whatever question she sought to ask, the Immortal only smiled, and laughed a strange, staccato laugh. "Heh. Don't worry, I'm a friend."

Good enough. "You can take my head later!" she said, to which the man only nodded as he pushed her along the plank, for there were many more to go.

And now, as Gabriela was jostled this way and that by the many people, the confused and burned Children of the Salamander, she felt yet another presence. She cast her eyes across the water to the prow of the *Gratiano*, and saw a figure climbing the anchor cable. His hands were burning as he reached the rail, and he was roaring a name, a name that spewed as fire from his Immortal mouth.

"Khordas . . ." cried Duncan MacLeod. "Khordas!"

But when Duncan reached the deck, Khordas was slipping away, through a door and down a ladder, for he had one last card to play.

Gabriela saw Duncan move in the direction Khordas had

gone, but not before he stopped, as if struck by a strong stench, and looked straight at Gabriela. For a brief moment she swore she saw a smile, but the look vanished, replaced by a look of greater anger than Gabriela had ever known.

Chapter 18

━━━

Duncan breathed in the smoke in the air and drew his katana, and felt its weight in his hands. *Where are you?* He caught a whiff of Khordas' presence as he passed a door under the bridge.

Oh, back where we started, Duncan muttered as he entered the door and stepped slowly down the ladder, two flights. When he reached the engine room, he knew it was true. In the dark, churning engine room, Khordas stood, waiting, and now he held something up in one hand, something that reflected the light in orange. The difference lay in Khordas' face, which was hidden, now, stuck to that deep blue mask. "We keep dancing the same routine, Khordas," said Duncan. "You've caused a great deal of trouble. And killing Gabriela was a bad idea."

"It was her destiny."

"No!" roared the Highlander. "Gabriela deserved to live a normal life. Her time would have come without your help." It was true. She would have had years. Time to get over Captain Savedra's death, time to enjoy the last of mortal love—hopefully with Duncan. Khordas had changed everything. Duncan moved forward with his katana and Khordas held up the item, and Duncan saw it to be a glass container. "What," Duncan smirked, "more 'petrol'?"

"You know better than that. This is naphtha, Highlander,"

said Khordas, holding up the glass vessel. In the dark the glass glowed slightly orange. There was a separation point at the top of the vessel, where a second, darker compartment butted against the first. "And next to it, separated by a thin sheet of glass, is black powder."

The steam process was churning behind him. "The ancients called it Greek Fire. It was used to excellent effect by the Byzantines, and against the Arabs attacking Constantinople. It is old-fashioned, but I like it. It has history."

"Is destruction the only history that interests you?"

"Mortal destruction is the only history that makes sense to me, MacLeod," said Khordas.

MacLeod stepped forward and Khordas raised the jar. "No! One move more, Highlander, and I throw this into the boiler. I've blown you up once already, so I know that's old hat to you. I can handle it, too. But there are a lot of people over our heads and I don't think they'll pull together quite as well, do you?"

"You're deluded as ever, Khordas. They're all gone. All of them. Even now, they're being ushered away by the Navy and by your own Companion."

The Salamander shook his head. "Bad bluff, MacLeod. The Companion you know is dead."

Duncan watched him for a second. "How does it feel, then, Khordas, to be alone?"

"I should ask you the same question, because it is no longer a problem. I have a new Companion, and together we will live out a long and fruitful life."

Oh, no. He had sensed another presence. He had known it wasn't Lauren even before seeing the Immortal Gabriela, had even *smiled.* Gabriela was Khordas' *companion* now? *She's gone, Khordas, I saw her leaving.* "And where is the new Companion?"

"Doing my bidding!" screamed Khordas. "Serving me! As is her duty! As is the duty of all!" The arms swung wide, and the jar came dangerously close to the churning pistons.

"Khordas. . . ." He would keep killing, no matter what anyone did to him. "You will never get what you want. What you want doesn't exist anymore. It's gone. There are no more Children of the Salamander. You kidnapped and drugged them. What is easily gained is also easily lost."

"No!" cried the god, enraged, and Duncan saw that Khordas was backing up to the bulkhead. Khordas reached behind him with his free arm and turned a circular handle, and a hatch fell open. He was standing under the escape trunk, the vertical passageway that led all the way up to the main deck. "No! It is you who are deluded, MacLeod! I am the guardian of the Children! My people are many, and strong!"

"Khordas, stop . . ."

Khordas had one hand on the ladder of the escape trunk and the other arm he drew back. Duncan saw the jar of incendiary liquid tumbling through the air, and Khordas was cursing him as the Salamander ducked his head into the escape-trunk shaft. "Hell be thy home, and that of all who oppose!"

The jar landed with a tinkling sound against the tubes, and fell into the furnace, and Duncan was moving towards the escape trunk as he saw the glass cracking, and the orange liquid spilling out, flaring. Khordas' legs disappeared up the trunk as Duncan grabbed the ladder and began to pull himself up.

Up the trunk shaft, Duncan could see the swiftly moving limbs of Khordas, taking several rungs at a time. The ladder went up for three stories at least before reaching the main deck, and now Duncan heard a great, cracking sound, coming up from the boiler.

Duncan's feet were just reaching the first rung when something groaned, loud and metallic, and the shaft itself was lit up by the great flaring light in the engine room. The Highlander scrambled to the next rung, then the next, and suddenly he heard a great, fiery roar from below, in the belly of the beast.

Duncan MacLeod cried out in pain as a wave of fire shot into the hatch below him. A wave of heat flew past him, and he knew it caught Khordas as well. And he prayed that he had been right about all the Children of the Salamander being off the ship by now.

"Khordas!" Duncan gritted his teeth against the heat. The air was drying out, the metal heating up and shuddering . . . *move*, *damn it, move!* Up above him, clothes blazing, Khordas was laughing again, laughing in pain, laughing at the destruction he wielded.

The shaft began to shake violently, and the hot metal seared Duncan's already burning hands as he pushed onward, gritting his teeth against the burn.

Rung after rung, Duncan chased Khordas, until they reached the first level above the engine room and the Highlander found the rungs to be a bit cooler. He looked up and saw Khordas' boots, not five rungs above him.

"Khordas!"

The Salamander looked down, and Duncan saw the mask, blue paint curling away with the heat. "Are you still with me, MacLeod?"

Khordas reached into his coat and pulled something out of it, a canister like the one that he had thrown into the boiler, and he shook it and threw it down the shaft.

Duncan winced as the canister hit his shoulder and bounced, falling down a few more yards before exploding below him, and hot liquid rose up and tore into his legs. "Oh, Khordas, you are going to pay for that," he growled. "And you're not getting rid of me that easily."

There was a rumble from below, and the bowels of the ship seemed to growl and whine as tons of metal shifted and cracked. Two engines were about to blow, and the Immortals still had two stories of ladder left to climb.

It was dark again in the escape hatch now, and Khordas had taken the moment's diversion to move up several more yards. And Duncan heard Khordas, somewhere above him, speaking to him, the voice of the Salamander echoing down the hatch.

"The Salamander does not tire, Duncan MacLeod. His home is in the dark, in the damp, and in the fire. These are his elements. What do you know of his power?"

"I know he is an Immortal! Just as I am!"

"No," came the velvet voice, and Duncan heard the boots move a few more rungs. Duncan kept climbing. "You are a young fool who has been blessed with a gift I cannot explain, but we are not the same. I became a god. You are simply an Immortal."

"I'm coming, Khordas," said Duncan. "You just wait right there." He looked down at his boots, the leather eaten through by the chemicals from the canister, and smoke was coming off his seared trousers. The blade of the katana batted against his side, waiting to be drawn. *Just give me room.* Duncan bit down and tried to ignore the pain of Immortality.

"You are coming, aren't you?" sighed Khordas. He sounded positively weary. "We can go on like this, you know. For centuries. You taking my Companions and I taking yours. You have not thwarted any grand schemes, Duncan. You have only interfered with me once again. But I will continue. And one day, I *will* receive the recognition, the worship I deserve."

"All you deserve," said Duncan, "is a very painful death." Two more rungs. And again. The sound of the grinding metal was growing in intensity, but here in the escape trunk it all seemed a world away. Duncan saw nothing but the rung to which his hands clung, and the metal in front of him. All else was pitch black.

Silence from Khordas. The echoing velvet voice had stopped, and now all he heard was the distant moaning of distressed engines. Duncan looked around and kept climbing.

Two more rungs, and Duncan put his hand on the next rung and screamed. There was something wet and thick on the metal, and it instantly seared into his fingers. The Highlander wrenched free his fingers and reared back, slamming his head against the metal of the cylindrical shaft. Duncan sucked in his breath and let his back rest against the metal. He tore away a sleeve from his coat and ripped the sleeve in half, and wrapped his hands in the cloth. Duncan looked up when he heard the breathing of the Salamander. He heard something move and a body uncoiling. With a *whoosh* something dropped next to his head.

There, half a foot from his own face, were the masked, burning eyes of Khordas. *What in . . . ?*

"My elements, Highlander!" Two hands came down and Duncan saw a dagger flying at his throat. He grabbed one of the wrists and looked up. Khordas had wrapped his feet around a rung up above and was hanging upside down. Khordas thrust at him with the dagger and Duncan twisted it, and now the other arm slammed into his head, banging it back against the metal.

There was no room to go for his sword. Duncan reached for his own dagger and brought it up, and felt the Salamander's blade slice into his ribs and glance away. The tip of Duncan's own dagger sliced into the funnel piece of Khordas' mask and it ripped away from his face, landing with a clang against the rung next to Khordas' head.

The Salamander turned a mud-lined face to Duncan and smiled. "Listen to the engines, MacLeod. Not much time," said Khordas. "She blows any moment now." The shaft was vibrating again, and Duncan was working hard not to slip.

"You're off balance," said Duncan, and he grabbed at Khordas' collar and tugged. He felt the Salamander's dagger slice into his face and growled as it tore away. Khordas did not budge, so well was he lodged in the shaft.

"Do you really think you can beat me at my own game?"

"Oh, Khordas, easily!" Duncan tore into the Salamander with his own dagger and felt part of Khordas' shoulder tear through, and the god cried out.

Something belched and whined, far below in the shaft, and a new wave of fire gurgled up, and Duncan was momentarily blinded as he looked down and saw the distant flash of orange flame. Almost instantly the accompanying heat wave tore past him, and Duncan looked up, but Khordas was nowhere in sight.

"Any moment now!" came the Salamander's voice up ahead on the ladder. "How far are you willing to go?"

"All the way," seethed the Highlander. "You're not getting away this time, Khordas."

Now a metallic, grating sound came from up ahead, not ten yards up, and Duncan wiped his face and looked up to see light. The shaft pitched, now, and Duncan slipped for a second, feet scrambling until he found a rung. He steadied himself as the shaft seemed to snap a yard in either direction and back into place. The metal was screaming, twisting to the point of breakage. Khordas was right, there was no time left. And Duncan felt certain that when this ship went, his head was sure to come away from his shoulders.

A circular vent was opening at the top, and Duncan could

see Khordas' silhouette against the night sky. "Adieu, High-lander!" The Salamander scurried out of the shaft and the vent fell closed once more, plunging Duncan into darkness. Duncan looked down and saw flames in the engine room, now far, far below. He looked up and climbed on. *Not far now.*

Duncan felt the shaft pitch again, more violently than ever before, and he climbed faster, until he reached the top of the shaft and began to turn the handle. Another cry of metal and flames, and the ladder began to buckle under him. Now a crack, and a distant booming sound, and Duncan turned the handle once more and pushed, and the vent fell open.

Duncan stuck his head out into the night sky and immediately cursed himself. It would be just like Khordas to wait and lop his head off when he emerged, like a gopher waiting to be shot. But the Highlander looked around and saw nothing, save a deserted deck. The belly of the ship gave another mighty groan and something heavy blew, and Duncan jumped from the shaft and onto the deck. Far across the deck, Duncan saw a mountain of fire erupt from the bridge, as sheets of metal flew in all directions. He stood his ground and kept from stumbling as the deck pitched underneath him. "Khordas!"

Duncan ran to the rail and looked out. Far below, on the water, he saw the Salamander at the oars of a lifeboat. *You're not going anywhere, Khordas. Don't kid yourself.*

Duncan looked around and spotted a lifeline, travelling from the first smokestack to the rail. He ran to the point where the cable connected to the rail and drew his sword, and part of him said, *Oh, Connor would love this.* The katana came down hard on the cable and bounced clear, but a couple of the strands snapped. Duncan drew back again and brought the blade down once more, and the cable was shorn through, falling back on the deck. Duncan sheathed his katana and grabbed the cable, and leapt onto the rail.

We are men out of time, are we not, Khordas? We are walking myths, you and I, the hero and the villain, except that all of it is true, the lives you have taken were real, they had souls that enjoy peace I never shall. Can you appreciate the battle you wage? I can.

Seared limbs restitching themselves even now stretched and rippled as Duncan MacLeod sprang from the rail with the cable in his hands. He gripped the cable tightly and tried to ignore the frayed metal digging into his palms as he flew through the air. Duncan looked down, using his weight to swing out and fly towards the lifeboat, and Khordas was looking up at him, amazed. *Do I amuse you, Khordas? This IS a Game, isn't it!*

All in a moment, all things at once, now: a shockwave, as the boilers blew, and Duncan felt a hot wind slam against him in midair as he was torn free from the cable and bits of his hands went with it. He tumbled through the air and saw the *Gratiano* behind him, her side groaning and pitching in the waves. Duncan was plummeting towards the lifeboat as the starboard hull of the *Gratiano* burst like an inflamed blister, and all at once the ship roared and flew apart, spitting hot chunks of metal and wood and glass.

Duncan slammed into the deck of the lifeboat and the boat flew forward with the force of the Highlander's landing.

Khordas dropped the oars and kicked at Duncan with his feet, sending him reeling back against the stern of the lifeboat. Duncan grimaced with pain, and grabbed his side. He had broken a rib or two, at least. Duncan saw Khordas drawing his sword, and Duncan jumped to his feet, but not before he noticed the smell of the water he had landed in.

Naphtha. The *Gratiano* belched flame and missiles once more, and bits of flaming metal flew. Khordas visibly winced as a burning fragment hit him in the forehead, and bounced off into the bottom of the lifeboat. Duncan drew his katana again and lunged at the Salamander as the deck of the tiny boat roared to life in flame.

"This is it, MacLeod. My elements!" Khordas in flames, Duncan seeing him through a wall of flame that engulfed both of them. Swords clashed and rang out and Duncan saw sparks fly from the blades as they met.

Duncan shifted to the left and winced, and realized that his ankle had been badly damaged in the flight to the boat, but there was no time to think on this. And in any case, the rest of him was burning.

Khordas lunged at him and Duncan raised his katana to

meet the rapier, and the Highlander stepped back and nearly tripped on the ribs of the boat. *No surprises. If you get flustered, rebuild.*

Khordas' shirt was on fire, a human torch wielding a sword, and Duncan ducked and slammed his head against the Immortal's breast, and Khordas fell back. *No room. No room to circle, no room to compensate. No room for mistakes.*

Duncan knocked Khordas' sword aside and brought his katana around and swiped at the Immortal's neck, but dislodged only a piece of flaming shirt material. Khordas seemed to laugh, somewhere inside the wall of flame, and Duncan barely saw him drop before the Salamander's black boot came flying and connected hard against his face. The wound on his cheek tore open and Duncan felt himself falling. The Highlander slammed against the ribs of the lifeboat, his hands landing in a flaming puddle of incendiary fluid, and the flames came up and sizzled the blood that flowed freely from his cheek.

With one hand he groped for his sword while with the other he scooped up a palm full of naphtha, feeling it tear at his flesh as he slung it upwards.

Khordas roared and staggered, tearing at his own face, which burned with the liquid. Duncan saw the rapier fall from the Salamander's hands and clatter against the deck, and Duncan jumped once again to his feet, ignoring his burns, ignoring his wounds, ignoring the flames that licked at his clothing.

Khordas fell to his knees and wrenched a hand free from his face and reached down for the rapier, which lay near his knees. *God, you regroup fast, Khordas.* Duncan found the hilt of the rapier with his foot and kicked, bringing it up and into the air. *But not fast enough.* Khordas cried out in rage as he watched the rapier spin through the air and disappear into the water. He seemed to take a breath, as if for once at a loss for what direction to take next.

"It's over, Khordas."

"Not yet it isn't, young one," said Khordas, as he drew his knife from his belt and let it fly, and Duncan felt it tear into his neck and he gurgled in shock. Duncan felt blood in his mouth and growled furiously, and brought the katana up in rage, and he heard Khordas laughing.

You are an abomination, Khordas. A mistake I should have taken care of long ago. You do not fit, you have no place, you are dangerous, and you will not be allowed to win this Game. And even if I have no idea if the Game is real, or if there is really a Prize, I know that if all these things are true . . .

"There can be," rasped the Highlander, "only one." The katana flew forward in the night air, through the flames, through the pain, and connected with Khordas' neck, and Duncan felt the familiar pressure of steel meeting flesh and the equally familiar lack of it as the blade came through.

The head tumbled off the Salamander's shoulders and into the water. For a moment, the head was staring, floating in the water as Duncan felt the strength drain from his legs.

The Highlander fell to his knees, hardly aware that the deck was still burning, and he tore the dagger furiously away from his own neck. He leaned back on his heels and let his arms fall wide apart, and his seared knuckles burnt against the burning wood.

I am Immortal. Born in 1592 in the highlands of Scotland. I cannot die. . . .

Seconds warping into hours now, every cell of the Highlander's body burning with energy that only came to him in one way . . .

Winds picking up, whistling, the fire around him dying down, ears popping the way they did when one sailed into the eye of a great storm, the lull, the pulse of blood, ready, waiting, before it hit.

This is your destiny, this is our gift . . .

The gift must be hidden, but do not be ashamed. You are Immortal!

It is Khordas who lies before you, remember the name, it is he who has passed his part of the gift to you, take it!

Visions now, flying into Duncan's brain, as the sky overhead rumbles and the clouds burst open and lightning cracks through the sky. Khordas, the god, and the dancing Children, in a time before numbers of years denoted the Return of the God.

Slake your Immortal thirst; do not fight, for this is what you are.

Lightning arcing wide and bright, flying into Duncan's chest, pounding through the Immortal heart, crisping his blood inside him, flaring out through his mouth and nostrils and eyes, connecting him to the fallen foe.

The lightning will speak to you as it burns through you, remember the name of the presence you have consumed, for he is part of you now, and you will go on with him. . . .

The drums of the dead, the dancers before Khordas, the god rises from the pit, happy in his role as king and savior. Remember! Remember!

This is the gift, receive it!

Duncan rears back his head and screams, knowing his foe—

Loneliness! Terror! The Children, dead, the land, changed, the truths, untrue! I am a god! I am a god! Damn you all who say it is not so!

I am Duncan MacLeod, the Highlander! I accept this tortured soul and give it rest! Great was his history, hard was his fight, terrible his loss! Deserving of death was he, but Khordas will be remembered!

Lightning tearing through clothing, fusing it to the Highlander's flesh, the body of Khordas levitating before him, the loser of the Game pouring out the gift.

Cursed! Cursed those of us who play the Game, that we know not who we are and whence we came!

Great are those of us who play the Game! Immortal are we, and in our hands lies the fate of all!

This is the Quickening!

Blue and white bolts swirled around the Highlander, pinning him to the ribs of the lifeboat. Visions whipping past like stallions at a race: Amber Lynn, the young one, Nerissa and all of the victims of Khordas, all the lost Children, all the hopes and dreams of the lost god. All these things racing alongside the visions of Duncan MacLeod, the villagers who cast him out, the father who betrayed him, the truth and the ignorance. Years. Centuries. Millennia.

Duncan MacLeod felt his eyes about to explode, and they

rolled back into his head as the lightning bolts ripped away from his body and flew back into the clouds.

And Duncan collapsed against the boards, unconscious and yet seeing all.

Great is the Prize. What is at stake?

Everything.

Epilogue

It was Connor MacLeod's turn to pay for drinks all around, so he, his former student, and Gabriela Maria Cuadra de Savedra gathered at the Ratter, not long before the *Dido* was to set sail. Behind them, through the frosted windows, the harbor outside the Ratter still bore the marks of the Salamander's rampage. The docks, still charred, served the usual offering of ships. But the wreckage of the *Troilus* lay in the harbor, the crow's nest sticking out of the water. It was being debated what would become of her; most likely the Navy would salvage the parts that could be saved.

Lauren, the Immortal with whom Khordas had consorted for so long, had blown up on one of the fireboats, Gabriela had seen that. But she was an Immortal, after all. Lauren herself was nowhere to be found.

"For that matter," said Connor, "she has a right not to be found. We all have a certain amount of rebuilding to do."

"Careful," said Duncan, "I wouldn't go looking for Lauren to turn over a new leaf just because she lost her religion. This is a pretty vicious woman. You yourself told me what she did to that Quaker."

Gabriela leaned forward, her brow knit with concern. "But she was under Khordas' power when she did that, doesn't that—"

"Excuse it?" Duncan asked. "I am convinced that line of

reasoning only goes so far. In any case, Lauren will have to deal with herself, *by herself*, for some time." The Highlander paused for a moment before asking, in mock nonchalance, "So. How does it feel to be Immortal?"

"Why didn't you tell me?" she asked. "You could have warned me."

"No," said Duncan. "I tend to believe that we should be allowed to live out our lives as normally as possible. What Khordas did to you, killing you before your time, was wrong. Even if he knew that you were going to become an Immortal." Duncan glanced at Connor, for he was reciting the facts surrounding the Elder Highlander's own death.

Gabriela nodded, gazing at Duncan. "So much has happened. How is it that you entered my life just before I . . ." she stopped, groping for a phrase.

"Turned? Crossed over? Died?" Duncan shook his head. "Who can say? I don't know what leads one Immortal to another, much less one to one who is not Immortal yet."

"Call it," said Connor, "a kind of magic."

"Aye," said Duncan.

Gabriela was looking down at the table now. "I never could find the mother of the child."

"Genevieve?"

"Yes." She cleared her throat. "I fear that Genevieve's mother was the poor woman substituted for me at the boarding house. At any rate, I cannot keep her." She pressed her eyes with her palms, the last vestige of mortal life and longings leaving her. "I left her at the hospital today. God knows. God knows what will become of her. I simply cannot look after her now. That's correct, isn't it? My god, Duncan, I'm supposed to be dead." She looked at him, huge, brown eyes that Duncan had known from the beginning would burn forever.

"You've been through a great deal," said Connor. "But what you have decided is best. You need to strengthen yourself for the Game, and it will be hard enough without the child."

"It was not a perfect time to become Immortal," said Gabriela, "but then, what is?"

Connor looked at Duncan. "Are you going to train her?"

"I'd thought about it," said Duncan. "But I don't think I should."

Gabriela looked agitated for a second and Duncan said, "Don't worry, I'm not leaving you right now. But I am not the most skilled mentor for you. And remember, it is vital you receive the proper kind of training. Immortals are basically lone wolves, we pair off every now and then, but we're not a good lot for groups."

"Right," agreed Connor. "I suspect that's because our very existence is dedicated to killing one another."

Duncan cocked his head. "He says that, but there are other theories surrounding the Immortals. I like to think you can have friends as well as enemies—and I think that Connor would be forced to agree to that."

Connor nodded, a wry, almost sad smile crossing his face. He was looking out to sea, but his eyes were full of vistas unknown to them both. The Elder Highlander said, "I envy you, Gabriela. You're just at the start of your journey. Your name is more than a dusty engraving hidden away somewhere. You have a head to protect now, and in the Game your head means as much as anyone else's. Yours could be the one that wins," he sighed. "And you will be weary."

"You sound as if you're ready to give it all up," said Gabriela.

"No," said Connor, "I am only very tired. There are older Immortals, and they tell me it will pass. I must warn you, Gabriela. Losing yourself is easy. To not do so, to remember yourself, to save a core of it so that who you are now is still with you, should you win the Prize—this is our greatest struggle."

Within three hours time Duncan and Gabriela stood on the docks and watched Captain David Carruthers fade into the distance aboard the *Dido*. Duncan watched him go, standing with his hands in his pockets, as if waiting for something. Gabriela looked at him and said, "Where to now, Mr. MacLeod?"

"Oh," he said. "I think we should go west. There's a teacher that I think will be perfect for you."

Gabriela put her arms around his neck and pouted. "Are you sure you want to get rid of me?"

Duncan laughed. "I didn't say I was in a *hurry*. You had a great deal of living to do, and I like to think you would have done much of it with me." He looked out to sea, where the *Dido* was fading in the distance, the Immortal presence of her captain long gone. "I was thinking we could find some place with no curtains and you could burgundy the Hell out of it."

"I'd like that," the Argentine said, wrapping her arms around his waist. "You mean you wouldn't mind travelling with a friend?"

"I mean," the Highlander said, "that sometimes I get tired of being alone." And with that, they kissed, and clung to one another like lovers, or mad sailors in a storm.

After a while, Gabriela left the docks and went ahead to her late father's house, but Duncan remained on the dock until the sun went down. He sat on the boards and dangled his feet and closed his eyes. He was listening to the ocean. The sound was old, older than the Immortals, a sound that Khordas would have known in his youth, and one of the few things that would not have changed. There were connections to that time that never changed: the sounds of wind, fire, water. All the old elements.

Duncan MacLeod, the Highlander, listened to the wind and the ocean and the seabirds on the pilings, and thought about Khordas and Connor and Gabriela, that young soul, at her father's house waiting to redecorate his world. And he felt, for the first time in a long while, at peace. For now, that was enough.

Skimming along the stream. Down through the centuries. No sign of plummeting.

Yet.

THERE CAN BE ONLY ONE. . . .

But not when it comes to new *Highlander*™ novels! On sale in January 1996 comes *Scimitar* by Ashley McConnell.

Joe Dawson, the Watcher, is visiting at the dojo when a package containing an ancient Arabian sword arrives for Duncan MacLeod. The scimitar obviously carries many memories for Duncan, and Joe returns home and searches through Duncan's Chronicle to find the references. . . .

From the year 1653, when Duncan is sold to the Immortal Hamza on the slave block of Algiers, to the year 1916, when Duncan meets Lawrence of Arabia on the Saudi Arabian Peninsula, the sword is the object of mystery—and murderous desire. Duncan persuades a minor Arab prince to support Lawrence's desert revolt by promising him the priceless sword of legend, which has been hidden in the ancient city of Petra. But Duncan is not the only seeker of the sword. . . .

※

By the year 2000, 2 out of 3 Americans could be illiterate.

It's true.

Today, 75 million adults… about one American in three, can't read adequately. And by the year 2000, U.S. News & World Report envisions an America with a literacy rate of only 30%.

Before that America comes to be, you can stop it… by joining the fight against illiteracy today.

Call the Coalition for Literacy at toll-free **1-800-228-8813** and volunteer.

Volunteer Against Illiteracy. The only degree you need is a degree of caring.

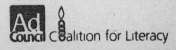

Ad Council   Coalition for Literacy